# SHERMAN'S EAGLE

Devin Blankenship

# SHERMAN'S EAGLE

NINE · ONE · SIX
publishing

ISBN 978-0-9856016-0-7

## ACKNOWLEDGMENTS

Copyedited by Darryl Arata. Thanks to Paul Blankenship,
Chris Clark, Alex Traverso, Jordan Traverso, Dayna Simondi,
and Andrea Hurst for your thoughts, edits, and time!
To DMay, thank you for the inspiration.

www.DevinBlankenship.com

## <u>DEDICATION</u>:

To my wife, Lori, and kids, Jack and Aly. Thank you for being patient and believing. Much love to my parents, brothers, family and friends who supported this endeavor and gave me words of encouragement. It helped more than you know.

## AUTHOR'S NOTE:

This is a work of fiction and any resemblance to an actual person or event is purely coincidental and a product of the author's imagination. Several of the historical persons, groups, and locations identified in this piece, although based in reality, have been enhanced or changed to fit the story.

Visit www.DevinBlankenship.com for more information or to send a thought or opinion. All correspondence is welcome!

-Devin Blankenship

# PROLOGUE

**Early Spring, 1865**

The Lieutenant shuddered as the blade slowly sliced through the initial paper-thin layers of skin above the victim's hairline, hit bone, then transversed the forehead, eliciting a primeval wail that awakened the night.

Its experienced master continued undeterred by the massive depressurization of blood vessels, exacting pleasure the farther the metal cleaved. He pulled upward with his free hand to separate the human felt from skull at a pace paralleling the increasing level of pain in the young victim, who began to babble incoherently as a wave of plasma rushed down his face and painted his pale chest crimson, one sentence standing out from the rest.

"Leave me, Lieutenant Joseph," the victim yelled before slumping against the giant elm anchoring his captivity.

The butcher finished guiding the D-Guard Bowie knife to its starting point and with a final tug ripped clean the scalp from its sinews as if it were no more than a prop wig glued to an actor's head, the sound of meat tearing distinct from any other.

"You're next, Yank," he cried out to the wilderness, holding up his prize in the firelight and whooping along with the rest of his comrades.

The true target of the sadistic act threw himself to the ground, concealed less than 100 yards away behind a dead tree. *The cargo. Must not give up the cargo. The mission is the sole responsibility. Leave him,* thought the Lieutenant.

He turned back to the wounded soldier, the last of his hand-picked unit still alive. The spastic shadows barely illuminated the 18-year-old from such a distance; enough to see his chest slightly rise then give. *I can't leave him, he's still alive. I've seen men with worse injuries survive. He is someone's brother, just like mine. I can save him, too.*

Lying flat as a rock, the Lieutenant pulled a pinch of tobacco out of his satchel, stuffed it into his homemade pipe and held it under his nose. He let out a big sigh and placed the business end into his mouth before reaching into the breast pocket of his jacket for the letter given to him by General Sherman in Atlanta.

Even in the partial moonlight the wax seal of a bear and snake with the words PARIO and PARADIUS underneath gave him chills.

*I should have never volunteered for this. It was a suicide mission from the start.*

He folded the letter away and slid both of his Smith and Wesson Model 2's out of his belt, rechecking all 12 chambers before cocking the hammers.

*At least the rest of the family will be taken care of, their property bought and paid for. I've lived a fine 28 years, no regrets. Time to do somethin' for somebody else for once. Hell, I'm gonna smoke this thing anyway.*

With a quick flick of his final wood match he lit the pipe and sucked deeply.

"The bastard is over there!" yelled one of the Southern guerrillas. "Behind that log."

Bullets began pounding his timber buttress with the cadence of a snare drum as the Lieutenant rolled on his back and looked up at the night sky.

*Time to earn my keep.*

He rose to his feet and immediately fired to the left, nailing an enemy square in the chest. He followed with two shots to the right and a dive into a somersault, rolling along the ground to avoid detection. Gun smoke from the volley of ammunition cloaked the area, leaving the fire a hazy beacon to advance on, bullets whizzing and whirring past his head.

Two more shots to his left found their mark as he quickly approached the young private, the butcher the only obstacle in his way, still holding the bloody scalp while wildly shooting through the fog.

"I believe you requested me."

"You son of a—"

Before the man finished the expletive a bullet resided between his eyes.

"Are you able-bodied?" the Lieutenant asked, stepping over the corpse and cutting the young man free before reloading.

"It hurts real bad, sir."

"Can you move?"

"I-I think."

"Good, we have to go quickly. The wagon is about half a mile east from here near where we camped, just . . . "

The Lieutenant felt a sudden pain in his back taking his breath away. He immediately recalled the sensation from a prior battle in Tennessee as his leg and buttocks were pierced in the same manner, dropping him to one knee.

*Getting shot feels like a goddamn snake bite.*

"Go, take this letter," he said to the private with a throaty yell, struggling to get back on his feet. "Get it to Hopkins and finish the mission."

The Lieutenant spun and shot haphazardly toward the remaining enemy, resembling a drunken beggar as he lurched; only he wasn't looking for money. He glanced back once during his bull run, spotting the injured private crawling through the dirt into the darkness to the wagon.

The fate of his mission and family was now in the hands of a living corpse.

# CHAPTER 1

**November 13, 2008 12:46 a.m.**

"**W**hy are we hiding, Nana?" the little girl asked in a whisper, her eyes struggling to stay open.

"We're playing a quick game of hide-and-seek with Grandpa," Lillian Dunning answered. "So we need to be as quiet as possible."

"But I'm sleepy. It's still night time."

"I know, but we won't play long, just until Grandpa finds us."

"Why is he talking to those men downstairs?"

"It's part of the game," she said, resting her trembling hand atop her granddaughter's head, the other firmly holding the doorknob to the closet. "Please, honey. Be quiet."

The little girl closed her eyes for a brief moment before speaking up again. "What do we get if we win? An ice cream?"

"Lily, please . . . "

"I mean, I want a cookie."

"Okay, you can have a cookie after, but right now you need to be as quiet as a church mouse."

"A church mouse? That's silly, Nana. Mouses don't go to church."

A series of clicks echoed off the hardwood floor just outside the door, prompting the little girl to giggle.

"Shh, Lily," said Mrs. Dunning to her namesake, covering her granddaughter's mouth and drawing her in. The noise climaxed, reminiscent of an angry typist pounding out a letter of discontent, then halted sharply.

The older woman held her breath and recited the Lord's Prayer in her head.

*And lead us not into temptation, but deliver us from evil.*

Just as the ligaments in her arthritic hand felt as though they may snap from the stress of holding back the unknown, her forearm stiff from overexertion, a series of loud sniffs beneath the doorjamb broke the silence.

"It's Fred," whispered the little girl. "He found us."

"Shoo, Fred," Mrs. Dunning said, relaxing her arm. "Go to bed."

"Does he win? He always finds me when I hide, I think he cheats because he's a dog and can smell good."

They both listened intently as the canine retreated, his pace interrupted after a few steps by a thump on the floor. Mrs. Dunning motioned for silence once again and placed both of her hands on the knob, gripping as tightly as possible, her knuckles white from the strain.

"Nana," the little girl whispered after a minute of waiting. "My feet are getting wet."

The older woman glanced at the slim crack under the closet door, focusing on a stream of liquid steadily invading their space via the bedroom and enveloping their feet. She paused, unfamiliar with the viscosity, when Lily reached down to touch it.

"What is this?" the girl asked, the dark color of red on her hand unmistakable even in the dimness.

The door handle suddenly ripped out of the older woman's grasp, their only escape route blocked by Sarah Palin and Bill Clinton, or at least two large men wearing their rubber likenesses. Palin grabbed Mrs. Dunning by the hair and heaved her into the bedroom.

"I got the Tar-Baby, you get the black bitch."

The 42nd President pinned Mrs. Dunning to the bed and duct-taped her mouth shut, her eyes fluttering as she struggled to make sense of the scene. Several more men in masks entered the room, including Dick Cheney dragging her semi-conscious husband. On the floor next to the closet lay the carcass of the family dog, the blood from the freshly-killed animal still flowing.

"Is this what you wanted, Dr. Dunning?" asked the tallest of the group, the distinctive mustache on his Adolf Hitler mask frightening in itself. He motioned to take the screaming girl out of the room. "I asked you nicely downstairs and your response hastened this reaction. Again, where is it?"

"I told you. I don't know," her husband struggled to answer.

Hitler turned to Clinton and barked an order in German, causing the man to pick Mrs. Dunning up by the neck and toss her into the nearest dresser, shattering its mirror. She listened to her granddaughter cry as the man continued the assault with a flurry of fists, hitting her so hard in the chest she heard her own ribs crack. The melee finished with a kick to the face, displacing her nose and nearly causing her to black out. Her assaulter left her crouched on all fours spitting blood, terrified for her granddaughter.

"Last chance, Dr. Dunning," Hitler said, storming over and adding a slap to her face. "Tell me or your wife is going to feel more pain than you can imagine."

"Please, I swear. Hurt me, not them!"

Mrs. Dunning looked up at the face of evil just as the flash from the muzzle of his gun ended her life.

# CHAPTER 2

**November 13, 2008 7:25 p.m.**

**K**al rubbed the side of his head and attempted to focus his eyes, but everything was a blur.

He choked back the deep recesses of his stomach desperately attempting to reach daylight, a sensation he had not experienced since childhood.

As his eyes adjusted to the darkness, the diminutive size of the room became apparent; the outdated wallpaper shedding from its plaster base while the shag carpet swayed from an infestation of ticks and other bloodsucking creatures. He managed to stretch his chained ankle and peer through one of the cracks in the nearest boarded window but saw only darkness. It was still night, not too much time had passed.

He clawed at the wood in a feeble attempt to pull it from the wall, only stopping when a series of footsteps halted outside the room. Before he could position himself into a defensive crouch, the lone door swung open releasing a blinding light.

"Mr. Boyce, how are you feeling?" a deep voice asked. "I hope you weren't roughed up too badly by my men. They can be a bit over-zealous at times."

"You got the wrong guy, I was just meeting a friend," pleaded Kal, his eyes adjusting once again, enough to surmise the person speaking was down on one knee within striking distance with another well-built man behind him in the doorway.

"Whoever you're looking for, there's been a mistake. You can just let me go and I won't say a word to anybody, I swear."

"Hmm. Wow, I apologize," the man said. Well dressed, he was lean and tall with short blond hair and steely blue eyes that studied Kal's every facial expression.

"So, you think I accidentally grabbed another Kalei Boyce who happens to also work as an assistant under Dr. T.A. Dunning, is also from Greeley, Colorado, is the son of Bob and Diane Boyce, and also attended Georgia Tech but is now at AMC majoring in history? You, this other Kalei Boyce that I'm not looking for, just happened to be at the Citgo off Hollowell Parkway at the exact time the Kalei Boyce I am looking for was scheduled to arrive? Stunning, the coincidences."

Kal's heart sank. "What do you want with me?"

"Oh, come now, son. We're not going to hurt you. We just need your help with a little project. It's in your area of expertise, you should be excited."

"Expertise? I'm a college student, I don't have any expertise. I play baseball, that's it." But Kal knew the man wasn't looking for tips on how to hit a curve.

"I'm talking about your work with Dr. Dunning."

"He's one of my teachers, I'm just in some of his classes."

"I think you underestimate yourself, son. Either that or you're trying to lie to me, which wouldn't be smart on your behalf. You're the lead assistant for T.A. Dunning, one of the most renowned Civil War professors in the country. I know a lot of people that would kill for that job."

*If they only really knew. It's not exactly paying dividends right now.*

"What do you want from me?" Kal asked, his voice cracking.

"Calm down, Kalei. How about I unlock you from those shackles and give you some ice for that nasty bump? We can continue after that."

Kal nodded and relaxed. The throbbing in his head was getting worse as his agitation level rose—ice sounded pretty damn good right about now.

# CHAPTER 3

**November 13, 2008 9:30 a.m.**
**10 HOURS EARLIER**

**O***ne.*

> *Two.*
> *Three seconds.*
> *Wait for it, wait for it.*

There it was, the body thick at first in appearance before quickly evaporating into nothingness.

> *Wait for it again.*
> *One.*
> *Two.*
> *Three.*

Again it developed, a shadowy dancer morphing from the top of the cup of black coffee. Its appearance for some reason brought a temporary sense of calm to Kal's brain, an escape from his immediate set of circumstances. He traced the outline of the cup's red Atlanta Metropolitan College logo with his index finger as another wisp of steam rose from the mug, the heat slightly stinging his skin.

A hand gently came to rest on his shoulder, startling the young man. "Alright, Mr. Boyce. The detective has just a few more questions and then you can go home," the uniformed officer said.

*Home? That's a funny proposition. Perhaps I'll just forget all about this and jump right back into that homework.*

He looked down at his cell phone and saw that Elle called yet again.

*Probably thinks she's breaking the news to me.*

"Can I ask you a question, just between us," the officer asked, fidgeting with his radio. "After you hit that ball, the college women must have been throwing themselves at you. You have some crazy stories, right?"

Kal just shook his head and avoided eye contact. "I don't really remember much about that time, to be honest. It's all a blur," he mumbled, using the same stock answer he'd been giving for years.

"Sorry, had to ask. Me and some fellas at the station always debated what it must have been like for you. You can follow me."

*It's funny*, thought Kal, half-heartedly slouching off the bar stool and following the officer out of the kitchen and into the hallway. *Just last night I was sitting in this same exact spot, on top of the world. Now? All of it's gone and I'm back to answering questions about that damn game.*

Entering the living room, Kal forced himself to look up the staircase as two coroners began their trek down to the first floor holding a stretcher containing the body of Lillian Dunning in a black body bag.

He abruptly froze and could feel his eyes well.

"Why? Why would someone do this?" he asked out loud.

"That's what we need your help with, son."

Kal turned to the lead detective, trying to wipe away the moisture from his cheek.

"I've told you everything. It makes no sense to me. None whatsoever. Everything was fine last night with the Dunnings."

"I know, I know," the detective said in tandem with a half-hearted nod, patting Kal on the head in the exact manner a cat lover might greet a big German Shepherd.

"So let's go over this again. We have a deceased African-American woman in her late 50's positively identified as Lillian Dunning, found in the upstairs bedroom with the family dog. Both shot at close range. She was beaten up pretty good before her murder. The room is a complete mess with lights overturned, mirrors broken, and one of the dressers on its side. Yet, you say the Dunnings have no enemies and their relationship was solid. And when you left them last night, things were copacetic?"

"Exactly," Kal said.

"Kid, do you know what kind of pressure this is going to put on me? I already have media crawling up my ass. I really need you to help me out here. How was the husband's state of mind?"

"He was happy. I'm telling you, there is no way Dr. Dunning could do this."

"No way he could do this? If that's the case, son, to be brutally frank, why the hell then did he kidnap his granddaughter and run off?"

# CHAPTER 4

Marcus Adler was a man of order.

From the part in his close-cropped, blonde hair to the neatly pressed shirt and slacks combination, everything in his world had a proper place to it. His leather wallet went in the back right pocket, a black BIC ball-point pen in his front left. And he always drank a cup of chamomile tea before bed, heated to exactly 75 degrees Celsius. Growing up as a young man his peers often referred to him as a control freak, a term he disliked but could not rationally argue against. It irritated him greatly whenever things were not organized, or plans did follow the path he specifically designed, which is why he was particularly vexed at the moment.

*Look at me now, though,* he would repeatedly reassure himself from time to time. *Those same men would die to have done the things I've done during the course of my career. To witness the things I've seen and accomplished. I'm a fucking American hero, and it's all because of the way I carry myself.*

He stood next to the kitchen sink and looked over his reflection in the window, rubbing his hand over his angular jaw, tracing his finger over his high cheekbones and around his sunken eye sockets. He hadn't eaten in quite awhile, and he could feel the damage all the recent stress was causing to his face—he looked as if he aged a decade in the last few months.

*I'm going to treat myself after all of this is over, maybe take a nice vacation. Perhaps find a girl to come?*

His cell phone rang in his shirt pocket just as his mind started drifting to images of a random Pacific island.

He looked at the number and quickly answered. "Yes, I took care of it. You don't need to know how, you'll find out soon enough. This was your mess to begin with. I specifically hired you to do a job, and you failed. I don't like chaos, and this just got substantially more chaotic. You've forced me to use methods I usually reserve for more dire circumstances."

Marcus walked to the refrigerator and grabbed a bottle of 100% whole milk and took several gulps as the voice on the other line talked—drinking straight from the bottle was an act he would normally never partake in, but because of his temporary living circumstances he had no dishware. The sweetness of the cream tasted good on the back of his aching throat as he listened to the blabbering.

"I'm in the process of tying up the loose end and moving forward," he finally interrupted. "I'll contact you as soon as we make progress. No more fucking surprises!" He hung up abruptly and neatly tucked the phone back into his breast pocket so as to not wrinkle the fabric. He took one more swig of the cold milk, wiped the lip of the bottle with a napkin and placed it back into the exact same spot in the dirty refrigerator.

*A tuna sandwich sounds good, I should have one of the boys grab one for me.* He picked his vintage Luger handgun up off the table, chambered a round, and placed it in the shoulder holster. *Maybe pastrami?*

He walked out of the kitchen and down the dingy hall of the one-story home still weighing which type of sandwich sounded best, finally stopping at the second bedroom on the right. He unlocked the deadbolt, stepped inside and flicked the light switch on the wall, startling the lone sleeping inhabitant.

"Dr. Dunning," Marcus said. "I need you to make a phone call for me. Your life and that of your granddaughter depend on it."

# CHAPTER 5

**K**al gazed at the back of the squad car as it pulled away from his apartment complex and checked his pockets for his house keys, reluctantly pulling them out. Sitting at home by himself with his thoughts didn't seem all that appealing. He took his time strolling through the sprawling compound and noticed a figure huddled on the stairwell leading up to his front door.

"Kal! Where have you been?"

*Elle. How long has she been sitting there waiting for me?*

"Hi, sweetie," he said, managing a weak smile.

"Did you hear about Mrs. Dunning? It's all over the news, I figured you were asleep or something."

"That's actually where I'm just now coming from."

"What?"

"Trust me, it's crazy. Dr. Dunning invited me over for dinner last night to talk about some school stuff and I didn't end up leaving until late. I crashed when I got home and had a nice early wake-up call from the police at my front door. I've been at their house all day. Sorry I didn't call or text you back."

He gave the petite girl a hug, holding on for a few extra satisfying moments before heading to the front door, his stomach aching imaging Mrs. Dunning's body coming down the stairs.

"Let's go inside, I need a beer."

She followed right on Kal's heels, mumbling questions to herself.

*Thank God for Elle.* It was one of those times he was glad his best friend showed up unannounced at his place. Not that he was ever disappointed when she came over, only that right now, to be very clichéd, he really needed companionship.

The two walked inside the darkened, one-bedroom apartment and Kal made a beeline past the single futon and his favorite ratty recliner to the fridge, grabbing two beers and ripping the caps off with his back molars—a trick he learned years ago that always seemed to be a crowd favorite, although this time he did it without even thinking. It was a bad habit by now.

Elle gently toyed with the row of dominos set up in a giant 'S' shape on the kitchen counter, the first piece begging to be tapped to start the chain reaction. It was one of Kal's favorite pastimes when coping with boredom—creating new and zanier patterns to knock over. He once setup a 500 piece formation complete with ramps and moving parts that took up almost the whole kitchen, only to accidentally brush one with his foot and start the process before the video camera could be prepped to save for posterity.

"You should have seen her," Kal said, staring off.

"You saw her body?"

"Yeah. I mean, well, she was in one of those bags the CSI guys put dead people in."

"I'm so sorry. That had to be awful," replied Elle. "Wait, they don't think you're a suspect, do they?"

"No. At least, I don't think so. I had to go back to Dunning's classroom at AMC to work on something after dinner that he needed for class, and one of the security guards let me in. The cops talked to the school and verified my alibi pretty quick. They just wanted to get an idea how things were at the house before I left. They still can't find Dunning or Lily, although I just can't believe he'd do this."

"That's good. At least you don't have to worry about people thinking you murdered someone, right? You didn't murder her, did you, Kal? Please tell me it wasn't you?" she feigned.

If it was anyone else, Kal probably would have taken offense to the timing of the joke, but it was Elle. "It wasn't I," he said with a smirk. "Anyway, you know the first person I'd come after would be you in a classic case of the jilted ex-lover."

"Aw, gee. Thanks. As I recall, though, it was you who broke up with me after a month, not the other way around, which would make me the jilted ex," Elle said. "But that would actually work out in the end because I wouldn't have to pay back that bet I owe you from the Falcons-Broncos game."

Kal shook his head in amazement and took a big swig of his beer before heading to the bathroom. *Worst mistake I ever made.*

"You know, Elle," he yelled back to the kitchen as he lifted the toilet seat and unabashedly relieved the pressure. "The whole thing is so weird. I mean, where could Professor Dunning be? His face is all over the news. I'm telling you, he just wouldn't kill his wife and run off. You should've seen them last night; there was nothing but love and respect. I mean, she busted his balls every now and then, but I've seen worse. Especially from you."

Kal stared at the half-burned candle resting above the toilet, mold beginning to form on the top.

"Hey, Elle. You hear me?" he asked, zipping up his pants and running the faucet to wash his hands. "Elle?"

Kal nearly jumped in surprise when he turned to walk out of the bathroom. Elle was standing in the doorway, her eyes hollow as if she just saw a ghost.

"Y-y-you need to come listen to your message machine. You're never going to believe it."

\*\*\*\*

"Play it again, Kal," Elle said. "Please play it again."

Kal obliged with a blank stare and carefully pressed the button, afraid to hit anything else on the outdated message machine.

*"Kalei, Kal . . . Oh my God. Please pick up if you're there. I-I-I need your help. This is T.A. Dunning, your professor. They killed Lillian. They killed her . . . (moan) . . . I need your help, you're the only one who can help me. We're in a lot of trouble. Please, please do not call the police. The number here is 404-867-5919. Please, Kal. Please."*

"Holy S," Elle said, rhythmically tapping her manicured nails against the countertop. "That's the third time I've heard it and I still don't believe it!"

"I know," Kal said, resting his head in his hands as he hit play once more.

"What are you going do? Call the cops, right?

"I guess so. I mean, I'm not sure."

"You're not sure? What do you mean, Kal? I'm pretty certain it's called aiding and abetting a fugitive and possible murderer if you don't tell them he called you."

"You heard him, though. He said someone else killed his wife and he's in a lot of trouble. How bad is it if I call him back first?"

"What if he did it and he's trying to somehow pin it on you? This could be some crazy plan to get you to take the fall. Think about it, you were the last one to see them," Elle said. "Just call the cops and cover your butt."

Kal was silent as he listened to the message once again, burning a hole through the machine with his gaze.

"What if I just call back and see what he wants? You know everything he's done for me. I can just talk to him and convince him to turn himself in, and then call the police right after."

"Are you insane? Why do you want to involve yourself in this at all? It's stupid and unnecessary. The police probably still consider you a partial suspect, and you'd make yourself look guiltier by sneaking around. You are such a typical guy, just call the cops."

Kal hesitated to respond and knew Elle could see the inner conflict raging over whether to betray the man who helped turn around his once unstable life.

"You've been through so many things the last few years, Kal. You're finally in a good place. I know you are loyal to Dr. Dunning, but you need to protect yourself."

He nodded but could not mask his facial expressions.

"Well, you're making me do this. I didn't want to," Elle said, pulling her pink cell phone out of her purse. "I'm calling in backup."

Kal groaned, realizing what she was about to unleash. "Don't call him, please. There's no need to involve him in this, let's just keep it between the two of us."

"Nope, you had your chance."

Kal got up to head to the kitchen. Having to deal with Elle's current boyfriend was hard enough when sober—this was going to require more beer.

# CHAPTER 6

"I think Kal should call him back," Benny Rebelski said after listening to the message. "He knows him better than anyone. If he thinks something is wrong, he can call the police after."

"What?" Elle asked. "Are you serious?"

Benny smiled in the same goofy manner that usually pissed Kal off, only this time he wasn't irritated. The truth was Benny annoyed him on a constant basis, ranging from over-the-top attempts at chumminess to satisfy his girlfriend's undying desire to unite them as buddies, to simple character flaws like the manner in which he spoke. Kal wasn't in a relationship with Elle anymore, but that didn't mean he enjoyed spending time with the man who essentially replaced him.

"Alright, let's call him right now then," Elle said, brushing off the surprise with a death stare to her beau. "Put it on speaker so we can hear."

"Fine, but be quiet," Kal said, turning the phone on. "I don't want to freak him."

Benny idiotically pretended to lock his mouth while doing the same to Elle's, sending him right back into Kal's bad graces. He slowly dialed the number, taking a deep breath before hitting the last digit. It rang all of one time before a breathless Dunning answered.

"Kal, thank God you called."

"Dr. Dunning, what the hell is going on? Are you okay?"

"We're fine. I don't know if you've been watching the news, but Lillian is dead."

"I know. It's all over the place. What happened?" Kal asked.

"A group of men. I don't know who they were or what they wanted. They broke into the house wearing masks after you left and tied us up. They took Lillian into the other room and they shot her, Kal. They killed her for no reason. I knew they were going to do the same to us but I managed to wiggle out of my restraints and get Lily out through the back door."

"The whole city is looking for you, Dr. Dunning. The police are crawling all over your house and even questioned me. You have to turn yourself in. Where are you now?"

"I'm at a pay phone off the Hollowell Parkway," Dunning said. "We're safe for now, but I'm scared. The police think I did it, don't they?"

"They just want to talk to you. I'm going to call the detective and have him pick you up," Kal suggested.

"No!" Dunning said, raising his voice. "I don't trust anyone, that's why I called you. You're the only person I can rely on right now. The men who did this were animals and are probably scouring the city for me as I speak. I know this is asking a lot, more than I've ever asked of you before, but I need you to come get us."

Elle shook her head and waved her arms trying to get Kal's attention.

"I don't know if I can do that, sir," Kal said, nodding to her in acknowledgement.

"Please, I beg you! You can drive us straight to the police station if you wish. I'm going to do everything to protect my granddaughter. These men were not amateurs, Kal. They came in with a purpose and possess capabilities you can't imagine."

"You have absolutely no idea what they want?"

"Nothing," he said, pausing for a brief moment. "But it could be something to do with my research. Please, son. I'm asking you as a friend, not your teacher. You're my last hope."

Kal glanced around. The idiot Benny stood with his mouth open as if he swallowed a fly while Elle shook her head, her eyes pleading with Kal not to give in.

"Okay, I'll be there in a half hour," he finally answered. "And then we're going straight to the police."

"Yes, of course. Just park close to the Citgo gas station and I'll find you. And please keep this between us, I don't want to involve anyone else. Thank you, son. Thank you."

Kal hung up the phone and immediately made eye contact with Elle. "What are you doing?" she finally asked. "Are you crazy?"

"I'm going with my gut, Elle. I trust him. You heard him, he didn't do it."

"Kal, think about this for a second."

"I did, back when no one in this city wanted anything to do with me, he took a chance. He risked his reputation to hire me as his assistant, and this is my opportunity to repay him. You read those stories about me—people always accuse me of taking the easy way out, but not this time. He needs my help. Besides, I'm not doing anything illegal, only taking him to the police station."

"You're wrong, Kal," Elle said, brushing her strawberry-colored hair behind her ear. "He wasn't the only one to stick by you, I was there, too. Through it all. Your mom dying, the arrest, when it seemed like the whole city turned on you. I was always right there, even when we weren't together, but as your friend."

Kal immediately shut up.

"The thing is, if you really believe you need to help him, we're not going to stop you. But just like back then, you're not going to do it alone. We're coming, and you have no say in the matter. Otherwise, I'll call the police myself," she said, turning to Benny, who reluctantly nodded. "Deal?"

Kal quickly mulled the offer. "Dammit, I hate you sometimes, Elle. Deal."

"You know you love me . . . both of you boys," she said, walking over and pecking him on the cheek, then doing the same to Benny. "Who's driving?"

\*\*\*\*

Kal glanced at his face in the mirror as he pulled a navy blue Georgia Tech sweatshirt over his head. For a second he thought he noticed a grey hair amongst the rest of its dark brown siblings and turned on the overhead light to double check.

*What the hell am I doing?* he thought to himself as he touched the bags under his eyes. *I look beat down.*

He flipped off the lights to his apartment, locked the front door and headed down to Elle's Jeep Cherokee, reflecting back on the sound of the professor's voice earlier in the day, how scared and frightened he sounded when he asked—no, begged—Kal to meet. It was the desperation in Dunning's voice during their short conversation that convinced Kal he was indeed innocent in the murder of his wife and needed his young assistant's help to save his granddaughter.

Kal was familiar with the gas station Dunning was hiding out near, just west of the Atlanta downtown, and tried one last time during the ride to spare Benny and Elle from becoming involved. "Guys, I really appreciate you coming. You didn't need to, though. I'll be fine."

"Stop it, Kalei," Elle said. "We always do things together. You can't expect us to just go away now."

"I know. But I don't want to get you involved in some trouble you can avoid. I mean, I know Dunning, but you don't know him that well."

"We're not doing this because we want to help Dunning," Benny said. "We're doing this because you're our friend and we want make sure nothing happens to you. You may trust him, b—"

Kal didn't even let him finish the sentence. He did not have a choice in involving Benny initially, but he'd be damned if he let the guy sit there and pontificate on their so-called friendship. "I think we're almost there. When we get near that senior center a few blocks away, just let me out and I'll walk the rest of the way. I don't want him to see you guys with me."

"We're going to park close, though," Benny said. "We've got to be able to spring with our cat-like reflexes in case we need to rescue you."

Kal stared at him for a good five seconds before opening the passenger door as the car slowed. "Just don't make it obvious."

"Stay strong. Remember, if he tries to pull anything he's only a 65-year-old grandfather," Benny said. He laughed and looked at Elle as Kal made his way up the street. "Who am I kidding? He'd kick Kal's ass."

****

Kal blew on his hands to keep warm. The sun disappeared long ago and the chill of the Atlanta winter was taking effect on his extremities.

He had been standing outside the Citgo for 15 minutes now with no sign of Dunning anywhere. The gas station/mini mart/auto repair shop was empty sans the lone employee manning the cash register inside and Kal could barely see Elle's SUV parked about two blocks down the street, sitting in the lot of an abandoned store with all of its lights turned off. There was the slightest hint of stirring inside every few minutes or so.

*That douche is probably trying to make out with her while I'm freezing my ass off out here.* Kal briefly remembered what it was like to kiss Elle before blocking it out of his mind.

A homeless man who looked as if he hadn't shaved for a year suddenly morphed out of the darkness and stumbled toward the store.

Kal tensed his muscles, ready for anything as he strained to make out the man's features. *Is this how far Dunning has fallen, reduced to dressing in rags and pretending to be homeless to avoid authorities? Maybe I did make a mistake in coming?*

But he realized it was not who he was looking for as soon as the light from the store reflected off the man's face; the paleness of his skin noticeable even through the layers of dirt.

"Hey, guy. You got any change for a vet?" the man asked as he staggered by.

Kal distractedly reached into his pocket and pulled out a couple of quarters.

"All I got."

"Thanks," the man said, turning and walking to the store's front door. Just before he reached it, he looked back and yelled.

"Hey, your name Karl, or Calvin, or some-thin?"

Kal's blood started pumping. "You mean Kal?"

"Yeah, that sounds right. There's someone looking for you in the back, paid me five bucks to come get you. I almost forgot."

Kal nodded, took a deep breath and headed around the store, stopping at the mouth of a barely-lit half-alley leading to the back lot where all the busted cars were stored for the night.

*Something is not right. Run. Just run away and don't look back. It's easier this way,* the familiar recess of his brain screamed.

He gathered himself before taking a step.

*Not this time, no easy way out.*

It took every muscle fiber in his being to walk the short distance, an intense fear gripping his psyche.

"Dr. Dunning? Dr. Dunning are you there?" he whispered loudly, careful no one else was in the vicinity as he entered the lot, which was littered with broken glass, empty boxes, and six beat-up cars in various state of restoration. One faint light flickered overhead every few seconds or so, providing scarce luminosity.

*If I was in a movie, I'd be screaming at myself to get the hell out of here,* he thought, his heart pounding inside his chest. Just as he began to embrace the concept of self-preservation by turning around and scrapping the whole idea, he heard his name called.

"Kal! Kal, over here. Behind the blue car."

He strained his eyes to see. The only blue auto he could semi-distinguish was almost flush against the back of the store wall, impossible to fully make out in the dark.

"Dr. Dunning?" he called out again, heading in that direction. "Where are you?"

"Over here, Kal. Look behind the trunk."

Kal followed the voice, feeling along the side of the late model Oldsmobile until he reached the back bumper, barely making out the silhouette of a man in a hooded sweatshirt crouching on one knee behind some crates.

"Dr. Dunning, I can barely see. Is that you?"

A second person from behind suddenly spoke in a clear and monotone pitch.

"Hello, Kal."

Caught off guard, he whirled to face the mystery voice and instantly felt a searing flash of pain on the side of his head, buckling his knees. His vision crossed and blurred as he tried to catch himself on the trunk of the auto, but he hit the ground with a hard thud, rendering close to unconsciousness.

The last thing Kal noticed before passing out was the familiar face of a homeless man glancing down at him.

"Sleep tight, chump. Thanks for the 50 cents."

# CHAPTER 7

**November 12, 2008 8:55 a.m.**
**ONE DAY PRIOR**

"**M**r. Boyce, did you happen to finish grading my quizzes?" T.A. Dunning asked, his reading spectacles gripping the edge of his nose as the pair walked through the hallway of Atlanta Metropolitan College toward room 'Science Lecture 218' and the start of 9 a.m. class.

"Yes, sir," replied Kal. He only skipped an opportunity to hang out at The Beacon House, one of Atlanta's best dive bars, in order to get them done.

Working for the famous Dr. Dunning so far had been a lot of effort with little reward for the 22-year-old. Reading papers, picking up dry cleaning, refueling the professor's car—it quite frankly had been nothing what he expected after enrolling in several of Dunning's classes and emerging as a top student, then beating out several other classmates for the student assistant position. Kal originally anticipated supporting the professor on his next award-winning novel or accompanying him on one of his famous Civil War research expeditions.

*But no, I'm basically just his secretary now.*

Still, he was in a better place than a year and a half earlier, and he constantly reminded himself of that fact.

As he walked with his professor he reflected on the very first day he enrolled at the local junior college and registered in one of Dunning's U.S. History courses by accident. He was never interested in the subject in high school; baseball held his only focus. But things clicked under Professor Dunning almost immediately, and aided by the fact he was immersed in so much past culture in Atlanta, Kal bonded with the subject matter and began imagining a future in teaching.

He initially felt self-conscious at AMC, not only because he was one of the few Caucasian students on a campus predominantly African-American, but he was also hard to miss at 6'3 with broad shoulders, dark hair and sharp features—features that almost every Atlantan had been bombarded with via TV and newspapers only a few years earlier.

"Listen, I know you've been working hard lately," the professor said, holding open the classroom door. "I want you to come by my house this evening for dinner. Lillian is making her specialty and I'd like to discuss something with you. Can you be over around six?"

Kal was hesitant to answer, having visited Dunning's house on several occasions in the past with high expectations, only to end up retrieving forgotten items the professor needed for school. However, this appeared to be the opportunity he longed for—logging some one-on-one time without office phones ringing or other students barging in.

*Perhaps Dunning is going to ask me to accompany him to a conference or on a research trip?*

"Should I bring anything?"

"Just an open mind . . . " Dunning said as the two walked into the lecture hall full of students.

" . . . just an open mind," he repeated with a wink before turning his attention to the class. "Alright, people. who of you have ever heard of the Old Hay House in Macon? Let's see how many know some local Georgia history!"

****

Dr. Terrance Alan Dunning was somewhat of a superstar in his field, and on most occasions Kal felt honored to be working for him, let alone visiting his home for dinner.

Dunning's resume was permanently imprinted on his brain, having provided it countless times to organizers of the speaking events the professor frequented. An Ivy league graduate, Dunning taught up and down the East Coast at several prestigious universities throughout his 30-year career before semi-retiring late in the nineties, only to grow bored and return to lecturing part time at the local junior college—in large part due to the urging of his wife, who couldn't stand having him at home all day.

Dunning coined a phrase he would repeat at the end of each class that most of his students thought corny. But Kal liked it for some reason, and repeated it to himself whenever he was nervous around the teacher.

*Respect and understand the past, but do not fear it. Never underestimate the power of something old, because it can always teach you something new.*

"Never be scared to learn something new," Kal muttered to himself, taking a deep breath as he walked up the pathway to the Dunning's two-story, brick home in midtown Atlanta, one of the nicest parts of the city with rich culture, diversity and proximity to downtown. It was an ideal place for a man like the professor to live. The Dunnings' front yard was beautifully manicured and in immaculate condition, full of rose and azalea bushes and a tightly-mowed lawn. A small peach tree stood next to the house, creating a living embodiment of the perfect Georgia residence.

"Kalei, how are you doing?" Lillian Dunning asked, opening the door to her home and simultaneously holding back the couple's giant yellow Labrador Retriever, Fred—aptly named after slavery activist Frederick Douglass.

"Great, thank you. I brought a little something for dessert."

"You didn't need to need to bring anything, I'm just happy Terrance finally invited you. I've been asking him for some time now."

Kal grabbed a hold of Fred's collar, allowing Mrs. Dunning to take the box of cheesecake and shut the door. "Thanks for having me," he replied as they walked through the entryway to the back of the house and the kitchen.

"Hello," a small voice chirped from the staircase.

"Hi, Lily," Kal said, looking up at the Dunning's grandchild perched on the top step with a doll in her hands.

"Lily Marie Dunning! I told you to get ready for your bath. Don't make me come up there. Say goodnight to Kalei and get your water running right now."

"Your name is weird," said the five-year-old before scurrying back up the stairs, only stopping at the top to wave goodbye.

"Don't mind her, she takes after her mother—a mouth on her. Terrance is in his study working on some school stuff, why don't you go join him for a drink. You're old enough, right? Dinner will be ready in a few minutes."

Kal gave Fred a playful head rub before heading down the hall toward Professor Dunning's study, the only place in the house he had ever spent any real time.

Dunning would occasionally forget lecture points for his classes, forcing Kal to rush over during the day and rummage through the room in an attempt to find them. It was as stereotypical of a college professor's office as possible, with several book shelves furnished in dark cherry wood and filled with Civil War collectibles surrounding an intimate fireplace. Artwork of famous military generals adorned the walls and two dark leather couches accentuated the cave-like atmosphere.

The professor was seated behind his huge desk, smoking a fat cigar and reading from a novel when Kal gently knocked on the slightly ajar door.

"Kal, right on time, my boy," Dunning said, turning down the sound on Richard Wagner's epic instrumental *Das Rheingold* playing through the sound system. "Come on in. Can I fix you a drink? Beer, wine, perhaps something a little harder?"

Kal noticed the professor holding a small glass that appeared to be full of extremely potent liquor.

"Whatever you're drinking, Dr. Dunning."

"You're a Scotch man? Nice, very nice."

Kal immediately regretted his decision.

The last time he ingested Scotch was in the ninth grade when he broke into his father's liquor stash and made off with a cheap bottle of the stuff. The aroma of it to this day nearly made him dry heave. But he had to impress his mentor, so Scotch it was.

"Alright, young man," Dunning said, handing Kal a tumbler— thankfully the drink was on the rocks. "How are things going for you? Are you fulfilled and have you learned everything you hoped by working for me?"

This was Kal's chance, a chance to request more involvement.

"Yes, of course sir. It's been great."

He wanted to punch himself in the mouth.

"Really? Because it seems to me like all you have been doing is running errands and grading quizzes. Not exactly the most exciting of work, eh?"

"Well . . . "

"You don't need to answer that," Dunning said, taking a long puff from his cigar and examining the rose tip.

"I'm sorry, would you like one? Actually, let's wait until after dinner. Lillian has been getting on me to smoke only one a day and these taste better after a nice meal, anyway. As I was saying, you don't have to answer that question, I already know the answer. I can see it in your eyes every day."

"Sir?" Kal asked, his voice wavering.

"Relax, Kal. It's a good thing. I would worry about you if you didn't want more. It's sort of a test I give to all my assistants."

Kal took a deep breath and a big swig from the glass, temporarily forgetting the piquancy.

"I have a project I'm working on that could use your help. It's very important and somewhat of a secret . . . let me rephrase. It needs to be treated with the utmost discretion. You cannot discuss it with any of your friends or family."

Kal nodded, a mixture of excitement and curiosity suddenly engorging his brain. *This is not just any old research project. This is major.*

"Do you think you'd be interested?"

He nodded again, chewing on a piece of scotch-flavored ice. Suddenly, a second drink was not out of the question.

"What do you know about L'Aigle de la Liberté?"

Kal scanned his memory, trying to recall it. *Was it something Dunning talked about in class? No, it couldn't be.* He transcribed Dunning's lectures for the records, one of the more tedious aspects of being his assistant, and would have remembered this. Relying on the little bit of French he retained from high school, Kal knew it had something to do with the word liberty or freedom.

"I'm sorry, sir. I can't remember it for some reason."

Dunning smirked and took another puff from his cigar.

"Okay, how about the Freedom Eagle?"

*This*, Kal knew.

"Of course, the Freedom Eagle. The old Southern myth about the pure gold statue of an eagle Napoleon III gave to Jefferson Davis for good luck in the Civil War. I read something about it online one time."

"Yes, but why do you assume the Freedom Eagle is a myth?"

Kal smiled in confusion. Many U.S. history scholars focused in the Civil War field had heard rumblings of the Freedom Eagle at one point or another, but most dismissed it as just that: a rumor.

"Let me refresh your memory," Dunning said. "As the 'story' goes, after the French initially pondered coming to the aid of the South at the start of the war, but remained neutral due to diplomatic pressure from the North, a French delegation traveled to meet with the Southern President Jefferson Davis. At that meeting in Montgomery, a solid gold eagle was given to Davis as a symbol of the South's struggle for freedom and France's sublime support for their cause. If you recall from some of your other history classes, Napoleon Bonaparte I, himself, was very fond of the eagle form, adopting it as the standard for his Grande Armée in the early 1800s. It was carried upon a pole into combat. Many other cultures throughout history used the eagle in battle, as well, including the Romans. Did you ever read The Eagle of the Ninth by Rosemary Sutcliff?"

Kal answered, "No, but I think my dad did. I remember him talking about how good the book was."

"Yes, well, it's a great fictional tale about the demise of the famed Roman Ninth Legion of the North, who many speculate was destroyed by tribes in Britain and Scotland in the first century, A.D. One of the sons of those soldiers, a young man not unlike yourself, goes on a quest to find the truth about his father and ends up discovering the lost legion's bronze eagle standard, which he returns to Rome to restore their honor. You should read it sometime—although it contains a few historical holes, it's quite a good story."

Dunning stood up and quickly scanned his massive wall of books.

"It's in here somewhere. Anyway, back to the Civil War. Napoleon III, Napoleon Bonaparte's nephew, coined his gift to the South as L'Aigle de la Liberté, or the Freedom Eagle. It was almost a foot and a half tall and had giant red rubies for eyes, as well as diamonds interspersed along the bird's spread wings. It was a formidable piece of artwork and was immediately embraced by Southern leaders as a figure of their cause. The bird allegedly traveled with Davis wherever he went—at speeches and rallies for the troops, even to church. It was supposedly guarded by a group of men whose sole duty was to know where Davis, and to a degree, the Eagle was at all times."

Kal nodded his head, the tale slowly coming back to him.

"The North allegedly sent spies several times in an attempt to steal the statue," Dunning continued. "Which they hoped would help break Southern spirit, but they never were able to gain any proximity to it. In fact, as you know, the whole story of the Freedom Eagle was thought by most scholars to be an old wives' tale. There are very few mentions of it in accounts from that time. One of the best pieces of evidence supporting its existence was an article chronicling a Davis speech that appeared in the Charleston Mercury."

Dunning reached into a large folder on his desk and handed a highlighted photocopy to Kal.

> As the slovenly Davis railed against the North's tyranny and pleaded for Southerners to bond together and strengthen their military numbers, the red eyes of an eagle statue poured of gold resting on a table behind Davis stared out at the crowd, almost challenging

Charlestonians to delve into their hearts and find the strength to fight off the invading forces. Unfortunately, our faith in our "leaders" has diminished to the point that no amount of golden eagle statues will allow true Southerners to blindly follow them any farther.

      -Charleston Mercury, August, 1864

"Scholars debated for years on the subject, with many pointing to the fact the Eagle seemed to disappear into thin air sometime near the end of the war as a sign it never existed and was merely a part of Southern legend meant to raise the spirits of the people. Those on the other side of the fence maintain the statue was hidden away by their leaders in an attempt to keep the North from finding it, much the same manner millions of dollars of Southern gold bullion earmarked for the war was hidden and forgotten, leaving some Confederate states a veritable wasteland of buried treasure to this day."

Kal realized he was on the skeptical side of the argument as he continued listening. He never bought into the whole treasure notion because there was such a lack of verifiable evidence. The idea of a solid-gold eagle sitting in the basement of a North Carolina home or somewhere else, passed from generation to generation didn't jive with him as a genuine possibility.

"I remember it all now, Dr. Dunning. But I really thought it was just a tale. The way you're talking about it, you sound like you think it's real."

Dunning laughed and took a big puff from the cigar, blowing the smoke straight up into the air. His features suddenly became stone-cold serious and he locked eyes with Kal.

"I don't think, I *know* it's real."

# CHAPTER 8

**November 13, 2008 5:40 p.m.**

"**H**mm, *Dumb and Dumber?*"

"No, but close."

"Let me hear it one more time."

"Okay," Benny said, contorting his face and adding a lisp. "Just promise me you'll never go bungee jumping in Mexico, they just don't have the regulations."

Elle raised two fingers to the side of her temple. "You said Jim Carrey, right?" she asked, buying time as she scanned her memory for all of the movies starring Benny's favorite actor.

"*Liar, Liar?*"

"Come on, Elle. I can't believe you don't know this one. It's *Cable Guy*. The guys would have gotten it in a second."

"Well why don't you go hang out with your buddies then, if movie trivia is so important."

"I'm sorry, let's do something else. You want to make out instead?"

"For the fourth time, no," Elle said, slightly smiling as she checked her watch.

"Have I showed you the latest incarnation of the Elephant?" he asked.

"No, Benny. I don't want to see the Elephant right now!"

The 'Elephant' was perhaps Benny's favorite party gag, which he unveiled only for a select group of friends. It involved him pulling the pockets of his pants inside out so they hung like elephant ears, then unzipping his fly and threatening to dangle his manhood to the world. "Viola," he would proudly proclaim upon completion, laughing hysterically. "The Elephant! Don't get hit by its trunk!"

Elle was not particularly fond of the trick, and often referenced it when describing the differences between her ex- and current lover. They couldn't have been more polar—Kal the intense, brooding type while Benny possessed a playful personality and always seemed to enjoy the fun in life. She often wondered if it was a futile attempt to make the two men bond.

"We're supposed to be on the lookout. How long has it been since we last saw him?"

Benny checked his watch and then the spot Kal had been standing in front of the gas station before disappearing down a side street—out of their line of sight.

"Ten minutes, at least. How long before we go look for him?"

"I don't know. You're supposed to be my big hero, you decide."

Before he could answer, a loud knock on his window startled both of them.

"It's just a homeless person," Benny said, cranking down the window slightly. "You scared the crap out of me!"

"Sorry, guy," said the disheveled man. "You think you could spare some change?"

Benny looked over at Elle, who was clutching her chest, trying to regain her composure after nearly jumping through the sunroof. "Just give him some so he goes away," she whispered as they both felt around the center console, trying to grab as many loose coins as possible.

"This is about all I've g—" he said, turning back to the man with a handful of nickels and dimes.

Elle, still feeling for any more out-of-view change, looked up to see why Benny stopped talking mid-sentence and instantly got her answer. The muzzle of a handgun was pointing at them through the open window, the expression on the man's face changed from emotionless to angry.

"Get the hell out of the car!"

"Oh my God, Benny!"

"Just do what he says."

"Out, now!"

The two slowly eased out of the SUV, the pistol still trained on them. "Gently toss me the keys, honey, or I'll put a bullet through his head. And keep your hands where I can see them."

Elle attempted throw the keys over the car but ended up bouncing them off the roof and on to the ground, next to Benny's feet.

"Be a good sport and hand those to me, carefully," the man ordered Benny, who slowly picked them off the sidewalk and placed them into his extended palm. The gunman raised his arm and waved to someone up the street.

"Take whatever you want, the car is yours. Just let us go."

"Shut up or I'm gonna shoot the girl," the man said, now pointing the gun at Elle.

An engine fired to life and echoed down the empty street. Within seconds a dark-colored van pulled up behind the Cherokee, the side door swung open and several men jumped out holding automatic weapons. They strapped blindfolds on Benny and Elle and herded them inside with the precision of an elite military unit.

"I'll follow you in the girl's truck. Keep your speed down—don't attract any attention."

"Please, no!" Elle said, eliciting a rabbit punch in the back of the neck from one of the gunmen.

"Just do what they say, babe," Benny said in a low voice.

Elle immediately thought of Kal as her instincts to survive took over.

*He'll wonder where we are at first, then he'll call the police. He'll know something is wrong.*

Crouched on the floor in an upright fetal position as the van drove, Elle reached to her left and felt for Benny's hand. Having grown up in the nearby suburb of Stockbridge and familiar with the area, she figured they were probably on the freeway now and could be on the downtown connector, followed by the Perimeter in minutes and therefore anywhere in the city and beyond.

The Perimeter, aka Interstate 285, was a beltway that encircled the city and provided Atlantans with access to every major road or freeway in the area, in every direction. Elle knew the chances of being found quickly by law enforcement were dwindling as quickly as the van traveled away from the abduction spot and it became apparent to her the situation they were in was not going to end swiftly. Unless the whole thing was a terrible mistake, whoever had gone through all this trouble wanted them badly.

After 15 minutes of erratic driving the van finally slowed and then stopped.

Elle could hear the sounds of men moving around as a garage door opened. The van jerked forward and slowly crept ahead a few feet before the engine shut off and the side door opened. Since it hadn't been a long ride, they were still most-likely in the Atlanta area. She had listened carefully for any passing noise that might give her a reference point to their location—church bells ringing, crossing of train tracks, tires bouncing over a bridge, but nothing sounded familiar.

Truth be known, it was hard to hear much over the moans coming from a third semi-conscious person in the rear, whom Elle noticed shortly after they were tossed inside.

*Another carjacking victim?*

Every time she tried to raise her head she got a hard kick in her side. The first one stung, the second one almost made her cry.

*Floorboard it is.*

Benny would later laugh at her for not figuring it out at the time, it was so obvious.

"Hind tit is 20-20," he loved to say.

"It's hind *sight*, Benny, not hind tit. Stop being gross."

Benny was never very good with expressions.

"Who are they?" a new voice asked, this one deeper than the

others, as they entered inside a building, the overhead light peeking through a crack in Elle's blindfold.

"Stragglers. They were hanging around the gas station."

"More complications. You should have just killed them and burned the bodies."

"Sorry, sir."

"Stick them in one of the other rooms. We'll see if they have any value to our target," the new voice said. "You two stuck your noses where they didn't belong. That was very stupid. My name is Marcus, and you'll be my guests for awhile."

# CHAPTER 9

**November 12, 2008 8:05 p.m.**

**K**al realized it had been a good amount of time since he ate a home-cooked dinner as he picked through the last remnants of pot roast on his plate. "That was as good as it gets, Mrs. Dunning. I haven't had a meal like that in ages."

"Thank you, Kalei. So please forgive me, because I'm not much of a sports fan, but Terrance says you used to play baseball for the Braves and won the Super Bowl? Or was it something else?"

Kal smiled as Professor Dunning chuckled at his wife's attempt to delve into a topic outside her comfort zone.

"Kind of. I played baseball over at Georgia Tech my freshman year and we were lucky enough to win the College World Series."

"Don't be modest, Kal. Tell her what you did," Dunning said, leaning back in his chair.

Kal grimaced. This part of his life was supposed to be easy to recap—a high point.

"I came into the championship game having barely played all year. I probably should have redshirted because of an injury, but the coach decided to keep me on the bench for the right opportunity. We were down late to Cal State Fullerton and I ended up coming off the bench in the top of the eighth inning and hitting the home run that won the series for the team."

"Well, that's wonderful," Lillian said while Kal stared at his plate. "What's the matter? Did I say something wrong?"

"No, no," Kal said. "The truth is I was just really lucky, and as crazy as it sounds, that wasn't a good time in my life. My mom died unexpectedly a few days after that in a car accident. Then a couple months later I got busted for taking some illegal supplements and everything else in my life went to crap. It was all over the news."

"I'm so sorry, I didn't know."

"It's okay. It's my own fault—not my mom, but the other part. I just stopped caring and was really angry at the world. The media attention was unbelievable after we won and I wasn't ready for the pressure of people recognizing me everywhere I went. I had a bum shoulder all year long that I played through, and I finally just decided to take some stuff to help it heal. I was so sloppy, though, the coaches caught me right away. A couple of weeks later I got into a bar fight and had to spend a weekend in jail for assaulting a cop. They kicked me off the team and took away my scholarship, so I dropped out. It's still pretty embarrassing for me. I'm just glad my mom didn't see any of it. From hero to villain in a few months time."

Kal paused for a second as his hosts continued to let him have the floor.

"I honestly believe it was a good thing, though. Baseball was always easy for me growing up, but I don't think I ever really loved it— bad stuff had to happen for it to dawn on me. After all, if it hadn't, I wouldn't have met your husband and taken his classes. I was persona non grata around Atlanta—the Journal-Constitution wrote a story on my struggles to go to a junior college, but Dr. Dunning didn't treat me any different. He took a chance on a cheater and now I'm here having dinner with you guys, so everything is good."

"You didn't give me a choice," Dunning said. "You were so voracious, I was forced to hire you to keep you from interrupting with all your questions."

"Well, I'm glad you are doing well, Kalei. And just so you know, you are welcome any time in this house. But please don't call yourself a cheater, we all make mistakes when we're young, it's how we grow. The important thing is to learn from them. Now, do you feel like having a piece of that cake you brought?" Mrs. Dunning asked.

"I'm so stuffed right now, I don't know if I can fit it in."

"The boy and I have some work to do, Lillian," Dunning said. "He'll have time for dessert later."

"Don't be rude, Terrance. Kal, I'll bring you some coffee and a slice later. How about that?"

"Thanks, Mrs. Dunning," Kal said, following the impatient professor out of the kitchen and down the hall to his office.

*Time for the nitty gritty.*

"How about that cigar now, Kalei? That'll be your real dessert," Dunning said, opening the box and handing it to Kal, after taking one for himself.

The two sat there in silence, slowly enjoying the taste of the smooth tobacco, which melded in Kal's mouth with the flavors of the just-completed meal, providing him a jolt of happiness. It had been a while since he had been in a home with such warmth and closeness, the bond that comes from a tight-knit family. Ever since the death of his mother there had been a noticeable emptiness in his own house back in Colorado, an irreplaceable void Kal was unsure would or could ever be filled again.

He felt terrible for leaving his father alone, a constant burden on his psyche. He contemplated moving back several times and attending nearby Northern Colorado or Colorado State, but his father insisted he stay in Atlanta and finish what he started in terms of earning a degree. And although that made him feel somewhat less guilty, only returning home for the holidays was extremely tough to handle. The house didn't have the same energy about it. It was as if it lost a piece of itself. That's why Kal took note of moments like these with renewed appreciation, and attempted to enjoy them to the fullest.

"So, where did I leave off," Dunning asked, breaking the tranquility. "Ah yes, Dr. Ashworth from the University of Virginia. Let's see, I was randomly contacted by him about six months ago via email. He told me he was working on a project in conjunction with a private citizen regarding several Civil War artifacts. It wasn't until a month after working together, engaging in mundane research he revealed what his true intentions were."

Dunning flipped a large file across his large desk to Kal. "Go ahead, peruse through it. I think you'll find a lot of interesting material there."

As Kal read, Dunning continued.

"Ashworth, it turns out, wasn't working on finding just any Civil War relic, but one in particular: the Freedom Eagle. According to him, he was contacted by a collector who had a veritable treasure trove of evidence proving the Eagle's existence. Newspaper clippings, drawings from that period by people who witnessed it first hand, even a photograph of Jefferson Davis with the Eagle in the background."

Kal had just gotten to that part of the file, and indeed, there was a very old, blurry shot of the Confederate president with what appeared to be a large eagle in the background. But the quality of the picture was so poor it was hard to make out any of the details. It could have been the Freedom Eagle, but it also could have been a generic statue.

"Do you know who gave him the info?"

"Ashworth was reluctant to get into that when we first spoke, and I never broached it again—probably just some wealthy, old connoisseur. More importantly, his research indicates the Eagle was last seen around the time General William Tecumseh Sherman began to cut through Georgia. The Eagle did not travel with Davis at that point in time due to safety concerns, but instead was shuttled from safe house to safe house, usually by prominent Southerners. It apparently made a public appearance in Macon only a few weeks before the Union army arrived, so Ashworth started looking at the connection between Sherman and the disappearance of the Eagle, and came up with loads of interesting data. For instance, what do you know about the route Sherman took to get to the sea?" Dunning asked, leaning back in his chair with a grin on his face.

Kal paused and looked up from the folder. "After taking Atlanta in mid-November, he pared his men down to just over 60,000 and sent the rest to keep the Confederate General Hood from getting a foothold in Tennessee. He split that 60k into two flanks, a right and a left. The right wing headed southeast in the direction of Macon, and the other took a more direct northeastern approach to Augusta, eventually taking the capitol of Milledgeville. Both wings reconnected in Savannah, but Sherman stayed with the northern-most group that headed to Milledgeville—"

"And that's the interesting part, Kal," Dunning said, interrupting his student. "Every Civil War historian knows that Sherman was never anywhere near the southern wing, that he was supposed to be with the more northern, marching with General Slocum. But Ashworth found evidence he actually was in the Macon area for a short period of time. The reason why is unknown."

Dunning now occupied Kal's total attention. He recalled how it was an established fact Sherman split his troops into two wings after leaving Atlanta to keep the Confederate forces guessing as to where he might march next. The right wing, or more southern, of which Sherman was not supposed to be traveling, originally feigned as if it were going to besiege Macon, but actually bypassed the city, confusing their enemy. And because a majority of the Georgian Confederate resistance was with General Hood attempting to take back Tennessee from the Union, Sherman faced little resistance during his infamous run through much of the state.

But now Dunning was proposing a theory that would contradict every history book ever written, including Sherman's own memoirs. He was suggesting that Sherman secretly deviated from his own plan.

"Ashworth has come across several unique and rare correspondence, some written by Sherman himself, one of which was to be given to the next in command should he be injured or killed. These letters indicate that he inexplicably broke off from the left wing before reaching Milledgeville and headed south to join the right wing, staying there for a short time before heading back."

"Wouldn't that have been dangerous to cross through enemy territory?" Kal asked.

"Certainly, but if you remember, he had his own personal escort in the 1st Alabama Cavalry Regiment—a group of loyal supporters from the south that protected him. Additionally, his army didn't face much resistance until after Milledgeville, when they headed toward Savannah. The whole operation was cloaked in total secrecy. Only the two majors directly below him and his personal cavalry knew."

Dunning took another puff from his cigar, and quickly exhaled the smoke.

"So what does all of that mean?" Kal asked, not fully understanding the connection Dunning was trying to make.

"It means there is evidence Sherman was in or around Macon at about the same time the Eagle was last seen." Dunning got up and walked to a painting of President Lincoln on the wall, pulling on it to reveal a hidden safe. He punched the combination and gave it a hard tug, popping the door open.

"I'm convinced the disappearance of the Freedom Eagle is not coincidently tied to Sherman's secret mission around the Macon area. We've looked at other options, but it always circles back to him. He is the key figure in the whole theory. Might I also mention Ashworth has interviewed descendants of Sherman, several who swore on record of a family legend claiming he acquired a valuable treasure near the end of the war and hid it so his family could be taken care of? Not one of those descendants ever heard of its discovery."

"Okay, all of this is great, but I thought the Union army never took Macon? They bypassed it and headed East. If the Eagle was in the city, how did Sherman get there without being detected?"

"Yes, you're correct. They never took Macon until near the end of the war, several months after Sherman's march—but they didn't need to. Sherman commanded a small and stealthy force and could have been in and out of Macon quickly. As the Confederates realized Tecumseh's army was moving past them, they would have shifted their attention to attack the rear of the right wing, allowing him to slip in behind."

"Damn. I mean, that sounds crazy," Kal said.

"Crazy? Yes. Impossible? No."

Flipping through contents of the safe, Dunning muttered some obscenities under his breath that Kal could not fully hear.

"Let's see here. Yes, here it is. I kept the important documents in the back. This is a copy of that letter Sherman wrote to his generals in the event of his demise, complete with orders," he said, handing over a photocopy.

"How do we know it's authentic?" Kal asked, quickly scanning the letter which was dated 11-28-64 and was indeed signed by a William T. Sherman.

"Ashworth has the original, which he carbon-dated. He also matched handwriting samples to confirm Sherman was, in fact, its author."

Dunning held another piece of paper up in the air. "But that has nothing on what I am holding here. What do you know about Civil War cryptology?"

"What do you mean?" Kal asked.

"Codes, Kal. Codes," Dunning said.

"Oh . . . I know the Civil War is considered the first modern war because the mobile telegraph was used in battle. It changed the way future wars were fought, showing communications were just as important as anything else. Commanders could receive instructions direct from Washington and reply back. Didn't you teach us that Lincoln himself used to spend a lot of time in the telegraph room of the War Department, monitoring the progress of the fighting?"

"Exactly," Dunning said. "The problem was telegraph lines were easy to tap back then. Both sides were listening to each other constantly, so both the Union and Confederacy devised ciphers to send messages. The Confederates' system was a simple code called a Vigenère—basically a series of alternating and corresponding alphabets. A keyword in the telegram would signal how to read a Confederate Cipher Key, and the operator would proceed with that knowledge. To the layman, a Cipher Key would resemble some sort of decoder toy a kid might dig from a box of cereal."

Dunning grabbed a piece of paper off his desk and quickly jotted down some words. "For instance, the Confederates would send a telegram that might look like this."

*VTCTGPA, the JCXDC will
be at GXKTG by IJTHSPN.*

"The operator would then use a code word to correspond the letters in the Vigenère and spell the words out so it read, 'GENERAL, the UNION will be at the RIVER by TUESDAY.' This system had several advantages—it didn't require a code book, it was easily memorized, and the only information the sender and receiver needed was the code word telling the receiver where to start in the alphabet. Unfortunately for them, it didn't take the Union long to figure out. They cracked it almost immediately."

Dunning quickly scanned his wall of books until he found a hardback and tossed it on the desk.

"Have you ever read Kahn's work on codebreaking?"

Kal looked at the cover and shook his head.

*The Codebreakers: The Story of Secret Writing.*

"David Kahn wrote the Confederacy relied upon three keywords exclusively, 'Manchester Bluff', 'Complete Victory' and a third that escapes me at the moment. Because of this, the Union found and decoded the messages routinely. On the other hand, the Union's cipher was never—I repeat—never cracked by the South during the war."

"What did they use?"

"They deployed a complex system developed by a civilian, Anson Stager."

Kal immediately slapped his forehead—he remembered hearing the name, meaning he should have known about it before asking the question. He had always been a fan of solving puzzles, Sudoku specifically, and this type of stuff was right up his alley.

"Stager basically employed a route and transfer system that rearranged words in a message so the whole text looked like a nonsensical sentence. Unlike the Confederate system, the reader could understand each word, only couldn't make sense of the message if they tried to read it normally. He also employed code words in the message, as well as language that meant absolutely nothing, which made it much harder for the South to understand. The only way for a person to break the cipher was to have a codebook."

"Friggen Hillbillies."

Dunning stopped talking and just stared at Kal, who immediately apologized.

"Sorry, Professor. Just making a joke."

If there was one thing Dunning hated, it was stereotypes, regardless of the target—white, black, brown, or green. It didn't matter if it was directed at his own family or a group of people who considered his race inferior, he felt stereotypes to be the biggest symptom fueling racial problems in America.

"Whatever the reason, Kal," he said, hardly missing a beat. "They were unable to understand how the Union cipher worked. I've read accounts in which the South even reprinted captured transmissions in their newspapers, advertising rewards to civilians if they could crack the North's code. But it never happened. Which leads me to this."

Dunning handed Kal the piece of paper he had been holding up in the air.

Major LeBay,
WINTER VENUS AS LOCATED SAGINAW
WAFER PLEASE AND SAMVFOUR GOLD
ARRIVE WILL WHERE IS EAGLE NELLIE
BLACK WAS WAYLAND PLUTO
WHARTON WILL WHARTON OUR SAFELY
THIRD ACROSS OF PLANTATION UNDER
ANOTHER WALDEN AND A GROUND JOSEPH
BANTERLY HEADING HOLT ON ARE
RAMSEY WAS RESIDENCE ADVISE

"What is it?" Kal asked, puzzled by the gibberish.

"It's one of Sherman's personal telegraphs."

"Don't tell me your guy magically found it at some garage sale?" Kal asked.

"No. The War Department kept every raw, untranscribed telegraphed message they could get their hands on during the Civil War and later boxed the entire collection into storage in Washington. The government then systematically categorized, photographed, and documented the messages sometime during the 1980s, placing them in a computer database with its own mainframe so they could be accessed easily for historical purposes. It's amazing really, but almost entirely unknown to the public. Ashworth has a contact in the State Department with access to it. By setting the database parameters to search for a telegraph originated from Sherman during the time frame when the statue was last seen, and cross referencing it with the words Eagle/Freedom/Statue/Gold and Macon, as well as other known code words, his man came up with three hits. We ruled two out by investigation. This third telegraph in your hand is another story, however. It seems to be an accidental message. Unlike the other telegraphs, the War Department is not certain whom it was sent to—they have no record of a LeBay, the name at the top. But it holds every key word we were looking for and was sent around the time Sherman could have been in Macon. I believe this is the evidence we are searching for that will tell us where to locate the Freedom Eagle, or at least put us on the right track to finding it."

Kal continued to examine the letter, which still appeared to be just a paragraph of gibberish. Although, the word "GOLD" did jump out at him.

"Why don't you just crack it, or take it to someone else to do it?" he asked.

"And therein lies the problem, Kal. We have tried. We've used all of Stager's known cipher systems and have had no luck. It's as if Sherman used his own custom version. It shares a lot of the characteristics with Stager's classic Ciphers 9 and 12, but it's missing something. We also don't have a complete list of all of the known arbitrary codewords for that time, which is a major factor. In order to decipher that message, we need to get our hands on a Union codebook, of which there is only one in existence—but it is not available to the public. And there is no one I would trust with this letter, since we came by it through less than official channels. The only viable option I can think of is to try and crack it through trial and error. That is one of the reasons Ashworth approached me in the first place. It's a process that could take days, months, or even years, and that's why I need your help."

"Wow," Kal said, shaking his head.

"I know, I know," Dunning replied, looking up at the clock on the wall. "It's a lot of info to process in one short evening. Why don't we call it a night? We'll talk sometime later this week. You're not working for me tomorrow, right?"

"No, tomorrow's my day off."

"Well, rest up. It's going to get very busy the next few weeks."

# CHAPTER 10

**November 13, 2008 7:00 p.m.**

"**M**ore, please! More!"

Kal grabbed the glass from his captor and chugged the water again, hardly concerned that the tap it was coming from looked as though it housed a million different strains of mold and bacteria. He hadn't realized how thirsty he was until he held the bag of ice to his head and felt the beads of sweat and water combine and roll down his forehead, hitting his lips and evaporating in the pink desert currently posing as his mouth. The water overflowed Kal's face as he chugged, spilling down his sweatshirt, but he didn't care. Every time he finished drinking, the thirst just grew stronger.

"Slow down, Kalei. I don't want to take you to the bathroom again," the man said, his face fully revealed in the well-lit kitchen of the abandoned house, the power generator humming outside.

In his late-thirties, the man appeared to be the leader of whoever was holding Kal captive. He counted at least four different armed guards performing perfunctory tasks when he was led from the back room to the kitchen—all dressed in paramilitary gear, complete with big guns and bigger scowls.

"Come sit down, Kalei. I've got something I want to show you," the man said, his shouldered pistol holder obvious, complete with what appeared to be a vintage handgun.

Kal settled with a wince in the chair alongside the table in the middle of the room.

"It's just Kal. What's your name?" he asked.

"Excuse me?"

"What's your name? You apparently know mine, I just wanted to know yours."

The man turned and smirked at one of his men.

"You're right. I'm sorry, how rude of me. My name is Marcus."

"Marcus. No last name?"

"No, just Marcus," he said, waving his hand to the guard, who quickly strode out.

"Now, about that item I wanted to show you. I think you're going to be very surprised."

The words barely left his mouth when T.A. Dunning flew through the doorway, landing on all fours in front of Kal.

"Professor!"

Dunning looked up at Kal and weakly smiled, his face badly bruised and cut.

"I'm so sorry to involve you, Kal. I had no other choice. They have Lily," his voice wavered as he put his head back down and looked to the ground, his clothes tattered and bloody.

"I believe you two know each other," Marcus said, smiling wide enough to show the gums surrounding his porcelain white teeth.

Kal raised out of the chair to get to Dunning before a pair of strong hands slammed him back down.

"He'll be fine. It's amazing the amount of punishment the human body can absorb, isn't it? These boys of African descent seem to be able take more than your average Joe."

The last comment sent Kal scanning the tattooed forearm of one of the closest guards until one symbol in particular jumped out at him—a swastika interlocked with a skull and bones.

"Let me formally introduce my colleagues," continued Marcus. "I represent a group of well-established businessmen here in the South who privately banded together because of similar interests and backgrounds. Because some of those interests are—how shall I say?—less than politically correct in this day and age, these men are forced to retain a modicum of discretion when dealing with certain matters. Decades ago these men wouldn't cloak their true ideologies, but due to today's disintegration of our culture, even the once sacred South has changed from the beautiful place these men, and I, grew up to love."

Marcus stood up and paced as he spoke.

"This group is well connected with an unlimited reserve of funds, and therefore hired my services on a full-time basis to make sure their goals and objectives, which on occasion are dealt with behind the scenes, are accomplished in a timely, and once again, discrete manner."

"What the hell does any of that have to do with me?"

"Patience, Kalei . . . or Kal. Patience. I'm getting there," Marcus said.

"This particular group of men is interested in preserving the history and values of the original 11 southern states of the Confederacy, which they feel have been oppressed and treated like red-headed, stepchildren by Northern Zionists and their mindless followers even prior to the Civil War.

"Through subversive means, occasionally using force," he continued, nodding to Dunning. "My associates and I, who share common ideologies with these men, sometimes in one particular area more than another, actively work toward keeping the creed of the true South alive and well."

"You mean through violence?" Kal asked.

Marcus stood up, marched to one of the burly guards and barked out a command in German, prompting the man to snap to attention.

"Yes, as I mentioned, in some instances my men are more enthusiastic about certain aspects of the Confederacy than others."

Marcus yelled another command, eliciting a smile from the guard as he walked over to Dunning, who was lying silently on the ground. Without uttering a word the guard reared back and gave a swift kick to Dunning's stomach with his steel-toed boot.

"Stop!" Kal said, raising his arms. "You've already done enough to him."

The guard pulled Dunning up by his ear and dragged him out of the room as Marcus settled back into his chair.

"Now listen, Kal, I don't want to use the same level of force on you as your Negro friend there. I've held off for now because you come from good Aryan stock, and I would hate to do something unnecessary. I'll be honest, I was concerned for awhile with a name like Kalei, until I researched your background and found out your parents lived in Hawaii when you were born and decided to give you a forename with some island flavor. Disgusting and offensive to our race in my opinion, but your blood is pure, so I will do everything in my power to keep you un-harmed. I just need your cooperation. I need you to lead me to L'Aigle de la Liberté."

# CHAPTER 11

Kal helped Dunning, who had been lying face down on the floor of the bedroom, up on to the bed and handed him a wet cloth, examining the bruises on the side of his chest. It appeared he was beaten more by the guard after getting dragged out of the kitchen.

"I'm so sorry, Kal," he whispered. "They killed her and Fred right in front of me. Told me Lily would be next if I didn't help them. I knew you would be strong enough to involve."

"Do you know where they are holding Lily? Is she here?"

"I have no idea. The truth is, I would rather they kill me, too, if it wasn't for the sake of that little girl. I'm the only thing she has, Kal. We have to do what they ask of us."

"I know. My friends were close by when I got kidnapped, hope-fully they were able to see something and call the police."

"No. No police! Don't you understand? They'll kill her. They'll do it right in front of me, just like they did with Lillian, I-I won't be able to take it," he said, before breaking down and sobbing.

Kal could feel his stomach churn.

"It's okay, it's okay," he said, gently patting Dunning's back.

He could hardly believe this was the same man he worked for. The tough exterior the professor exuded inside the classroom was stripped bare—the man had been reduced to a bubbling mass of wounded flesh and muscle with some tears thrown in for good measure.

Dunning stopped crying and sat upright. "I'm sorry. Listen I've got to control my emotions and we've got to do what they ask. It's our only option. What did they want from you?"

"They want me to find the Eagle, which I'm not convinced is possible. Honestly, sir, I'm still not 100 percent sure it exists. I played dumb and they threw me in here with you. Told me to take a look at you and think about it."

"It exists, Kal. You need to believe that or else we have no prospects of finding it. I need you to find the faith."

"Why should we help them?"

"It's our only option at this point. Dammit, son. I need you to trust me. You're privy to intimate knowledge of my work and will have to perform the legwork crucial to our plan. My face is probably plastered on every television screen in the city right now, and I can't go out in public, or the police will grab me. That's why I led them to you."

Kal's face dropped as he realized what Dunning was implying.

"I'm sorry. I had to do it, I had to. They would have eventually come after you because you knew too much. However convoluted it appears, I did this to protect you. I made them swear to not hurt you!"

For some reason Kal did not believe these men could be held accountable by simple promises.

"Let's just do what we need to and forget it. What's done is done."

"Kal, I need you to know I am sorry. Just please acknowledge that."

"Fine, fine," he responded, quickly changing the subject. There was no point in faulting anyone at the moment. "What do you need me to do?"

"This is not going to be easy, but . . . " Dunning took a deep breath before blurting out the next sentence. " . . . I need you to break into my house and steal those files I showed you last night."

Kal's jaw dropped. "What? That place is crawling with cops. I'll be arrested for sure, not to mention it'll look suspicious returning to a murder scene where I was one of the last people to see the vict—"

He could see the hurt in Dunning's eyes, the reminder of his wife's death less than 24 hours earlier cutting him to the core.

"Sorry."

"Just stop. I can't think about it right now," Dunning said. "I've got to put all that away, lock up those emotions."

He took a deep breath and winced, grabbing at his ribs. "That file has all of my information and notes, plus the contact info for the man I told you about with the State Department connection: Ashworth. We need to get in touch with him, he's the only one who can help us. He has a wealth of information we need.

"I—" Dunning said, catching himself. "We must have it."

"Are these guys going to let one of us just go get it? Why would they?"

"Because they want this as badly as we do. And this is the only way they're going to be successful."

Kal couldn't believe what he was agreeing to. "I hope you hid an extra house key somewhere, because I'm no good at picking locks."

****

Dunning had finally fallen asleep on the bed, collapsing from sheer exhaustion, leaving Kal alone in the room with his thoughts.

*How is this going to end?*

*I can't simply escape and go to the police, they'll kill Lily. Judging by what these guys did to Mrs. Dunning, if we don't find what they want, they'll do the same to us.*

*How can I contact the authorities without them knowing?*

Kal pushed himself up off the ground and went to the window, which was blackened on the outside with paint. He could hear the pitter-patter of rain gently falling against the pane of glass as he tapped along with his finger. The hum of the generator outside combined with the downfall to create a steady and entrancing rhythmic beat, and he closed his eyes to try and match the tone, resting his battered head on the sill.

"Kal?"

He heard the sound of his mother's gentle voice call his name, faintly at first, until he was suddenly back in his upstairs bedroom in Colorado.

"Kal? What's the matter, honey?" she asked, her face coming into focus.

He didn't respond immediately, but rather looked at her in the doorway as she gazed back with a worried expression. Her skin was perfect, her hair smooth and shiny. There was a hazy glow to her silhouette, as if she weren't fully there.

"Not sure what to do mom, I'm scared," he finally said, although his lips never moved. She walked into the room and sat down on the edge of the bed next to him.

"Oh, honey. Don't be frightened," she said, sweeping his bangs back. "Things will work out, they always do. You just need faith. You were always my little worrier."

Kal smiled. His mother's touch sent chills down his spine, and the smell of her perfume warmed his heart.

"How do I know I'll make the right decisions?"

His mother smiled. "Go with your heart, Kal. I know I've raised you the right way and you'll make the best choices in your life. Believe you're doing the right thing. Things will get tough, honey. But you have to persevere, no taking the easy way out."

He sighed and looked around his room.

"I miss you, mom. I miss you a lot. So does dad."

"I know," she said, kissing him on the cheek. "Now close your eyes and rest, everything will be alright. I promise."

Kal got under the sheets of his bed and took one last look at his mother before shutting his eyes and falling back under the trance of the rain. When he opened them he was back in Atlanta with Dunning, who was now lightly snoring.

He tried to focus back on the situation at hand, but his heart was heavy.

*If we help them, I'm going to need Dunning's files from his house. I'm the only one besides him who knows where the safe is and how to access it. If I can somehow convince them to let me go alone, maybe I can alert someone?*

Kal adjusted his back just as a key rattled in the lock and the door swung open, startling Dunning out of sleep. A blonde guard stepped inside and immediately moved to the right, allowing the trailing Marcus to enter.

"So, have you two decided which course of action you'd like to take?"

Kal nodded. "We'll do it. We'll help you find it."

"Excellent!" Marcus said with a smug look. "I knew you were a smart boy."

"Before we do anything, though, I need to go back to Dr. Dunning's house and retrieve all of his research. It's locked in a safe in his office."

Marcus smiled. "Fine. Why don't you and the good doctor come into the kitchen and we can discuss the logistics of our newly-founded partnership? Perhaps we can get you a bite to eat?"

\*\*\*\*

Dunning weakly lifted the spoonful of chicken noodle soup to his mouth and drank the warm broth. They were once again sitting at the same table in which Marcus and Kal first formally met.

"So you think I should just allow you to leave, trusting you to enter the professor's home and get these documents without alerting anyone to your situation? You see, we have to reach some sort of understanding in which I feel I can rely on you," Marcus said. "I would prefer sending my men to obtain the information by force, but on the other hand, I do understand the need for discretion as well. We don't need any dead police officers or destroyed property drawing attention to what we're trying to accomplish."

"You are holding Dr. Dunning and Lily. As long as you have them I'll do whatever you say. I swear I wouldn't do anything to put them in harm's way."

"Perhaps. But I need something . . . something more to ease my admitted neuroticism. As you can probably understand, in my line of work, it doesn't pay to blindly trust without some collateral."

Marcus rested his chin on his hand and looked around the room. "You know what? I know how to make myself feel better about this."

He turned to one of the guards and snapped his fingers, pointing to the garage. "I think this will probably give you an added incentive to work with us in good faith."

Kal looked to the door. The last time Marcus surprised him a beaten Dunning came flying through. This time Elle and Benny were led into the room, their hands bound behind their backs and eyes blindfolded.

"Elle!"

"Kal!" she responded, her head turning toward the sound of his voice. "Kal, is that you?"

Benny was noticeably silent with his chin down and crusted blood around his mouth.

"It's gonna be okay, guys!" Kal said, turning to Marcus. "They haven't done anything. Let them go!"

"Oh, I beg to differ . . . I believe the good doctor told you to come alone earlier tonight. Instead, you chose to involve your friends by having them wait outside the store for you. They are now just as much a part of this as you and him."

The familiar urge to flee rather than fight overcame him, only there was no place to run to. The situation was deteriorating by the second, and the well-being of his best friend was now jeopardized. "I swear," he said. "Please just leave them alone. I'll do whatever you want."

"I know," Marcus said. "I know you'll do whatever I say. That's why I'm allowing you to get those files on your own."

# CHAPTER 12

The van stopped a few blocks short of the Dunning home, allowing Kal to jump out on the run and adjust the small headset in his ear, which crackled to life.

"Remember, there is a single squad car parked in front of the residence. Your best bet is to go through the alley in the back and hop the fence."

"Okay. Do you know if the cop has been going inside at all?" he responded.

"Don't know. We'll meet you outside the alley after you retrieve the information."

Kal pulled the hood of his sweatshirt over his head and started slowly walking in the direction of the house. His mind was fully focused on Elle, and to a lesser extent, Benny. His only hope of escaping had been based on those two calling the authorities after his abduction, but now things were complicated substantially. He had absolutely no choice but to play by Marcus' rules—the lives of not two, but four other people depended on it. There would be no contacting anyone. No leaving a note or message at the house to alert someone. It was too risky.

Kal turned down the alley intersecting the Dunning's block

and counted the houses until he reached his target. Careful no one was watching, he hoisted himself up over the fence and into the Dunning's backyard. The house was dark inside, but the landscaping lights in the garden were on thanks to a timer, giving Kal a direct line of sight to the elevated wood deck running to the back door.

*Third rock from the lawn gnome, looks like a turtle. Should be a spare key underneath.*

Kal replayed Dunning's directions in his head as he counted the rocks twice to make sure.

*That rock doesn't look like a turtle, it looks more like . . . like nothing.* Sure enough, there was a key underneath the boulder wrapped in a plastic baggie, right where Dunning said it would be.

Kal crept to the back door and peered in, making sure the place was indeed vacant. He could see clear down the main hallway through the middle of the house to the security panel by the front entryway— the red light was blinking, meaning the alarm was set and active.

*Another obstacle, although not impossible to overcome.*

Because he was required on occasion to visit the house when no one was home, Kal had the code memorized. It was a matter of trekking to the front in the dark and punching it in within the allotted 60 seconds before the alarm triggered.

He took a deep breath, counted to 10, then slid the key in the lock and opened the door, quickly stepping inside and closing it behind him. He turned on the mini flashlight Marcus' men provided and made his way through the kitchen and down the hallway, stepping around the bench and coat rack separating the corridor from the foyer. Once he was to the front of the house, Kal looked out the peephole to make sure the cop was still in his car.

*Check, on to the alarm system.*

Kal played out the sequence in his head. *The code is 69760, then #.* He opened the panel face and punched the numbers in carefully.

UNAUTHORIZED PASSWORD, PLEASE TRY AGAIN

*What? I must have hit it wrong. It's okay, I have two more chances.*

Kal slowly re-entered the same code, realizing he probably only had about 35 seconds before the alarm was activated.

UNAUTHORIZED PASSWORD, PLEASE TRY AGAIN

*What the hell? It's always been 69760#! Did Dr. Dunning change it for some reason?*

"Is the alarm deactivated yet?" his captors radioed.

"Working on it."

Kal started to panic—he only had about 20 seconds now to figure the new code before the security company started the process of alerting the authorities. If that happened, he would be forced to make a mad dash into Dunning's office, open the safe, grab everything he needed and get out before the police officer walked the 20 feet from his patrol car to the entry way. The probability of that happening successfully without getting caught was not high—he needed to remember the code.

Kal racked his brain and suddenly recalled the professor mentioning the alarm system getting an overhaul a few weeks earlier.

*That's right, he said he had to change the code to—damn, what was it? It was something about the date he considered the biggest event of the Civil War.*

In all the confusion back at the house, Kal forgot one of the most important details.

*It's too late to radio the van to get the code from Dunning.*

*Was it the day Robert E. Lee signed the Confederate surrender at Appomattox? Or the day the Emancipation Proclamation was delivered?*

As he went to punch in the date of Lee's surrender, the answer came to him with the subtlety of a sledgehammer.

Kal suddenly knew exactly what the code was.

$$0 - 4 - 1 - 5 - 6 - 5$$

The alarm system beeped three times as Kal held his breath.

PASSWORD CONFIRMED, Thank you.

He pumped his fist in the air and leaned against the wall, covered in sweat. Dr. Dunning considered the most defining moment of the Civil War an incident that did not actually occur until after Lee and the South surrendered: the death of President Abraham Lincoln on April 15, 1865.

## 04 15 65

He was rattled, but in good shape. The police officer was still in his car and the alarm was down.

Kal walked to the back of the house, passing the stairwell where it seemed days ago Lillian Dunning had been brought down in a body bag. In reality, it was only hours earlier. "I'm heading to the office now, the alarm is taken care of," Kal said to the van, carefully moving through the kitchen and turning down another small hallway toward the office, the door still open.

He shined his flashlight into the room causing the paintings on the walls to morph into ghostly apparitions, the dark wood soaking in the ray from the little light. Kal could still smell the aroma of the cigars from the previous night, and oddly enough, taste the Scotch in the back of his throat.

He moved to the oil-painted canvas of Lincoln and reached around the lower, left corner, releasing the hook that kept it fastened. Swinging the painting on its hinges revealed a Gardall SL4000FE model safe, one of several Dunning concealed in the house.

Kal punched in the code and waited several seconds before pulling the lever.

This time there was no drama—the safe opened easily, exposing all of Dunning's research on the Freedom Eagle. Kal put the flashlight in his mouth and quickly scanned through the pile of folders, shoving them into his backpack as he read to make sure he had everything. Wasting as little time as possible, he zipped up and started to close the safe when a sound from the front of the house made him pause.

*What the hell was that?*

Kal strained to listen for a few seconds and heard the bang

again. He slowly inched his way to the door of the office and peeked down the hallway out into the kitchen.

*Nothing there.*

Creeping out of the office, Kal made it barely halfway down the short corridor before freezing at the sight of a light cutting through the cooking area.

He almost hyperventilated as he spun around and tip-toed his way back to Dunning's office, quietly closing the door behind him. A walkie-talkie squelched and echoed throughout the empty residence, confirming Kal's only escape route was blocked—the police officer was in the kitchen, the room in which Kal had to go through to get to the back door.

"Dispatch, this is 214. I'm in the rear of the house now, it appears the back door was unlocked—not sure if it was locked previously. I don't see any sign of anyone in here, though. What exactly did the neighbor say they witnessed?"

*Dammit! Someone saw me.*

Kal leaned against the door and looked around to find a possible hiding place.

"A flashlight in the kitchen? Alright, I'm headed to the back of the house and then upstairs. Can you find out if the detectives or CSI had the security company arm the alarm before they left, because it was deactivated."

Kal ran his fingers through his drenched hair, figuring he had a few moments before the officer came in and arrested him. He ran to the lone closet in the room and yanked it open, only to find it piled to the ceiling with boxes and files.

*What excuse can I use to get out of this?*

*Working on a research project and had to get into the office . . .*

*Forgot cell phone and was forced to break in to get it . . .*

Even if he was able to miraculously talk his way out of the situation, his mind raced ahead and knew his captors would surmise he was conversing with a police officer and immediately cover their asses by killing everyone back at the house.

Almost as if on key, the men in the van began calling. "Kal, the cop is on the move and is in the house, get out immediately! Kal?"

He could hear the officer walking down the short hallway now, only a few paces from the door. Kal frantically looked around the room one more time.

*The desk!*

The opening under Dr. Dunning's big oak desk was his last resort and he practically dove into the small space, pulling the chair behind him just as the officer stepped in. He was now fully entombed.

"Whoa, nice office," the officer said out loud, scanning the room and taking a few steps before walking over to the mini-bar and clanking through Dunning's collection.

*Please do not have a drink.*

"Kal, you copy? Respond," crackled his earpiece.

He could hear the officer stop dead as he frantically grabbed for the volume button. Even though the earpiece was small, in the silence of the abandoned house the officer heard the muffled noise and was now coming to expose his hiding spot.

# CHAPTER 13

This was the worst part of being a peace officer: security detail.

While on most occasions the sophomore member of the Atlanta Police Department would welcome sitting in his patrol car and catching up on paperwork, he was in a mood to cruise the city, not babysit an empty crime scene.

"Unit 214, are you still on scene at 694 Penn Ave NE? One of the neighbors just reported seeing a suspicious light in the residence."

He perked up immediately.

"This is 214. I'm still on scene, looking at the residence now. I don't see anything, but will enter and check it out."

"Copy 214," the radio responded as he got out of the car. It felt good to stretch his legs and get some brisk southern air into his lungs.

He walked up the pathway to the residence of Dr. T.A. Dunning, whose wife was murdered almost a day earlier in an upstairs bedroom, and shined his light though the glass pane next to the front door, noticing the alarm was deactivated.

*Strange, I thought dispatch told me the alarm was on?*

He made his way into the house and checked each of the front rooms with one hand resting loosely on his sidearm—the place was vacant.

*God, murder scenes give me the creeps. Feels like a haunted house.*

The officer entered the kitchen and made a straight line to the back to make sure everything was locked up.

Only it wasn't.

"Dispatch, this is 214. I'm in the rear of the house now, it appears the back door was unlocked—not sure if it was locked previously. I don't see any sign of anyone in here, though. What exactly did the neighbor say they witnessed?"

"Copy Unit 214. The neighbor says she saw what appeared to be a flashlight moving around the kitchen about five minutes ago."

"A flashlight in the kitchen? Alright, I'm headed to the back of the house and then upstairs. Can you find out if the detectives or CSI had the security company arm the alarm before they left, because it was deactivated."

The officer could smell the cigar aroma waft down the hall as he walked to the last room on the floor. He didn't particularly like cigars, but the smell brought back favorable memories of his grandfather's pipe.

Everything in the office appeared to be in order at first glance, a small library in its own right, nothing extraordinary. But when his flashlight caught the bar in the corner of the room, his heart fluttered. The officer was in the process of building his own at home for his wife's cocktail parties, and he loved gleaning ideas from others' alcohol stands.

*Not too shabby. Has a nice collection. Macallan, Johnny Walker Blue. Reminds me, I have to pick up some grenadine after my shift.*

The officer put down a bottle of Scotch and headed out to finish his sweep when a peculiar noise caught his attention. He quickly turned to the desk and shined his light on the oak monstrosity, figuring it was just a misplaced cell phone or an alarm clock buzzing. He waited a few seconds, listening intently before walking over to investigate.

The owner had a lot of junk strewn all over the top of it—papers, books, colored pens—but a giant gold coin encased in glass drew the officer's interest, causing him to temporarily forget the noise. He walked to the back of the desk, pulled out the chair and plopped down to carefully examine the antique further, suddenly aware the entire room was filled with similar items.

*Some guy in fancy digs on a horse, another guy on a horse—*

The officer froze when he came to the third canvas, which was pulled halfway off the wall, an opened safe behind it. Alarm bells went off in his head.

"What the hell?" he said out loud.

The officer immediately dropped his feet off the desk and grabbed for his radio, but before he could utter a word, a cacophony from the front of the house startled him, nearly causing him to topple out of the chair.

*Bzzzzz*
*Bzzzzzz*
*Bzzzzzzzzz*

He jumped up and quickly darted through the hallway and kitchen tracking the sound, temporarily forgetting the safe.

*Bzzzzz*
*Bzzzzzzzzz*

He recognized as he ran that someone was pushing the doorbell trying to get in. Moving as fast as he could without knocking furniture over, he unholstered his weapon and braced himself, slowly opening the front door.

Only no one was there.

He stepped outside and looked around, positive the doorbell just rang. But he was by himself, save his unattended patrol car in the street. The officer shuffled back inside and slowly made his way through all of the downstairs rooms, checking each thoroughly by flipping on the overhead light. He crept down the hall into the kitchen, his adrenaline and heartbeat slowly restoring to normal with the realization he had probably been the victim of a simple doorbell ditch, only to have them jolted back to heightened levels. The back door, which he personally re-locked moments ago, was wide open and slowly swaying back and forth with the outside breeze.

Someone just came through it.

\*\*\*\*

Kal ran down the alley screaming into his radio.

"I'm coming! The cop is on me!"

The van roared to life as Kal exited onto the street and jumped into the moving vehicle. Two of Marcus' men helped him in and he threw the backpack to the floor, gasping for a breath.

"What happened, my friend? We were about to write you off," the driver said, looking back as he weaved through the streets of mid-town Atlanta, leaving Dunning's neighborhood behind.

Kal shook his head and stared at the roof of the vehicle.

"Someone must have seen me or something . . . the cop came inside . . . I hid in the office."

The men all laughed.

"Did you kill him?" the driver asked in a sarcastic tone, eliciting another round of snorts.

"No, I was under the desk and he was inches from me—I think he was about to step on me, but I remembered Dr. Dunning has a buzzer under his desk that unlocks the front door for times when he doesn't want to get up and let someone in. I buzzed it and when the cop took off to check it out I ran out the back door."

This, for some reason, made the men laugh even louder as the van turned onto the freeway onramp, passing a police cruiser heading the opposite direction with its lights and sirens blaring.

Kal reached into his pocket and felt around for his trusty and al-ways present iPod, placing the buds into his ears. He leaned back against the side of the van and closed his eyes as one of the guards placed the blindfold over him, the same one he was forced to wear on the ride over. Kal had been trying to place the driver's face and it now came to him in the pitch black: he was the homeless man who knocked him out behind the Citgo station.

The soulful melody of RadioHead's *Reckoner* queued up, helping Kal shut out reality. There were times when he loved thinking of his life as a piece of cinema playing out on an imaginary big screen in some bizarro universe, millions of viewers watching his every move, accompanied by some of his favorite songs—a soundtrack to his existence. This was one of them.

# CHAPTER 14

Elle wiped the dried blood from the corner of Benny's mouth.

He had been noticeably silent since hearing Kal's voice in the other room.

"What's the matter, Ben?" she asked as she moved over to check on the older black man lying on the bed. They had just been escorted into his room, and he appeared to be badly beaten. She assumed it was T.A. Dunning, although his face now hardly resembled the one she saw on the television earlier in the day.

"He didn't listen to you," Benny said, barely audible. "And I was a fool for siding with him."

"What?"

"He didn't listen. You told him to go to the police, but he didn't. I only agreed with him because I thought that's what you wanted. But he chose him over you," he said, motioning to Dunning.

"Oh, Benny," Elle said, turning back. "He tried to do what was right. He didn't know this would happen to us. If he had any inkling, he would not have put us in harm's way. You know that."

He just shook his head and looked away. "Is there any time when he doesn't do anything right in your eyes?"

Elle could see the anger and felt guilty for making excuses for Kal once again. No matter how hard she tried to mesh her former and current boyfriends it never seemed to work, and not for a lack of trying on Benny's part. Now Kal had been reckless with not only his own safety but theirs as well. She hoped bringing Benny along would have helped convince Kal to go to the authorities in the first place, but it instead backfired in the worst way imaginable, and she was left making excuses for him . . . again.

Plus, her head ached from getting smacked around.

Benny sat back down on the floor and messed with his shoes as Elle continued to dote on Dunning, who was waking out of his deep sleep.

"Kal? Where is Kal?" he mumbled, looking around the room and at his watch.

"He's gone right now, we don't know where he is," Elle answered.

"Is my watch right? Is it really midnight?" he asked, gingerly raising himself up. "He better return soon. I hope nothing happened to him while getting my files. You're his friends they captured?"

"Yes. My name is Elle, and this is my boyfriend Benny."

Dunning angrily looked them over. "Why did you come with him? I told him to show up alone."

Elle broke into a smile and glanced at Benny, who was shooting death stares at the professor. "Kal and I have been through a lot together Dr. Dunning. We couldn't, or wouldn't, let him try this without helping in some way."

Dunning shook his head in disapproval.

"Look what's happened, though. The two of you are now captive and your lives are in danger. I wish that boy would have listened to me."

"That makes two of us," Benny said.

Dunning studied the young man before responding.

"Listen, son, I know you're probably angry about being in this situation, as am I—"

"You don't know anything about what I'm feeling. As far as I'm concerned, you're to blame for this entire mess. Why didn't you just turn yourself in? Instead, you fooled Kal, who unnecessarily roped the both of us into this."

"Benny!" Elle said, shocked by his outburst. She had never seen him so irate—he was nearly shaking.

"It's okay," said Dunning, taking a second to collect his thoughts. "He's right. He's absolutely right."

Elle gave Benny a stern look and turned back to the professor.

"I'm sorry, he's not really himself right now."

"No, young lady. He has nothing to apologize for. Your involvement in this situation is entirely my fault. I should have known Kal would have people that care for him and wouldn't let him run willy-nilly into dangerous circumstances. The fact of the matter is that I had no other choice. These men killed my wife and have my granddaughter held hostage somewhere. I don't even know if she's still alive, truth be told. Because of this I panicked, and unfortunately, the only way I thought I could save her was to contact Kal."

Elle was taken aback by the frankness of his response, which also wiped the scowl off Benny's face.

"I want to assure the both of you I will do everything I can to make sure you get out of this alive. In fact, I already know how this episode will end, and though it's a bit more complicated with your involvement, you will all be fine," Dunning said cryptically, leaning back on the bed with his hands behind his head.

Elle sat down next to Benny and wrapped her arms around him. Kal couldn't get back to the house soon enough.

# CHAPTER 15

"So, Mr. Boyce, did you retrieve the items you needed?"

"I'm pretty sure I got everything."

"Good," Marcus said. "Then you and Dr. Dunning should be able to continue your work, which the professor indicated he made significant headway on recently. I was told you had some trouble at the house. Nearly caused an incident requiring my men to become involved?"

Kal nodded sheepishly.

"I think we'll need to be more careful from here on out to preserve the integrity of our operation. That will be the last time you will be left out of the sight of my men. Now get to work."

Kal decided to push the envelope. "We need a computer."

Marcus started laughing. "Really? I can't believe you would have the balls to even think of asking me."

"Listen," Kal said. "There is no way for us to find this thing if we can't research. There are people we have to contact on the outside who specialize in certain aspects of this subject material. We'd almost be blind without their help."

Marcus motioned to one of the guards, who gruffly picked Kal up by the shoulder and led him back to the room he originally woke up in upon his initial arrival to the house.

"The Major is considering your request," said the guard before locking the door.

Buoyed by his minor victory, Kal immediately began pulling the files out of the backpack and spreading them out on the floor. He had momentarily entertained the thought of trying to smuggle some sort of object at the house to use as a weapon, but ruled against it, which proved to be a prudent move when his belongings and person were thoroughly searched in the van on the ride back—twice.

He managed to lay everything out neatly and started leafing through each folder when the door jostled back open.

"You got company," said the guard, herding in Elle and a hobbled Dunning with the aid of Benny, slamming the door behind them.

"Guys!"

"Kal," Elle said, grabbing and nearly squeezing the breath out of him as if it had been years since they last saw each other. For a brief moment he forgot their circumstances.

"I'm so glad you're back. Are you okay?"

"I'm fine," Kal said as Benny helped Dunning ease down into a seated position against the wall.

"Were you able to get the files?" the older man asked, already looking better than the last time they spoke.

"Yes, but it was a really close call. It's a long story. I'll tell you later. I think we should get started."

"Good boy. Hand me the file that reads 'Macon.' Benny and Elle, dig in. We could use your eyes as well. Let's try and figure out where this blasted thing is."

\*\*\*\*

Kal woke up with a pile of papers lying all over his chest. They had been reading material for hours, asking questions and bouncing ideas off each other—until the sandman came calling.

Dunning was asleep again as well, snoring loudly between pained breaths, and Elle was curled up in a little ball next to Benny, who was wide awake staring at Kal.

"Benny, what's up? Did you guys fall asleep, too?"

Nothing but silence.

"Benny?"

Benny continued to look at Kal with a blank stare.

"You're not even going to apologize to her, are you?" he finally offered.

"For what?" Kal asked, although he had a pretty good idea what Benny was talking about.

"She told you to go to the police, she told you not to get involved, and now look at where we are. What the hell else would I be talking about?" Benny said in a somewhat hushed yell to get his point across without waking the others.

"You know I didn't want any of this to happen, you agreed I should call him."

"We shouldn't have even been anywhere near that gas station. We should have been sitting at home watching Dunning get arrested on TV. The only reason I sided with you in the first place was because she wants us to be friends so badly. I've done nothing but try and be cool to you since we started dating, but the truth is you're an arrogant prick who can't get over the fact she's seeing me."

"But he's innocent! You see that now, he didn't do anything," Kal said, glossing over the last statement.

Benny was practically foaming at the mouth. "That was someone else's job to find out, not ours. Look around. Look at the position you've put your 'best friend' in."

Kal wanted to punch him in the face, but he was in the wrong and knew it. In a past life he might have tried to argue with Benny.

"I probably did screw up," he said, attempting to be apologetic. "I've known Elle since freshman year. She came with me back to Colorado when my mom died, even after we broke up. She was there for me when the whole steroid thing came out and every person in this town wanted to crucify me—I couldn't go anywhere without getting called a fraud. When I finished the jail time she was there with my dad waiting. You're right, I should have trusted her over Dunning. I'm just tired of getting accused of always taking the easy way out. People say I didn't want to do the hard work so I cheated, that I couldn't take people heckling me so I sucker-punched that kid in the bar. This is the one time I didn't want to quit. I wanted to follow through on my word."

"Those are people who don't know you, Kal. She never felt that. You never had to prove anything to her." Benny said. "I feel sorry for you. Your whole life is based on trying to keep up this fake image of yourself. In the end, you're a fraud, just like that home run you hit."

"What did you say?" Kal asked, jumping to his feet. There was only so much he could take, and Benny crossed the boundary.

"You heard me fine. Elle might be scared to hurt your feelings, but I could give two shits."

Kal took a menacing step toward him, deciding which part of his face he was going to work on first, when Dunning, stirred by the noise, interrupted. "Boys! Please tell me you are not about to waste your energy fighting each other? Right now we have more important things to deal with. Please check the testosterone!"

Benny smirked and gave Elle a sickeningly sweet kiss on her forehead as Kal unclenched his fists and returned to the floor, picking up where he left off. He was seething, but drained both physically and mentally, and they had barely started.

****

"If I even think you're trying to deceive me or you are somehow alerting someone in an attempt to facilitate a rescue, we will immediately take control and shut the computer down. I will then shoot this lovely little lady in the forehead," Marcus said, pointing matter-of-factly at Elle. "Don't even give me the most minute reason."

It appeared he finally decided to give Kal what they asked for, a laptop with wireless access. But there were safety measures in place.

"We have a master computer linked to this laptop that has total remote access. We can see everything you do, every email you send, every person you talk to, and someone will be constantly watching, so don't try anything," said Marcus as his tech man worked on the laptop, finalizing the settings. He was substantially dissimilar in build from the rest of the men, apparently a part of the crew for his brain more so than his brawn.

Kal nodded in understanding. "Thank you."

"Don't make me regret this, Kalei," were Marcus' last words before he and his men stalked out of the room.

Elle made immediate eye contact with Kal.

"No, we're not even going to try. It's not worth the risk," he said, glancing at Dunning, knowing full well what she meant. "We're just going to play this by the book and get everyone home safe."

****

Kal scanned Google, looking for anything that might be slightly helpful.

"You're right, Dr. Dunning. There seems to be only one of them in existence. I'm hitting dead-ends everywhere else."

Dunning looked up from the papers he was trying to read without his glasses. "I could have told you before you even turned that thing on. Let's all stop what we're doing and regroup. So what do we know so far?"

Benny took a gulp of bottled water and gargled. "Well, we know the Eagle was in or around Macon the last time it was supposedly seen."

"And there is separate evidence supporting the theory General Sherman may have secretly been in the area at that time as well looking for something important," Elle chimed in.

"Good job, Elle," Kal said, secretly impressed with how much they both learned during the short crash course on the subject. Hell would freeze over, however, before he would publicly offer Benny the same compliment. Their uneasy truce was now all but gone after the mini dustup.

"Right. The fact remains all the evidence is pointing to Sherman being involved in this thing. We have interviews and letters from his family talking about a legend of valuable gold treasure. Strong circumstantial evidence, but nothing concrete. I guess we could start backtracking where he was from the end of the war until the disappearance of the Eagle."

"Do you think we should make contact with that Dr. Ashworth guy to see if he might be able to help?" Elle asked.

"That's not a bad idea, actually," Dunning said. "I usually only communicated with him via email, though, and once or twice over the phone. But I don't remember his number and it's not in any of these files, like I'd hoped."

"It'll take too long to email him," chimed in Kal. "What if he doesn't check it for a while?"

"True, true," said Dunning. "Wait a minute, I talked to him on the instant talker thing once or twice."

"Do you mean Instant Messenger?"

"Yes, that was it!"

"Do you remember which one it was? Yahoo or AOL—something else?"

"Yahoo, it was Yahoo. I'm pretty sure. He had his email through that."

Kal opened a new browser and quickly downloaded and installed Yahoo Messenger to the desktop of the laptop, allowing them to instantly communicate computer-to-computer via the internet.

"Do you remember your info, Dr. Dunning?"

"No, I don't, I'm afraid," he responded. "Lillian always set it up for me."

"Let me try and log on. It's been a while since I used my account, though." Kal entered his username and password several times but received an error message saying the account was expired. "We could just try and create a new one."

"We could, but . . . wait a sec. Benny, don't you have a Yahoo Messenger account?" Elle asked.

"Yeah," he enthusiastically responded at first. "It's, uh . . . you know what? I don't actually have an account anymore. We should just make a new one."

Benny's face was red for some reason.

"What? You just told me you were chatting online with one of your buddies from high school the other day," Elle said.

"You must have heard me wrong. Let's just drop it and start a new account."

Everyone just stared as he nervously fidgeted with his hands. "Alright, I have one, dammit. The login is BUTTMAN00," he finally admitted, his voice trailing off in embarrassment.

The others just looked at each other for a few seconds, speechless.

"God, you are pathetic," Kal said finally, breaking into a mocking laugh.

"Oh, my," Dunning added.

"That's just gross, Benny," Elle said.

"I made it in high school and at the time it was funny. I just haven't changed it since then. Can we just log on and talk to this guy?" pleaded Benny. "It's not really that big of a deal."

"Okay, okay. BUTTMAN00 it is. Wow, Elle, you really got yourself a winner here," Kal said, shaking his head and typing the name and password as Benny stewed. "Do you remember his account name, Dr. Dunning? We'll try and search to see if he's online right now."

"This I do remember because it was so easy. It was just his name: Robert.Ashworth."

"Let's hope this works," Kal said, biting his nails nervously as he typed Ashworth's user name into the recipient box.

**BUTTMAN00:** Dr. Ashworth, this is T.A. Dunning. Sorry about the strange user name, am using a student's account—it's a long story. Had a couple of questions about the Eagle.

"All we can do now is wait and hope he's online," he said to the others.

After thirty long seconds, the messenger box flashed—Ashworth was there.

**Robert.Ashworth:** Hahaha, how am I supposed to know this is you T.A.?

"Tell him I know about his connection in the State Department, the one that procured the copies of the telegrams," Dunning said impatiently.

**BUTTMAN00:** I'm the only one who knows about the telegrams you illegally obtained from the State Department.

**Robert.Ashworth:** Touché. Jesus T.A! Your name is all over the news, even up here. What the hell is going on? Are you ok?

**BUTTMAN00:** It's another long story, everything is ok and will be sorted out, I need your help though. That's why I contacted you, seeing if you had anything new on the Eagle?

**Robert.Ashworth:** OK, I'll take your word on it. Unfortunately, no. Same story as where we left off before. I thought I had a good lead on a copy of an 1860s story from Harper's Weekly that mentioned something about the 'South's Eagle' being in Montgomery after the war ended—which would have totally thrown off our Sherman hypothesis. But it turned out to be a false lead.

**BUTTMAN00:** Thx. I haven't been able to break through that last issue we were dealing with: Sherman's telegraph. Have enlisted the help of my teaching assistant, but time has become an issue. Still think it's the best lead we have.

**Robert.Ashworth:** Agreed. Continue to focus on

finding a solution for that. Let me know if I can help you with anything. Are you sure you're alright? Do you need me to call anyone?

**BUTTMAN00:** I'm fine, will be in touch. Thanks. Please do not let anyone know I contacted you, my freedom and the future of the Eagle depends upon it.

Kal logged off the site as the rest of the group, who had been reading over his shoulder, went back to work. Dunning reached into his pile of folders and picked up a piece of paper, holding it up for all of them to see.

"Everything leads us back to this—our dead end, our mysterious coded message from Sherman. This is the key to finding the Eagle and unlocking the puzzle. The problem is it could take years for us to figure it out. Considering the Confederacy spent thousands of man-hours working day and night on doing just that without success, we might need to find an alternative plan."

"An alternative plan? We don't have the time to try and solve this by hand. The only other way is to," Kal trailed off, realizing what he was suggesting.

"Yes, my boy," finished Dunning. "We're going to need a Union codebook, and as you found out earlier via the internet, there is only one in known existence. Unfortunately, it is in the hands of the NSA."

"Well, we're screwed then, right? I mean, I liked Mission Impossible with Tom Cruise, but I don't know how realistic it is to break into a high security government facility, even with Major Dipshit and his men over here," Benny said, pointing toward the door.

"As I was about to add," smiled Dunning. "The good news is the codebook is not specifically at NSA headquarters but at a public museum down the street. A lightly-guarded museum that is not on the same property."

"Yeah, the National Cryptologic Museum. I saw a picture of the codebook on their website," Kal added, scrambling to pull the page back up.

"Normally I would never endorse using physical force as a

means to achieve success, but in this case, our hands are tied. Perhaps our captors would not mind taking part in a breaking and entering exercise if it meant helping us get closer to the Eagle?" Dunning asked.

Benny felt his swollen lip and laughed.

"I don't think they'd mind."

"Well, let's see how dedicated this Mr. Marcus is to finding the Eagle. Elle, be a dear and knock on the door will you? We need to ask for another favor."

# CHAPTER 16

The security guard set the alarm and shut the panel before dimming the lights around the National Cryptologic Museum until the building was cast in a very ominous glow.

He headed back to the office and tucked the key to the alarm box in the breast pocket of his uniform, which had the name tag "STEVE" pinned to the front. The place could get spooky at night with all the old cryptology machines, and it didn't help that the lighting played tricks on his poor vision. There were times when he would jump in surprise after catching one of the retired military displays out of the corner of his eye, believing a real person was watching from behind the glass.

Just as the guard settled into his favorite chair and comfortably positioned himself for the long evening, he was startled by a knocking sound emanating from the museum entrance.

"Who the hell could this be?" he muttered out loud, slowly unfolding out of his seat and shuffling off to investigate.

Stepping into the front area he realized this was a first—in two years working there he had never seen another soul on the night shift besides his morning replacement, and now his initial guest appeared to be a homeless man.

"Hey, guy. You got any change? I'm trying to get something to eat," yelled the man through the glass, running his hands through his long, greasy hair. His Atlanta Hawks sweatshirt had yellow stains all over it and it appeared his skin hadn't been graced by the presence of a bar of soap for many weeks.

"Sorry, I'm all locked up here. There's a gas station about a half mile down the road you can try," the guard yelled back.

"Damn, man! Not even a quarter?"

"Listen, buddy. I can't open the doors once we lock up. Sorry."

The homeless man shook his head and stomped off.

"I don't understand kids these days, just get a job," the guard said, cracking his back and returning to the safe confines of his office. But before he could resettle to dine on the leftover meatloaf his wife packed, the knocking resumed at the front. "I'm going to murder this guy," he said, angrily tossing down the Tupperware.

"What the hell do you want?" he yelled to the same homeless man who returned and was now angrily banging his fists on the glass, marking them up. "I told you I can't open up. Get out of here before I call the cops."

The man moved this mouth as if he were responding, but whatever he said was inaudible.

"What?"

Again, the homeless man appeared to mumble something the guard could not hear.

"What do you want?" he yelled again.

The man motioned for him to come closer to the door to hear what he was saying. The guard obliged out of curiosity and cautiously approached, slowly cupping his ear to the glass, only to see the man break into a smile and start laughing hysterically.

For some reason—the guard would later wonder why this particular detail struck him at the time—he noticed the man's teeth were impeccable. Glistening white and in perfect order, not what you would expect from a person who looked like he dined out of a dumpster on a regular basis and smelled of rotten milk.

The man abruptly stopped laughing, smirked, and pointed at something behind the guard, twirling his finger for him to turn around.

The guard hesitated, initially fearing a trick, but slowly obliged and immediately sensed there was someone behind him—four persons, to be exact, all dressed in black with ski masks and pointing automatic rifles at his head.

"Th—this isn't really about some change, is it?"

One of the masked men slowly moved his head side-to-side before lifting the butt of his rifle and smashing it into the guard's face, sending him into a crumpled heap on the floor.

"Let's get the book quickly, and get out of here."

# CHAPTER 17

"So, let me get this straight. You think the Eagle is still in the Atlanta area?" Kal asked Dr. Dunning.

It had been a solid eight hours since they requested the book from Marcus and informed him of their dead end. In between trips to the restroom, meals of cardboard-quality microwaved pizza and the occasional nap, the group had not progressed much. Everything kept coming back to Sherman's coded letter. If they couldn't translate it, they were stuck and staring at the end game. If they did manage to translate it and it turned out to be nothing more than a letter home to his family, they had nothing else and would be forced to go to Marcus empty-handed—an option that didn't sound appealing considering the damage he and his men inflicted on Dunning.

The letter had to be the key to unlocking the secret. There were no other alternatives.

Kal noticed Marcus' mood getting darker as hours passed with no news of progress. It was a full day since they were first taken and the only people he knew that might be looking for him were locked in the very same room. And as far as he could guess, no one was looking for them, either.

"I just don't see how Sherman could have gotten the Eagle out of the area at that time. It was too high profile and I doubt he would have trusted anyone else for assistance. If his intention was to keep it, the best play was to hide it in the area," Dunning stated.

"Hey, Professor," Benny said, "What is this symbol? I've seen it a couple of places now."

He held up a piece of paper that had a crudely drawn crest of a bear's head with something in its teeth.

Dunning squinted and examined the symbol.

"Ah yes, I've seen this a couple of times recently in my work, but to be honest am not entirely sure of what it is. It could be Sherman's personal crest or family insignia. I've been meaning to ask Ashworth if he recognized it."

"What's in its mouth?" Elle asked.

"Looks like a snake. Those are very common symbols for that time."

"I think I saw it on one of his other papers, too," Kal said, rifling through a stack. Before he could find what he was looking for, though, the door to the room burst open and Marcus strode through with two guards close behind. He had a surprise with him—Dunning's granddaughter—and he forcefully pushed her to the front for his captives to see.

"Grandpa!" shrieked Lily, desperately trying to reach him. But Dunning only looked back in shock.

"I believe this is the codebook you requested," Marcus said, tossing a very weathered book to Kal, who carefully cradled it in astonishment.

*This is a one-of-a-kind piece of American history he just carelessly chucked as if it were some ordinary, used paperback. These guys are incredible. There isn't anything or anyone they can't touch.*

"I have to be quite honest, though, I need to start seeing tangible progress from you and the professor, Kalei. Time is not your ally right now, and at some point my men and I must cut our losses and move on to the next opportunity that will eventually lead us to the Eagle. The men I work for are many things, but patient with their time and money is not one of them."

Kal nodded in acknowledgement and looked to Dunning, who was still locked on Lily.

"It's gonna be alright, baby girl," he managed to barely whisper as she finally broke free and ran to him, clamping around his waist. The reunion was short-lived, however, thanks to one of Marcus' henchmen, who almost immediately pulled her off and led her back out of the room, kicking and screaming.

Kal knew this was their final warning—either solve a mystery no one had gotten close to figuring out in over a century, or face the consequences. It was a literal life and death deadline.

"There will be no more requests fulfilled. I implore you to use your time wisely. I don't want to start this process all over again with someone else. But I will."

Marcus finished talking and held out his extended hand, as if he were a doctor waiting for a nurse to place a surgical instrument in his palm, only in this instance, one of his men handed him a large hammer. He walked over to Dunning, forcefully grabbed his wrist and bludgeoned his knuckles several times—instantly crushing the bones to pieces. Kal and Benny were helpless to prevent the assault and could only catch the falling professor and help ease him to the floor in agony.

"I felt I needed to remind you of what the stakes are here," Marcus said, calmly examining the bloodied claw before handing it back to his guard.

"I don't understand all of this over a stupid statue," Elle cried. "Why?"

"It's bigger than you or me. It's bigger than all of us," Marcus yelled back. "It's an ideal, a way of life. In this day and age, this is what remains of our culture. Don't you understand? Something like the Eagle can be displayed to future generations of Southern children to show them the truth behind the Civil War and what we fight for today. This subhuman ape will be fine. But the next time I come in here and you are empty-handed, that hammer will be laid to that little girl's head, and then yours, and on and on down the line. And I will make you watch all of it, my good professor. There will be no more help."

Kal grabbed a spare blanket and wrapped it around Dunning's

hand, which was mangled and had already swollen to the point it looked like it could double for a boxing glove. Glaring up at Marcus, he felt a murderous fury for the first time in his young life.

*I'm going to hurt you, I swear.*

"I suggest you spend your next few hours worrying less about him and focusing more on finding me that damn Eagle," finished Marcus, stalking out of the room.

Dunning buried his face in the carpet and quietly moaned as Kal molded the blanket like a soft splint. "He's right," Dunning finally said, struggling to sit up and talk. "We now have what we need to decipher the letter. Stop worrying about me, I'll be fine. The pain is already subsiding."

Kal watched him look longingly toward the door for a few seconds, presumably burning the image of his granddaughter into his memory, before refocusing and grabbing the old book. He propped himself against the wall and examined it, gently opening the leather cover, which appeared so fragile it could disintegrate into dust at any moment. The sickly yellow pages inside weren't in much better shape and reminded Kal of his elderly, jaundiced next-door neighbor back in Greeley.

"Look at this thing. This book is a living example of our history. It helped decide the fate of this country and end slavery. Be a dear and put a piece of scratch paper in my lap," Dunning said to Elle as he grabbed the copy of Sherman's letter with his good hand and carefully laid it next to him so as to not smear any blood on it.

"Ah yes, here it is," he said, several pages into the book. "Look at the top here. It breaks down ciphers by each regiment. See these up here? This is what we needed."

At the top of the page were the names of all the top officers in the Union army with either the number 5, 6 or 7 printed next to them.

"The person the telegraph was addressed to indicated how many columns of text there should be in the decoding. Since LeBay is the first name in Sherman's letter, you would look up to the top for his name and see the number. Although there doesn't seem to be a Major LeBay in this case. Let's just go with six, since most of the Majors look like they used that number. So each row should have six words, followed by a new row of six words and so on."

Dunning slowly rewrote Sherman's letter verbatim onto the blank piece of paper, starting a new line after every seventh word, which confused Kal.

"I thought you just said six—"

"I did, but remember what I told you before? The Union cryptologists were so tricky, they actually added a column of nonsensical words in case the South managed to crack the code this far. Whatever the indicated number was, like the six because of the Major, the telegrapher would add an extra column filled with phony verbiage. Once the paragraph is laid out, the very first word 'WINTER' becomes the key to the whole puzzle—it basically gives us a road map to rearrange all the words into the real message."

He continued with the lesson, pointing to a grid of jumbled numbers about midway down the Union codebook page that ranged from 1 to 36 with Xs above and below.

## Six Column Route

| X | | | X | X | X |
|---|---|---|---|---|---|
| 6 | 17 | 27 | 36 | 26 | 16 |
| 7 | 5 | 28 | 35 | 25 | 15 |
| 8 | 18 | 4 | 34 | 24 | 14 |
| 9 | 19 | 29 | 3 | 23 | 13 |
| 10 | 20 | 30 | 33 | 2 | 12 |
| 11 | 21 | 31 | 32 | 22 | 1 |
| X | X | X | | | |

"This is telling us the route to take when decoding the message, how to order the words properly. Each number stands for that word in the letter. Six means sixth word, et cetera. Whenever an X follows a number, you throw that word out. Like I expressed to Kal previously, we've been able to get this far before using widely-known methods without much success."

Dunning looked down at the piece of paper, studied it intently and then looked back at the book.

"The rest of this is filled with hundreds of keywords and their meanings. For instance, President Lincoln's keyword was Adam Asia. They would use this instead of his real name."

He went back to work on the piece of scratch paper, placing a number sequentially above each word, then alternated between studying the book and transcribing, breaking only to look up the definition for possible code words. The others watched Dunning intently as he progressed, interpreting every facial expression as either a good or bad sign. They all knew their fates rested on him finding the answer.

"Shit!" he finally cursed out of character, flinging the papers off his lap with his one good hand. "I'm sorry, I truly am, but it's a dead end. It's the same problem as before. It's just nonsense. I was hoping the codebook would shed some new information on how to break the telegram, but it doesn't."

"No," Elle said. "Please, you have to keep working. At least try and fake something. You saw him, they're going to kill us!"

"I wouldn't even know how to fool them at this point. I . . . I'm afraid it's over."

The will to keep searching had been sucked out of Dunning—Kal could now see it in his body language and empathized. His shoulders sagged and his face looked haggard. He had seen the death of his beloved wife and faithful, family pet in person, he had been beaten mercilessly, and now the lives of his precious granddaughter and three innocent people appeared in serious jeopardy. He was a victim, but would also have blood on his hands for involving them.

Kal grabbed the book and the papers to see exactly what Dunning had written.

"We're not going to let you do this, T.A.," he said calmly, surprised it was he of all people trying to convince another to persevere.
He reviewed Dunning's translation, but nothing made sense, so he took
a sheet of paper and transcribed it himself from the beginning using the
codebook . . . only to reach the same result after several minutes. This
did not appear to be a normal Union cipher—it was not following the
rubric.

"Stager's number 9 cipher should break this letter, but it doesn't,"
repeated Dunning. "I've tried all of Stager's others as well; numbers 2,
12, 7, et cetera, with no luck. I'm afraid we're out of time."

Just as Kal put the scratch paper down to try again, he noticed
a word in the null column jarring his memory to a correspondence he
examined earlier in the day. He stopped everything to look through one
of the files until he located a specific photocopy, placed it aside and did
the same with another file. After a few minutes he had four different
pieces of paper stacked neatly on the floor.

"Look at these telegraphs and letters from Sherman," he said,
holding them up for everyone to see. "All of these are correspondence
he wrote during the war that Ashworth has marked as coded. Tell me if
you see anything in common."

Everyone took a turn looking over the papers, but it was Benny
who noticed it first. "This word 'samvfour' or whatever it is—it's in
every one of them."

"Yes!" Kal said. The same, made-up gibberish both Kal and
Dunning initially dismissed as a null word acting as a space filler appeared in each letter.

"Hear me out, Dr. Dunning. What if Sherman placed a cipher
within a cipher? What if he used the traditional Stager method to initially code his letter, then added another technique after to further con-
ceal the real message? In every one of these four letters he has this word
'samvfour' placed somewhere. What if this is a key to deciphering the
message further?"

Dunning cocked his head and looked over each of the letters
Kal pulled, placing his index finger on the word samvfour each time
it appeared as if it were in Braille and he were feeling the contours of
each bump.

"I guess it's possible," he finally admitted.

Kal wasn't sure if Dunning was hesitant because he did not want to admit the pupil outfoxed the teacher or didn't want to allow the possibility there was still a slim chance to save his granddaughter to creep into his consciousness. Having hope reemerge after acceptance of failure, only to be wrong in the end, again, was tantamount to psychological torture.

"We would need to figure out what 'samvfour' meant, first of all," Dunning said.

Kal swore he could almost see the professor's mind halting the process of disconnect and reengaging himself to the problem.

"If we can do that, than it will open the key. Elle, please log back online and contact Ashworth. See if he's ever seen that word or knows of Sherman or other Union officers using a different type of cipher within a cipher during the war. Most likely not, but it's worth a shot. Kal, I want you and me to run through a few possibilities to see if we can break this ourselves. Benny, go through the rest of these files and see if you can find anymore instances where samvfour appears. Let's go, let's go!"

Kal smiled—T.A. Dunning was back.

He also felt his ego flex just a twinge. Perhaps he would play a major role in solving this mystery after all.

"Man, I'm the one who noticed the word," muttered Benny under his breath to Elle as they turned to work on their assignments. "Why do I always get stuck with the crappy job?"

"It's a very important job, Benny," she said. "You're the one who saw what Kal was trying to point out, doesn't it make sense you should be in charge of finding the rest of them? What if you see something with that word, sami- . . . however you pronounce it, which ends up helping us solve this?"

"Yeah," he said. "Yeah, you're right. Stop messing around Elle, we have work to do, get busy. Let's go, toots!"

\*\*\*\*

"Ashworth wasn't online, so I left him a message he should receive next time he logs in," Elle said, not looking up from the computer to see who was listening. It was a good thing, because no one was. Benny was meticulously scanning files, pulling out papers left and right, while Kal and Dunning huddled around their scratch pad.

"Okay, let's assume it's a code of some sort. But what kind? Perhaps it's a simple transposition key corresponding to an alphabet?" Kal offered, showing off his new-found knowledge of cryptology.

"Could be," Dunning said. "But there aren't enough letters to figure out the entire alphabet. The sender and receiver would have to consult a key of some kind. Doesn't seem likely."

"What if each letter corresponds to a number?"

"Again, we would need a key because there aren't enough letters in 'samvfour' to figure it out by itself."

Kal stared at the word, hoping it would trigger something in his brain.

"I didn't find anything else with samvfour in it," interrupted Benny. "But, I found some other weird words that were close. Maybe they're related? Look at these telegraphs from Sherman. There is the word 'samviithree,' and then on this one 'samixfour.' "

Kal grabbed the letters out of his hands.

"This is huge, good job!" Kal said, momentarily forgetting his contempt for Benny, who beamed with pride and winked at Elle.

"Are you thinking what I'm thinking?" Kal asked the professor as he examined it. "They all start with the word 'sam.' "

Dunning was already a couple of steps ahead of him. "Yes, the 'sam' in the word must be the trigger. It signifies to the reader it's the code word. And because it always looks like it appeared in the null column and was supposed to be ignored, no one ever paid attention unless they were specifically looking for it, including us," Dunning said, gingerly rubbing his crushed hand and looking up to the ceiling in thought. "Sam . . . Sam . . . yes, of course! Sherman's most prized war horse was a stallion named Sam."

Kal penned down all the different variations of the trigger word Benny found on a piece of paper, then crossed off the 'sam' portion.

"It kind of looks like the next few letters could be Roman numerals. You have V for five, VII for seven, and then IX, which is nine."

"Yes, followed by another number written out in plain English. When you break the word apart, it becomes clear. Put together, it jumbles into something unintelligible. We just need to figure out how to apply it to the message," Dunning followed, turning to the others. "Everyone, we need your full attention. You've seen how the code worked before, grab a piece of paper and try and figure out how these numbers could translate the message."

They all moved with purpose. Something seemingly went their way for the first time since the whole ordeal started and Kal felt revitalized. He took a break to look around and catch his breath as everyone worked feverishly.

Benny's tongue was out and sticking to the side of his mouth in deep concentration, his eyes glued to his paper. Elle on the other hand looked as relaxed as she always did—nothing ever seemed to frazzle her. A few strands of her hair fell onto her freckled face as she jotted something down, and she quickly blew them off, looked at Kal and smiled. She was striking, and Benny was a lucky man to have her. When Kal turned to look at Dunning, he had to remind himself this was his professor. The man was so worn it would have been hard to place him on the street had Kal not already known his identity.

"Wait! I think I figured it out," Dunning said, snapping Kal out of observation mode. "Yes, I think just solved it. It's really quite simple, but ingenious.

"Once you decipher the original message using the codebook, I believe any word that appears in the null category that starts with 'sam' and ends with a number spelled-out tells the reader there is a second message hidden. The Roman numeral signals the reader to start over and break the original message into sentences of a certain number of words. For instance, in this particular case 'samvfour' was used, so the Roman numeral is five. That means you take the first five words as a line, then the second five, and so on. Understand so far?"

Everyone nodded their heads.

"The spelled out number then tells you which word to highlight in each sentence. Because this particular one is four, you would take every fourth word. If you do that to our Sherman message, you end up with this result."

He held up a piece of paper with the message scribbled boldly:

LOCATED GOLD EAGLE MACON SAFELY
UNDER GROUND HOLT RESIDENCE.

There was silence as they all read it simultaneously, followed by pandemonium, shrieking, hugs and kisses. After a few minutes of celebration, Dunning tried to calm things down.

"Okay, people. Okay," he said with a huge grin. "We still need to figure where this could be in Macon."

"I think I might have the answer," Elle said, pointing at a webpage already pulled up on the laptop. "I just did a simple internet search of Macon, Holt, and the Civil War, and this hit: the Old Cannonball House in Macon. It's now a museum, but it was formerly a mansion owned during the Civil War by a Confederate named Holt."

Benny pounded his fist on the bed.

"Yahtzee!"

\*\*\*\*

"How confident are you?" Marcus asked.

"Extremely," answered Dunning, leaning on the shoulders of Kal and Benny, still struggling to stand on his own for an extended length.

"Fine then. This is how things will play out: Kalei, you and the girl will go with two of my men to Macon in the morning to scout out this Cannonball House, check the grounds and find out as much information as you can. I will keep the professor, the little girl and your friend here with me. If the Eagle is indeed in the basement or underground somewhere as you propose, we will move forward from there. Understood?"

Kal nodded and made eye contact with Elle. Once again it would be just the two of them.

"I really don't think I need to overemphasize your stakes in this, folks. Let's just find this blasted thing so we can all move on with our lives."

Kal could sense Marcus' insincerity in the last half of his statement but at this point had no choice but to trust he was a man of his word. Marcus possessed total control over the situation and was presently dangling a carrot, forcing them to do his bidding.

"Weston and Schuler here will be your escorts," he said, motioning to two beefy men standing by the door leading to the garage. One of them was the fake panhandler/driver of the van. "Oh yes, one more thing, Kal. They will shoot you on the spot, no questions asked, if anything goes remotely wrong in their estimation. Now get some sleep and then find me that fucking bird."

# CHAPTER 18

It worried Kal that he and Elle weren't blindfolded leaving the safe house. He had previously been prevented from seeing every time he entered or exited the ranch-style bungalow, and the fact Marcus now didn't care whether or not his prisoners knew the location was unsettling. He thought back to the last thing the professor said to him before they left.

"It's okay if we find the Eagle and Marcus gets it. What he doesn't realize is the same evil that allowed him to kill my wife and commit his crimes against us will eventually be his downfall. There will be a judgment day, and his is coming soon."

Kal managed to nod to Dunning as they were ushered out of the bedroom and they both shared a moment of understanding. Elle had her own brief goodbye as well, kissing Benny passionately and running her fingers through his curly hair before she was jerked away. "We'll be fine, I promise," she mouthed to him as the door slammed shut.

Everyone in Elle's Jeep was presently silent, including Kal, who stared out the back seat window in a trance. It was morning—probably 8 or 9 a.m.—and as he blew a blast of warm breath on the glass, he began to recognize his bearings the farther they drove, leaving behind the isolated wooded region for a more populated neighborhood. They were in Fairburn, a small community 30 miles outside of Atlanta, heading west via back roads and through small communities toward the freeway.

He also, once again, noted the size of both of his captors.

*Big enough to easily handle Elle and me.*

"So why Macon?" asked the slightly older, balding mercenary who was driving, breaking the silence.

Kal looked up at Elle in the front passenger seat before responding—she was staring back at him though the mirror on her sun visor.

"What?"

"Why are we going to Macon?"

"Didn't your boss tell you?" Kal asked.

"We know the gist of it. I just want to hear it from your mouth."

*Is this some kind of test?*

"Okay, fine. We translated a telegram from the famous General Tecumseh Sherman saying he found the Freedom Eagle in Macon during the Civil War and he hid it in a house damaged by cannon. The telegram said the house was owned by a man named Holt and there is only one like it in the country."

Kal tried his best to recall the story of the Cannonball House, which he only learned earlier that morning. "When the Union was taking Atlanta in the summer of '64, Sherman had one of his generals, George Stoneman, move ahead of the army and attack Macon with the intent of freeing Union prisoners held in the city. He set up his battery just outside of town, across the Ocmulgee River and fired away. Unfortunately for him, he was rebuffed by the Rebs and later captured, but one of his cannon shells managed to hit the home of Judge Asa Holt, damaging an exterior column on the front porch and landing unexploded inside—that's where the house gets the name. We think Sherman tracked down the Eagle to the Holts' later in the war and hid it, perhaps in the basement."

"What makes you think it's there?"

Elle spoke up this time.

"Dr. Dunning says the Eagle statue was constantly moved and

hidden in homes of rich and loyal Southerners, which the Holts apparently were. According to him, the family fled Macon after the shelling when they felt the Union army might take the city, so they mistakenly headed to their plantation outside Jefferson Country—right smack in the path of the right wing of Sherman's Army. The very wing we have evidence indicating Sherman was secretly riding with."

Kal finished the story as the car entered the I-75 onramp, heading southeast to Macon.

"The Union army spared the plantation, but looted and burned everything else. Legend has it the soldiers hung Judge Holt several times in an attempt to find a 'hidden gold treasure' they were positive he possessed. We think Sherman was behind this and later discovered the Eagle was not at the plantation, but back at the Holts' original home in Macon—the Cannonball House. Once he doubled back and retrieved the statue, it would have been too risky for him to move it because they were in the middle of Confederate territory. Hopefully it's still there, hidden."

"Hopefully," the younger mercenary said, pulling a SIG Sauer 9mm out of his coat pocket and loading the clip.

*Subtle*, thought Kal, suppressing a guffaw at the scare tactic. *I owe you one for that sucker punch.*

"What was that?" the man asked.

"Nothing, we should be there soon."

\*\*\*\*

The older man was obviously in charge.

"I want you two in front of me at all times. We're just going to go inside and check the place out. See what we can find. I don't want you drawing any attention," he said, leaning back over the driver seat.

They had made good time to Macon and were presently parked in a small lot behind the historic house, waiting for the museum to open.

"You don't think it's going to look weird that all of us are chomping at the bit to visit an obscure Civil War museum as soon as it opens?" Kal asked. "What's our back story?"

He had studied their captors on the two hour ride from Atlanta and figured out the younger one next to him was Weston, the faux homeless person.

"Yeah, Kal is right. Isn't it going to draw some unwanted suspicion?" Elle asked.

"I don't really care," Schuler said. "We're on a tight schedule and need to get moving. Let's go."

The group exited the lot on to Mulberry Street and walked a short distance along the fence line to the front gate of the museum. Kal immediately noticed how pretty the place was, slender and reminiscent of a much narrower version of the White House in Washington, D.C. The two-story home was accented in black shutters and iron work, common of houses throughout the South built before the Civil War using popular Greek revival architecture, but not as big as it looked in the pictures. Four giant columns stretched from the entry porch to the second story roof and were the most noticeable aspect of the home, with the exception of the 145-year-old Napoleon Cannon resting on a stone pedestal in the front lawn.

"I guess we just go through the front door?" Weston said, lowering his nose to peek above his aviator-style sunglasses. Kal could feel the sliminess exude but ignored him to check out the house's second column from the left. The mended spot where General Stoneman's cannonball bounced off the ground and broke through the pillar was still apparent to the naked eye. It was occasions like this that made Kal appreciate history—not necessarily hunting for a mythical Civil War treasure, but experiencing the environment in person. Never lost on him was how surreal it was to touch and bring life to an object or place he previously only read about in a book. And even though the circumstances were less than ideal for soaking in the past at the moment, he savored it briefly before going inside.

Luckily, they were not the first visitors there. A group of mixed seniors were talking to the hostess of the house, who was standing halfway up the stairs on the right. "Hello, my friends! Welcome to Macon's famed Cannonball House. You folks here for the guided tour?" she asked, waving them in.

"No ma'am," Schuler said. "We just wanted to check the place out for ourselves, if that's alright."

"Well, sure. Although I will tell you I give one heck of a sight-seeing experience that you're not going to get by just bumping around the place," she said, patting her over-sprayed bob with her bright red acrylic nails.

"We'll be fine, thanks."

"Alright, just pay Sheila over there at the front table there and enjoy," she said with a sickeningly sweet smile.

Schuler paid for everyone and motioned to head into the front parlor, which was bathed in rays of sunlight full of dancing dust specks so large it appeared as if the fairy Tinker Bell had just flown through. The room was a perfectly-preserved example of 19th Century interior decorating, complete with red-patterned cloth wallpaper, an antique carpet and several vintage sitting chairs, paintings, and tapestry-clad windows. The focal point of the room was a fireplace adorned with a gold-leafed mirror, as well as a massive glass chandelier hanging from the ceiling.

"Weston, go ahead out back and see how many people are actually on the grounds. I want a head count of the employees in case things turn south. You two follow me," Schuler said to Elle and Kal, beginning the search process for a downstairs basement or crawl space. They walked through the house, room-by-room, some of which had display cases filled with old uniforms and Civil War artifacts, pausing only in the presence of other visitors.

"What if they don't have a basement?" Elle whispered to Kal as soon as they slightly separated from Schuler.

"Then we're screwed," Kal said quietly, shaking his head. "Seriously, we'd be in it deep. I don't know."

"Over here," Schuler interrupted. The group had made a loop around the bottom floor of the house and were now in a parlor next to the front hallway, from which Kal could hear the hostess cackling upstairs with her tour group. Weston had returned from sniffing around and joined his partner in focusing on a locked door in the room—this one much more masculine than the first with blue walls and dark oak furniture.

"Get out your pick, and open it," he said to Weston, who whipped out a small case filled with what looked like dental equipment.

Within seconds he popped the lock, but despite tugging, couldn't pull the door open. Schuler joined and both men used their legs against the wall as leverage until the hinges finally groaned and gave way, swinging open to reveal nothing more than a brick wall. The door was purely cosmetic, hiding a dead end.

Schuler closed it, brushed his pant legs off and looked at Kal. "You're running out of options here, kid. Not many other places to look. We need to head back soon and report to the Major."

"Wait a second," Kal said, walking back out to the main hallway where Sheila the cashier was stationed.

"Excuse me," he asked, "Do you have a basement here?"

"No, we sure don't. Just the first and second floor," she said, not even bothering to look up from the novel she was reading.

Kal turned to Elle, who had followed him, and shook his head. *Game over.*

" . . . but we do have a storm cellar outside," the woman added. "It's off limits to guests, though. Used for storage mostly."

Kal thanked her and briskly headed back down the hallway to the back door with Elle on his heels, only slowing to brief Schuler and Weston.

"They have a cellar outside, that's got to be it."

The group rushed out of the house into the back courtyard, scanning for anything resembling an underground entrance.

"Well hello, folks. I do reckon you might be from the North. Say it ain't so!" interrupted an elderly, bearded man dressed from head to toe in an authentic Confederate military uniform, a musket resting on his shoulder. Kal recognized him from the website as a part of the house's living history tour, where costumed actors played roles of real citizens from the Civil War—this guy was supposed to be an injured Rebel.

"Uh, no thanks, sir. Just doing our own thing," Kal said, trying to politely brush the man off.

"Now listen hear, sonny. You best follow me into the kitchen so I can show you something proper how we feed ourselves on the battle-field when we fight those Yanks. I won't take no for an answer."

Before Kal had a chance to again decline, Weston leapt directly in the poor man's face. "Listen here, you old bastard," he said with a menacing growl. "Leave us the hell alone before I gut you like a fish. Now turn around and walk back into that kitchen. I don't want to hear another peep from you."

The old man slowly backed away with a look of pure terror, as if Weston were the devil himself. It was obvious this was the first time anyone had declined his offer in such a manner.

"You're an animal," Elle said after the man retreated to the steps of the kitchen to confer with a few of his fellow actors, no doubt instructing them to steer clear of the rude tourists.

"Shut up and do your job," Weston answered.

"Fucker," Elle whispered to Kal as they rounded the side of the house and headed down a path toward the front yard. She didn't cuss very much and the vulgarity sounded very unnatural coming off her tongue, almost causing him to laugh out loud despite the circumstances. This particular walkway on the west side of the building was narrow and littered with weeds and bushes, an area intended to be off limits to museum guests. Kal's intuition was telling him to continue, however, and he was rewarded when he spotted the underground entrance ahead nearly covered in ivy.

"There it is! Come on, don't worry about him. He's just trying to intimidate us."

The cellar was similar to the one Kal had back home in Colorado with two giant wood doors built on an angle, jutted up to the base of the house. A lock and chain looped around the handles, presenting another obstacle.

"We have to shoot it open," Schuler said, looking back to make sure no one followed. "No time to find the combination."

Weston pulled out his handgun, quickly screwed a silencer on the muzzle, and pumped two rounds into the lock, sending sparks flying as it bounced off the wood and into the dirt. "You two first," he said, tossing Elle a flashlight—the gun now aimed at them.

Kal managed to take two steps into the dark and musty space before he was tapped on the shoulder by Elle, who pointed to something over the doorway. Carved into the wood was a circle with a squiggly line running through it. Kal focused the flashlight directly on the shape and immediately recognized the details. Although it was rough, it appeared to be the head of a bear-like creature holding a snake in its mouth—the same thing the group saw throughout their research on Sherman.

*This has to be it, it has to be down here,* he thought, trying to contain his excitement. *Could we be on the verge of discovering the Eagle?*

He looked back at Elle and nodded, pointing it out for the others to see. "This was on all of Sherman's letters—this sign. We're on the right track."

He continued his descent into the dark, carefully picking his way down the narrow steps, heedful not to trip over his own feet while he held onto Elle's hand.

The smallish cellar was filled with sundry items, from broken chairs and mattresses to old furniture covered in protective tarps, and harbored a distinctive smell of mold and decay. Elle coughed from all the dust kicked up and stumbled off the last step, nearly felling Kal as Schuler closed the cellar doors behind them and turned on his own flashlight.

"What are we looking for again?" Weston asked.

Kal scanned the room, focusing on the foundation walls and the columns that held up sections of the house. "It has to be buried underneath us somewhere. Look for any kind of marking similar to the one outside."

He made his way through the obstacle course of junk with Elle still clutching his hand, the two gunmen breaking off in the other direction. As he squeezed himself between two dressers, Elle once again rammed into him from behind, this time knocking Kal through the tight space and onto the ground on the other side.

"Whoa, you been lifting weights?" he asked, brushing the dirt off his pants.

"Sorry," she answered, laughing nervously. "I keep looking up for that symbol and forget you're in front of me."

He wiped the sweat off his brow and suddenly realized something.

"Elle, hold the light for me," he said, swiping at the floor with his foot.

After brushing an inch or so of soil away and tapping the ground, he grabbed the light back and quickly glanced around the room, moving to several different spots and performing the same task.

"What's the matter, Kal?" asked Elle, following but confused as to what he was up to.

"Follow me."

He hastily picked his way through the maze of furniture back toward the stairs, passing Weston and Schuler, and stopped in front of the staircase to again kick the dirt.

"What are you doing?" she asked in an excited whisper.

"We're screwed," Kal responded.

"What? Why?"

"Look," he said pointing to the hole he carved out. "It's solid concrete underneath the whole thing, including the walls. I just checked everywhere. This storm cellar is not an original, it was added on, probably sometime in the last century. This whole structure is solid as a rock. If the Eagle is actually underneath, which I now doubt considering someone would have found it when they built this, there is no realistic way for us to dig up all the concrete and search."

"Shit," Elle said. Again, the cussing seemed oddly funny to Kal, except he didn't have time to fully enjoy it because their two armed captors were making their way over. "They're coming, what do we do?"

Kal looked around.

"Follow my lead." he said. "Guys, I think we found it! Over here!"

The two mercenaries picked up their pace, almost smashing through a table in their haste to see what Kal was pointing at.

"Is it the Eagle?" asked Weston.

"I think so," Kal said, casually moving himself and Elle out of the way so the two men could see for themselves. Schuler crouched down on one knee and examined the small crater for a moment with his light, even reaching down to touch the concrete foundation.

"What are you trying to pull?" he finally asked, looking up at where Kal had been standing. "Are you trying to get yourself—"

Before he could finish the question a pipe smashed across his face, the force of the swing breaking his jaw with a loud crack and sending the light flying. Kal followed through as if he were in the batting cages, although the metal on bone didn't feel as clean as a bat and ball connecting. Turning to take a hack at Weston he realized the younger man reacted quickly enough to move out of harm's way and now had him dead to rights. Kal slowly dropped the pipe and put his hands up, catching a shadow out of the corner of his eye.

*Elle.*

She slammed into Weston's side with a tackle that would have made any football player proud, sending both onto the stairs in a tumble. A single round fired from his gun as he tried to handle the smaller woman, the bullet ricocheting off a piece of metal ceiling flashing and flying inches from Kal's ear.

With both lights rolling on the ground, he could only listen to them struggle and figured it was a matter of seconds before Weston used his superior strength to gain control of the situation and kill her. Kal stumbled to his feet and attempted to move to the action but tripped on his freshly-created hole, landing on his side as another shot lit up the room.

Then there was nothing but silence.

"Elle?" he yelled, sitting still to listen for any sign of life. "Elle, are you okay?"

But there was nothing—neither person was moving.

After what felt like an eternity, Elle finally called out, "Kal!"

"Elle, talk to me!" he frantically responded, picking up one of the lights and moving to the sound of her voice before finding her on top of an unconscious Weston, wiping blood off her sweatshirt.

"I don't know what happened," she sobbed.

"Are you hurt? Where are you bleeding?"

"It's not me, it's him," she said, pointing to Weston. Kal trained the flashlight on the man, revealing a bloody hole in his chest.

"I couldn't hold him, he was too strong. He had the gun and threw me off, but I don't think he knew where I landed. He shot and all of a sudden fell on top of me."

"You didn't get hit, though? You're sure you're alright?"

"I'm fine."

"The bullet must have ricocheted off something and come back and hit him. I almost got it the same way."

Kal felt for Weston's pulse but could not find it.

"It's too late for him," he said to Elle, helping her up. "We need to get out of here before his buddy wakes up."

She was nearly inconsolable, however, and shook so hard her teeth began to chatter. Kal sensed she was losing composure fast and grabbed her around the shoulders, hugging tightly. "You were amazing just now, okay? I don't know how you did it, but if it weren't for you we'd both be toast, as well as the others back at the house. But we have to move right now, we have to get out of here."

She nodded and wiped her eyes. They quickly stripped the men of everything, except for a single pistol, and tossed the rest of the weapons into the neighboring yard, keeping only the keys to the car and the cell phone. Kal figured that Schuler would be unconscious for awhile, but for good measure broke off a solid oak leg from one of the tables and lodged it underneath the handles of the cellar doors, wrapping it with the broken chain.

They quickly made their way down the side yard and back into the house, heading for the front door and exit. Elle's sweatshirt was flipped inside out in an attempt to keep the blood stain from being too obvious, but she was still shaking.

"Thanks for coming," said Sheila the cashier, barely acknowledging their departure as they carefully closed the door on the way out, not wanting to raise suspicion as to where the others were. After Weston's encounter with one of the staff, Kal was positive the whole place was watching them. But before they could traverse the front stairs and reach the street, the front door re-opened with the obnoxious tour guide hot in pursuit.

"Folks? Folks! Where do you think you're going?" she asked.

Kal's stomach sank as he turned, seriously contemplating just cold-cocking her. His gut told him she saw the blood, put two and two together and called the police.

*How am I going to talk my way out of this?*

"Folks, I don't know how you thought you were gonna get away with this, but I won't let you!" she said, rushing down the steps to them. Kal couldn't believe after everything that just transpired, they were about to be caught by a 55-year-old grandmother.

*If only this lady knew what she was about to cause.*

The woman stopped and eyeballed both of them before breaking into a big smile

"You forgot to pick-up your free 'I Visited the Cannonball House in Macon' stickers. These puppies are collector's items around here—your family members will never forgive you if you come home without them."

Kal's mind went blank as he tried to process what she was saying. Indeed, she held two white bumper stickers in her hand plus a coupon for a 'buy one, get one free' sandwich at a local sub store.

"Oh, I'm sorry. Thanks," he mumbled, grabbing the loot and following Elle out the front gate.

"I hope your trip here was a memorable one!" she yelled to them as they turned the corner toward the car.

Elle looked at Kal and feebly laughed. "I'd pay a million dollars to see her face when she realizes what is down in her basement."

"Wow, that would almost be worth this whole ordeal," Kal said, shaking his head. "Maybe not."

****

"What are we going to do now?" Elle asked, readjusting her seat as they hauled ass on I-75 out of Macon back to Atlanta. "We could call the cops, like Benny said."

The phone they took off Schuler had been ringing nonstop with the same number—probably Marcus trying to reach his men. If they didn't do something soon, they ran the risk of him assuming the worst and murdering the others.

"Not enough time," Kal said, swerving to pass a slow-moving big rig. "Besides, Benny's a jackass—and I mean that with all due respect. By the time we call the police, explain and convince them of everything, then try and remember exactly where the house was, Marcus will have killed them all."

Kal at one point actually considered calling the authorities, but was sure it wasn't the right strategy.

"Why are you so hard on him?"

"Who? Marcus?"

"You know who."

"Do we have to talk about this right now?" Kal asked.

"Yes. Yes we do, Kalei. I don't get why you hate Benny so much. He looks up to you and tries so hard to be your friend. But all you do is dump on him every chance you get. Is it because you're jealous of him?"

"Wow," Kal said with a chuckle. "Getting a little full of ourselves, are we? I mean, you're a great girl and all, but we had our time together. Can't it be something as simple as I just don't like the guy?"

"That's B.S., and you know it, Kal," Elle said, crossing her arms. "There's more to it."

"He just annoys me, that's all."

"Is it because he reminds you of yourself in some way?" Elle continued.

"He is nothing like me. He's short, got a beer gut and doesn't take anything serious."

"Okay, so what does that tell you?"

"It tell's me he's a douche."

"No! It means the guy I could end up marrying someday is almost your complete polar opposite. He's low-key, is always laughing at life, and isn't constantly holding back his emotions. That doesn't make you wonder at all?"

Kal went silent. She scored a blow right to the gut.

"You're thinking about marrying him?" he finally asked.

"Maybe."

"Well, if I'm such an asshole, why are you still my friend? Why do you spend almost as much time with me?"

"Because you mean the world to me—you always have. I love you as a person, Kal. I know how big your heart is and I cherish our friendship. But you have to grow up and be the bigger man here. I can't keep doing this, spending all my time trying to make you guys get along. Don't make me choose between you two."

At this point Kal was done talking about Benny, the conversation too tedious. "Can we please table this for now and try and figure out how to get out of our situation? We kind of have some bigger issues to worry about."

"Fine, but we're not done with this, Kal."

"Sure, whatever," he said. "Anyway, speaking of Benny and being a fake person, I was thinking we could fake this."

Elle shook her head in disapproval at the joke. "Fake what?"

"Well, we know we didn't find the Eagle, but Marcus doesn't know, right? His guys are in the basement back at that house and won't have the means to contact him for quite awhile. We call him and explain we found the Eagle and overpowered his men and escaped, and we want to make a deal for Benny, Dr. Dunning, and Lily."

"Okay, let's say he actually bites for a little bit," Elle said, playing devil's advocate. "What happens when he realizes we don't actually have the statue and his buddy is dead, thanks to us?"

"You didn't let me finish. We tell him to meet us in a busy public place where there will be a lot of people. We go ahead and find something, a statue of a bird or anything that looks like the Eagle that will fool him just long enough so Dunning and the others can get away. There is no way they are going to start shooting with a bunch of witnesses around—at least they're less likely to."

"You know what?" she added. "My mom has a big statue of an owl in her backyard to keep critters from messing with her plants and tomato bushes. We could take it, spray it with some gold paint and bedazzle it. It's pretty heavy, but if we put it in a backpack or something they might actually buy it for a second."

"Yeah, that's perfect. We don't need it to be exact since no one really knows what the Freedom Eagle looks like. It might even fool them longer. We have to somehow convince Marcus to let everyone go when we first hand it over. All we need is a few seconds to guide them away from him and into the crowd before he realizes it's a fake."

"What about the other guy we left in the basement? What if he somehow gets in touch with Marcus?"

"We'll have to chance it. He's not waking up anytime soon, and when he does it's going to take him time to find a way out of there. I'm not even sure he's going to want to answer to his boss."

"Okay," Elle said, getting excited. "Why don't we meet them at that fountain in front of Underground Atlanta in a few hours? You know, by the big whale mural, next to the old World of Coca Cola? The lunch rush should just be ending. A ton of people milling around."

Kal smiled. "Let's do it, this is our best shot. Are you sure you're totally down with it? Because I won't do it unless you're okay."

Elle smiled and gave him a high five of approval, just as Kal picked up the buzzing phone and answered it.

"This is Kal, I need to speak to Marcus. I have something he wants."

# CHAPTER 19

Marcus sat alone on the floor of an empty room, his eyes closed and hands crossed in front of his face. He breathed deeply, took in the essence of the space and quietly hummed a monotone note, trying to channel the rage building inside him. There would be a price to pay for Kal's actions, a heavy price—until then he had to remain sharp-minded.

*Tangier, the Philippines, Oslo, Boston. Every time I've faced adversity I've succeeded, it's the way I was raised. I never give up. This is but a boy, he cannot stop me.*

"We're ready, sir," said one of his guards from the doorway, interrupting the meditation session.

Marcus did not acknowledge him, instead continuing with his relaxation and breathing. He would have beat the man severely under normal circumstances for breaking his concentration, but because he was shorthanded and did not know where Schuler and Weston were at the moment, he had to spare him.

*Your worst enemy cannot harm you as much as your own unguarded thoughts. But once mastered, no one can help you as much . . . Your worst enemy cannot harm you as much as your own unguarded thoughts. But once mastered, no one can help you as much . . .*

He repeated this particular phrase, attributed to Buddha, over and over. As a student of war, there were certain aspects of other cultures Marcus came to grudgingly respect, even assimilating some into his own lifestyle despite a steadfast belief in the purity and dominance of his race over other 'subhuman groups.' The Samurai of Japan and their code of honor was a field of particular interest for him.

"Have they returned yet?" he finally said, opening his eyes and unfolding his long, skinny legs to stand up.

"No, sir. They are two minutes out."

"Fine. Start loading the prisoners into the van. I want everyone in with me, fully-loaded and ready to go in five."

"Fully-loaded, weapons-wise?"

Marcus turned and grabbed his face, squeezing as hard as he could. "Did I stutter? We are on the brink of Armageddon. I want that statue, no matter what it takes!"

****

Dr. Dunning, Benny, and Lily were herded out the garage and into the back of the same van they were kidnapped in, just as a car pulled up the driveway.

"Did you find them?" asked Marcus, bounding out of the house

"Just Weston," said the driver, who had been sent to contact the missing group. "Schuler was gone."

"Okay, well where is Weston?" he asked, looking at the empty backseat.

The driver pointed to the trunk. "In there—he's dead. No sign of the Eagle, either."

Marcus bit his lower lip so hard a trickle of blood ran down his chin. "Do you know who your friend is fucking with?" he screamed at Benny, punching the side of the van and making a huge dent.

"Throw the body in the back with them and torch the house

after we leave. We'll regroup downtown and ride together to the drop off."

Lily began sobbing in her grandfathers arms as he sang one of her favorite bedtime lullabies.

"I swear to God, this kid is pissing me off," Marcus said as he hopped in the passenger seat. "Drive!"

# CHAPTER 20

The little boy watched his grandmother with a laser gaze, holding for the slightest, split-second distraction that would turn her head the other direction. He patiently played possum while she read, remaining angelically still for at least several minutes until a car alarm in the parking lot provided the perfect diversion.

Acting on the small window of opportunity, the boy jumped off the bench and ran to the lip of the fountain, careful to keep his jacket dry as he made contact with his prey. The particular quarter that initially caught his attention in the pool was slimy and tough to secure with his undeveloped dexterity, yet he persevered and after several failed attempts achieved success, pinching it tightly in his forefingers. He raised the piece of metal from the water's depths and dried it off, imaging the bounty he could purchase while readying it for the confines of his pocket. But before he could safely hide the coin the collar of his shirt was yanked backward.

"Alexander!" the grandmother yelled. "That belongs to someone else! I told you to leave it alone. That's it, we're done, let's go."

The grandmother led the wailing boy by his arm to the parking lot, passing Kal and Elle, who were anxiously sitting on another bench, watching the whole episode unfold.

"Well, here's five bucks," Kal said, pulling the bill out of his wallet and handing it to her.

"You know you can't beat me," she teased.

After witnessing several failed attempts to pirate the coin and in an attempt to keep their minds off the impending exchange with Marcus, they decided to wager on whether or not the boy would escape with his fortune.

The weather had warmed and the cool mist spraying from the main spout of the fountain felt good on their skin—if Kal closed his eyes he could have easily been fooled that he was at the ocean. But they were not so lucky to be enjoying a day at the beach. They were at the entrance to Underground Atlanta, in their current predicament.

Kal looked across the street at a beautiful old brick church and allowed himself to say a quick prayer before quickly dismissing the notion there was a higher power listening. The truth was even though it was now, in this moment, he yearned to have trust in God, he couldn't bring himself to do it. He considered himself an atheist despite growing up in a loving Catholic household where he was baptized, confirmed, and attended mass every Sunday, staying the religious course into early adulthood and regularly attending church even after moving out on his own to Atlanta. But the death of his mother caused him to question his involvement in organized faith, enough so, that he eventually quit going altogether—just another of the many effects of her passing on his life.

*Just in case you're up there,* he thought.

The fountain where they sat marked the entrance to the Underground—a place presently teeming with people coming to and from the shops and restaurants.

"Did you know this was originally constructed as a train depot to replace the one Sherman destroyed when he ransacked the city?" Kal nervously asked. "The city raised the roads to create a better flow of traffic through the area, so merchants started building vertically as well, shifting their main floors to the second story and leaving the original level as basements, creating what ultimately became the Underground.

Over time this entire five-block radius below was covered and forgotten, left to bums and thugs—it wasn't until the city made improvements and rezoned it for entertainment that it took off."

"Yes, Mr. Tour Guide. I grew up here. I know," Elle said with a chuckle.

The courtyard that surrounded the fountain also looked out over the former home of the World of Coca Cola, a giant history and exhibit center for the soft drink giant whose corporate headquarters were in Atlanta. The museum recently relocated to a beautiful new facility in Centennial Park, and the giant red Coca Cola sign Kal remembered looming over the area like a red sun was gone.

He nervously tapped his foot and clutched the backpack holding the fake statue, the only thing they could find to carry it. It hadn't taken very long to drive to Stockbridge to get the stone owl out of Elle's parents' backyard. Luckily no one was home at the time, although a vulnerable part of Kal wished her mom and dad had been. Even though he was now 22-years-old, he secretly welcomed an 'adult' intervening in the conflict he was about to enter.

"Did any of it rub off?" asked Elle, anxiously looking at her watch to see how much longer they had to wait.

Kal reached into the bag and gently touched the statue to make sure the gold spray paint had fully dried, but instead knocked off one of the fake red rubies Elle skillfully glued on.

"The jewels are coming off."

"Here," Elle said, pulling a container of super glue out of her pocket and reattaching the small piece of plastic to the concrete bird.

"This looks like shit," Kal said. "Marcus is never going to fall for it, what the hell are we doing?"

"Come on, Kal. Stop stressing. This is your plan, remember? It's going to work."

He took a deep breath and tried to calm down.

Marcus was enraged when he learned Kal and Elle escaped from his men and initially unleashed a verbal shit storm over the phone, threatening to kill anyone and everyone slightly associated with the two. Kal never wavered, though, and waited patiently until Marcus stopped screaming to negotiate. The terms were simple: Marcus and his men were to meet Kal in front of the fountain with the hostages. Once the Eagle was handed over, everyone would immediately be freed. Kal was going to hedge his bets by having Elle sit in the nearby Johnny Rockets restaurant underneath Central Avenue near the lone pay phone, out of harm's way and ready to dial 911 if the exchange went wrong. The plan was a long shot to work—both Kal and Elle knew it. But it was their only shot.

"Alright, they should be here any minute, you should go over to the restaurant now. Remember, do not call the police unless I signal you or it looks like things are going bad. This can't turn into a shootout at the O.K. Corral, we need to get everyone away safe."

"Gotcha, can I get you anything? A burger? Shake?" Elle joked.

Kal got up and gave her a bear hug. "Thank you again for back at the Cannonball House," he said with a peck on the cheek. Her hair brushed his face and he felt overcome by emotion, enough so that he decided to press his lips to hers.

He could feel her attempt to resist initially, but continued forward until she relaxed. After several seconds she finally pulled away with a confused look.

"I love you," he sheepishly admitted.

"I-I love you, too," she stammered. " . . . as a friend. We can't do this now. Please, Kal."

"I know, I'm sorry. I just had to let you know."

"We'll talk about it later. I have to go now before they come, remember the plan."

"You're right. Follow the plan."

"Are you sure you don't want the gun we took off those guys?" she asked one last time.

"You keep it. It won't do me any good. I'll see you on the flip side."

\*\*\*\*

Kal sat alone on the bench facing eastward toward the parking lot, intently watching the black Dodge van as it pulled into the lot and headed his direction, finally stopping a hundred yards short of the fountain. A football field's length behind him in the opposite direction sat Elle, alone at a table watching the entire area with binoculars and poised to make the call to the police.

Kal tried to slow his increasingly spastic breathing and clutched the bag tight.

*I can't believe this is happening. Thank goodness there are still a lot of people here for lunch. It should make it harder for Marcus and his people to come out firing.*

Two men in dark trench coats jumped out of the van and scanned the area for several seconds, then signaled inside. Kal could tell they were heavily armed under their coats—the outline of automatic machine guns as well as grenades and other weapons was obvious. They were ready for a war.

Benny was the first to get out, holding the hand of little Lily and helping her leap to the ground. Dunning followed gingerly, initially trying to take his time before Marcus shoved him. Even from a distance Kal could tell his face was twisted in anger, forced into this position due to a group of college kids.

Benny immediately noticed Kal across the courtyard and gave him a nod to signal they were fine.

*Here goes nothing.*

Kal dialed Marcus on the same cell phone he took off Schuler and his mind's eye flashed to the scene of Elle throwing herself at Weston. It made him smile.

"We're all here like you wanted, Kal. The whole merry band," Marcus said into the phone, having now spotted him. "As you can see, they are no worse for wear. Where is my statue?"

Kal held up the bag.

"You know, you are a ballsy cocksucker," Marcus said. "What makes you think I won't just gun you down right now and take what I want?"

"Look at all these people around, I'm pretty sure there is a

MARTA cop having lunch over there at the restaurant," Kal said, lying through his teeth. "I guess you could do it that way, but it seems messy. I'm sure your clients would be less than thrilled with any negative publicity surrounding the Eagle if innocent bystanders, including a child, were gunned down in broad daylight over it. There'd be no way to cover it up, no matter how hard you or they try. I don't want this thing, or anything to do with it. I just want my friends and you can take this stupid bird and be done with it all."

"Very well. Once I take the Eagle and verify its authenticity, we'll let everyone go."

"No," Kal said. "That's not what we agreed. I give this to you, you give them to me. The second I hand you the Eagle, you let them go. I'm not going to let you renege on the deal—you have no reason to release them once I give it to you."

"You know what?" Marcus said, now yelling into the phone and demonstratively waving his arms. "To hell with what we agreed, I'm tired of playing your games. This is how it's going to go down or I'll just shoot everyone, including the cop and all these goddamn people walking around. At this point, I could care less about collateral damage— seeing your skull shattered all over that fountain would almost be worth the trouble. Now do you want your friends or not?"

Kal looked back to the restaurant. Things were not going exactly the way he planned, but at this point he had to agree. He was too far in to turnaround.

"Fine, come get your statue."

"No, no. Bring it to me . . . boy," Marcus said.

It had become a power struggle, and it was evident to Kal that Marcus wanted to rub his nose in the fact he still had some control over the situation. He once again glanced over his shoulder and slightly shook his head at Elle—he didn't want her to get antsy and make the 911 call prematurely.

Kal walked deliberately toward the van with the bag slung over his shoulder, analyzing everything. It amazed him that no one had the faintest idea what was really transpiring. Business people, tourists and regular Atlantans moved around the fountain and square with purpose, so engrossed in their own existence they were oblivious to the danger right in front of them.

When he was within 15 yards of Marcus, Kal abruptly stopped walking and held the bag out in his hand.

*You come get it.*

"Defiant to the end," Marcus said with a laugh, motioning for his man to retrieve it. "I had higher hopes for you, Kalei."

He wanted to retort but was scared out of his mind watching the bag leave his possession and head back to Marcus. He glanced over at Benny, Lily, and Dunning standing next to the van looking pitiful and scared and a horrible feeling suddenly crept over him. *This isn't going to work, this is bad, this is very bad.* Realizing his judgment had been clouded by overt optimism and there was no real chance to fool Marcus, he quickly turned to the Johnny Rockets and tugged on his ear multiple times—the signal for Elle to call the police.

*Please God have the cops come fast. Please hurry.*

Marcus took the bag from his man with a crooked smile and feverishly untied the knot, struggling to pull the statue out. His own mission was nearly complete and his handlers would be happy.

# CHAPTER 21

Having chased the legend of the Freedom Eagle for more time than he cared to admit and having paid a price worse than anyone could comprehend, the moment was bittersweet to T.A. Dunning. This inanimate object was the root cause behind the death of his wife, the reason his life was in shambles, and now held the future of his cherished granddaughter in a precarious position. It was not at all what he imagined the discovery of the Eagle would be like; holding it by its outstretched wings to a sea of media broadcasting around the world and proclaiming a final victory over the haunting past of the Confederate South and everything it represented. A black man had discovered the very propaganda tool the kinfolk of those who enslaved his forefathers coveted enough to shed modern blood over.

So it was no surprise that before Marcus pulled a third of the statue out of the bag Dunning recognized whatever Kal provided was a fake. Time began to slow down to a crawl for him as he watched the head mercenary hold the bird up in the sunlight and carefully examine it. His senses came alive and overly hyperactive. He noticed the air had a sweet smell from the nearby jasmine bushes, which were oddly blooming in the winter, and there was a crisp wind blowing over his skin, giving him goosebumps and dulling the pain from his multiple injuries.

He felt rejuvenated and revitalized as he turned to his granddaughter, looked at her and smiled. He did know how it would end.

"What is this?" Marcus muttered. "This isn't right."

Sensing it was his time, Dunning lunged at the closest guard and drove his shoulder into the man's solar plexus, leaving him on the ground gasping for air. He staggered to keep his own balance and screamed at Benny.

"Go, run!"

It took Benny a few seconds to comprehend before he finally grabbed Lily and headed through the square to Kal. The professor straightened himself and turned toward his secondary targets, who were still intently examining the statue and just noticing the unfolding action. Before either could react, Dunning flung himself like a Tasmanian devil on top of the second guard, knocking Marcus to the ground and shattering the false artifact into hundreds of gold-painted plaster and concrete pieces.

"Kill him!" yelled Marcus, his hands covered in white powder. By now Benny and Lily had almost reached Kal, who was pointing for them to head to the restaurant.

Dunning held onto his opponent for dear life even though he was outweighed by at least 60 pounds, desperate to buy time for his granddaughter and not allow the mercenary to get a clean shot. They wrestled in a bear hug, twirled like two clumsy dancers and slammed violently into the van several times before falling through the open door into the cargo area. The driver, the same man who set up their laptop and was seated with the engine running, jumped into the fray to try and pull Dunning off, but was knocked back into the dashboard by both men's thrashing legs.

Pure physics eventually won out, however, and within moments the guard gained control and used his strength to hold the professor down, smashing his head into the bed of the van several times with blows that should have crushed the strongest of skulls. Dunning instead began laughing hysterically and lifted his uninjured hand for the man to see. In it lay one of the several MK3A2 grenades previously strapped to the mercenary's utility belt, only this one had no pull ring securing it—Dunning had yanked the explosive off and activated it during their scrum. It was now cooking live in his hand, ready to blow.

"See, I always knew how this would end," he gurgled through a blood-streaked smile before dropping the explosive onto the floor and passing out.

****

Twenty yards from the van, Kal pushed Benny and Lily ahead of him toward the restaurant, only stopping briefly to check on the professor. He was instead distracted by Marcus, who picked himself off the ground and stumbled in angry pursuit attempting to pull his handgun out of his shoulder strap.

Kal could hear Elle screaming at Benny and Lily from behind to follow her as she ran full speed from the Johnny Rockets.

Kal turned his head and made brief eye contact with her as she raced to them. *What is she doing? She needs to get out of here!* He raised his hand to motion for her to turn around, but before he could utter a word he was cut off by an explosion.

It was small initially, followed by an enormous wave of heat and light that picked him up and threw him through the air more than thirty feet like a doll, the back of his head bouncing off the ground upon impact and knocking him unconscious for several seconds.

When he came to, his ears were ringing and he was lying on his side, a strange, heavy sensation emanating from his right leg. He groggily looked down and saw his calf bent underneath his thigh at the knee and twisted at a grotesque angle . . . yet he felt no pain. As the ringing noise slowly dissipated, replaced by a chorus of screams and cries from those in the courtyard who were either down or running to find cover, Kal raised himself by his elbows to look at the spot where Dunning, Marcus and the van had been just moments before and instead saw a giant fireball generating a massive amount of smoke. He leaned his throbbing head back over his shoulder toward the fountain and saw Lily huddled by herself, Benny running to someone crumpled on the ground.

It was Elle.

She lay prone on her back with her eyes wide open, emptily staring in Kal's direction as a stream of blood trickled from a red dot on her temple, staining her hair. Benny dropped to his knees and embraced her, screaming for help.

Kal reached his scraped hand to them and tried to yell, but nothing came out. Resting back on the ground and looking directly up into the partly overcast sky, he felt a sudden rush of warmness that slowed his heart rate.

"It's going to be okay, honey," said his mother, her face appearing above him with a loving smile. She brushed his head and kissed his cheek.

"Sleep now."

# CHAPTER 22

**September 3, 2009**
**Nine Months Later**

"**W**hat can I get ya, buddy?"

"Bud Light and a shot of Cazadores," the patron replied, plopping down on the stool and gazing up at the baseball game on TV. Within seconds of the room temperature shot of Tequila hitting the wood surface it was gone, down the man's guzzle, chased by a huge swig of ice-cold beer.

"Wow, it is coming down out there," said the portly, middle-aged man, his clothes partially soaked. "I was working on my front yard and damn near got dumped on. Decided to cut it short and head over here."

"Good idea," said the long-haired bartender, fiddling with the bottles of liquor behind the bar and adjusting them so their labels all faced outward. "Don't want to get a cold in the middle of the summer."

It was a typical hot and muggy early September afternoon in Atlanta, where the stickiness and humidity clung to the skin like mosquito spray, only to be followed by an afternoon deluge. Manuel's Tavern just outside of downtown was deserted on this particular Sunday,

U2's *One* playing in the background for no one in particular as the rain poured down in bucketfuls outside.

"I don't think I've seen you here before. You new?" the man asked.

"Kind of. Been around about a month picking up odd shifts to make some money. You know how it is."

"Sure. I try to get over here as much as possible to escape the old lady. She thinks I'm at the hardware store right now."

Both men laughed as the bartender slowly limped to the kitchen to break down some boxes, moving gingerly with one hand on the rail to steady himself.

"How'd you hurt yourself?" the man asked.

"Playing pickup basketball over at the college. Jacked my knee up."

The man smiled with a puzzled look.

"Hey, correct me if I'm wrong, but you look a lot like the kid from the bombing at the Underground."

It was the local story that dominated national headlines nearly a year earlier—a local college professor taken hostage with his granddaughter and a group of students after the murder of his wife, culminating in an explosion downtown killing six people, including the teacher and a young woman. And now the kid who ended up playing the hero appeared to be serving him drinks.

"No, not me," said the bartender, laughing. "I get that all the time. I need to start passing myself off as him, though. Might get me laid more."

"Wow, you could be his twin. You know if he is still around Atlanta? I haven't heard much about that story in awhile."

"Got no idea, didn't really follow it too closely," said the bartender, noticing the cook was waving to get his attention. "Excuse me real quick, looks like I'm needed." The bartender made his way toward the kitchen, stopping to check the score of the game and straighten some of the tables on his way.

"What's up?" he asked, peeking his head around the corner.

"Nada. Just seeing if that dude was gonna order food. I'm bored off my ass back here," the cook replied.

"I don't think so, sorry. Sounded like he had to get home pretty soon. Why don't you go in the back and have a brew? I won't tell anybody. Hell, I might come join you."

"Maybe next time, I'm off in an hour. Thanks anyway, Kal."

The bartender limped to his post up front, stopping briefly to adjust his knee brace. No matter how hard he tried to ignore the events of nine months prior, they always seemed to track him down.

# CHAPTER 23

**B**enny Rebelski shrugged his shoulders and sighed.

Standing next in line at the local Starbucks having waited an inordinate amount of time to get a plain coffee, he reached into his rear pocket for his wallet and realized it was still back home. *That's just perfect,* he thought as he discretely canceled his order and shuffled to his car, more amazed as his string of luck than angry. Even the simple task of buying a decent cup of java had become wrought with obstacles. *Not that it really mattered. I'm not sure I even have enough in my account to buy a cup of plain black.*

Benny pulled out his phone and checked for recent calls—no one other than his younger sister since last week. Tears suddenly began streaming down his face as he closed the door to drive home. "Fuck!" he screamed, pounding the steering wheel over and over with his fists until they became raw.

He closed his eyes seeking temporary refuge from the world but was bombarded by images of Elle's face, panicked as she attempted to get his attention before the explosion. It was ingrained into his psyche forever, and not a day went by that he wasn't haunted by her or some other part of that tragic event.

Things seemed to spiral downhill almost instantly after Kal and Marcus' exchange. The explosion from the van stopped everything and everyone in their tracks. Benny was thrown to the ground, initially more confused than hurt as the courtyard descended into chaos with throngs of screaming and injured attempting to escape the terror. He made his way to the spot Elle had been standing and found her on the ground, motionless, with a bullet wound to her head. Her eyes were wide open but when Benny picked her up, he knew the life had left her body.

He cradled his girlfriend in his arms and took in the amount of damage caused by the blast, immediately assuming the worst for those nearest, including Kal. It wasn't until later Benny learned he survived, albeit with major injuries.

Everything past that moment was a whirlwind.

Police and fire swarmed the scene and shut everything down for days. Kal was rushed to the hospital and underwent surgery for a broken tibia, fibula and shredded ligaments in his knee. Benny and Lily were sequestered by the FBI and Atlanta PD as the incident quickly became a national story and officials tried to sort through the mess to find out exactly what transpired. Six deaths, multiple injuries at a popular daytime tourist spot—people immediately assumed foreign terrorism.

It turned out Benny had been right in that no one within the immediate vicinity of the van, sans Kal, survived the explosion, including Dunning or Marcus. Identifying all the bodies became a herculean task and in the end authorities were only able to positively ID Dunning and one of the hostage-takers. The others were ghosts—no records, no fingerprint matches, no proof of their existence. For a short period the FBI even hypothesized that Benny and Kal lied about the existence of Marcus, but in the end were forced to accept limited evidence that the shadowy figure who left behind zero clues had been the mastermind, eventually discovering the burned-out remains of the safe house where the group was held.

Because the single deceased mercenary the FBI identified had ties to an Aryan resistance group, the government finally decided to run with it, tying up the entire incident in a neat little bow under the explanation of a hate crime directed at Dunning because of his race and status in the community. They attributed Elle's death to a single stray bullet, impossible to trace the origin of because of the vast amount of ordinance that showered the area after the fireball, although Benny was positive it intentionally came from Marcus' gun—a last act of horror. The Freedom Eagle was only briefly mentioned as a side note in the final reports.

The funerals of Elle and Dunning became a city-wide event, with their families deciding to honor the two simultaneously in a touching ceremony attended by hundreds, sans Kal, who was still confined to a bed at the time. He almost immediately rejected the FBI's version of events with fervor, making media rounds only a month after his surgery to relay his account of the story and accuse officials of a cover-up, all with the intent of illustrating the work Dunning did to save them. It was clear to Benny that Kal wanted the professor's legacy celebrated as that of a true hero and to make sure Lily was provided for, which was assured when a cousin of Dunning's eventually took custody of the little girl—all of her parents' estate and wealth left to her.

Benny found it slightly ironic that even though he had been initially mad at Kal for involving he and Elle, he did not hold him responsible anymore. He finally learned to accept the event as one of life's grand tests. He was just waiting for it to end and things to resume with some semblance of normality. He was tired of being down and out. Tired of waking up each morning, looking at his worn reflection in the mirror and feeling sorry for himself. Elle was gone forever, he had lost 20 pounds from all the stress, and most of the people involved with the previous chapter of his life were either dead or out of it permanently.

That's why he was so shocked when Kal rang his cell phone on the drive home from the failed coffee run. It had been almost six months since they last talked in passing.

"Benny, this is Kal."

"Kal?" he said, wiping his face and taking a deep breath to gain composure. "Kind of surprised to hear from you."

"Really? Why?" Kal asked.

"It's been a long time. To be honest, I didn't even know you had my cell phone number."

"I managed to track it down. How have you been?"

"Honestly? I've been better," Benny said, still confused but surprisingly happy to hear his voice. "Finished school in May and moved back home with my parents. Just hanging out right now, not real sure what to do with my life. Not exactly dominating things."

"I know exactly what you mean. It's been a rough year. I still have trouble sleeping at night."

"How is your leg?" Benny asked. "I know you were on crutches the last time I saw you at the benefit dinner for Lily."

"Pretty good, it's getting stronger all the time, just have to wear this brace now. I'm bartending part time over at Manuel's, you should come by some afternoon."

The invitation stunned Benny. It was the first time he had heard from Kal in months and now he was inviting him to hang out.

"Manuel's? I remember that place, I think I went there a few times with . . . " he said, catching himself before he said her name.

"Yeah. Actually, that's what I wanted to talk to you about," Kal said. "Can you meet up for lunch later today?"

"I think so. What's going on?"

"I'd rather talk to you in person. I wouldn't believe it myself if it hadn't happened to me."

# CHAPTER 24

**K**al took a big swig of Coke, ran his hand through his hair and hesitantly looked around the McDonald's. He always possessed an insatiable appetite for chicken McNuggets and figured they could blend with the restaurant's normal clientele free of disturbance. Trying to avoid recognition was his newest main goal in life, hence the longer hair and the job at the small, out-of-the-way bar. Even though it had been almost a year since the bombing, he was still stopped occasionally, which was about as comfortable for him as a severe sunburn.

He had been filling Benny in on his rehab and his withdrawal from school, unable to continue to study on the same campus where he and Dunning worked, actually moving to Greeley to temporarily live with his dad until a sense of unfulfillment beckoned him like a tractor beam back to Georgia after only a month.

Now he was about to divulge the real order of business.

"First off, I just wanted to apologize to you for being an asshole," he said, raising his hand to keep Benny from protesting. "I was. You don't have to lie. I treated you horribly, and for that, I'm sorry. We both lost a lot that day, and I think we . . . or, I, specifically, should try and mend fences. She would have really been happy with that."

"Thanks. It actually means a lot. It's been kind of a rough go lately."

"I should have done it a long time ago. But to be truthful, that's not the reason I wanted to meet up. Something happened recently and I wasn't real sure how to deal with it. I've been struggling with it in my head. Like I said, I haven't been able to sleep real well for awhile, and I thought you might be able to help me."

"Okay," Benny said hesitantly, dipping a handful of fries in a package of barbecue sauce.

"Well, it's about some old . . . stuff. You know, with Professor Dunning and everything."

Benny shoved the fried potato in his mouth and grabbed a napkin to wipe the grease off his hands. "Hey, if you are still feeling horrible about what went down, that stuff is over, done with. We don't have to deal with it anymore. What happened, happened, and it wasn't any of our faults, especially not yours. I don't blame anyone except Marcus."

"I know. Trust me, it took me a long time to accept it. It's something else, though. Someone came to visit me the other day at the bar."

"Was it more media? Those guys just won't quit, they're like, they're like . . . " Benny said, now licking the sauce packet. Before he could finish searching for the proper metaphor, Kal blurted out the answer.

"It was Ashworth. It was Robert Ashworth from Virginia."

Benny sat stunned for a few seconds before composing himself. "Are you kidding me? What did he want?"

"I'm not really sure," Kal said. "It was on Sunday afternoon, I was alone at the bar when he came in. I had no idea who he was, and he bought a few rounds so we struck up some bullshit conversation. Finally after about a half hour he finally told me his name and that he knew all about me and what I did for Dunning in trying to find the Eagle. He read the story in the Journal-Constitution—which I knew I should have never done—about cracking the code. But he started to tell me how much he always respected Dr. Dunning, and that because of our work he found more info from Sherman proving the Eagle really did exist and where it was."

"Are you kidding me?" Benny asked. "That thing was a myth,

we proved it. It's over, case closed. Didn't he read about that historical society performing one of those ground penetrating scans at the Cannonball House a couple of months ago and finding nada? Why is this guy trying to stir this up again?"

"I don't know," Kal said. "I started cussing him out. Told him to get the hell out of the bar, that I didn't want to hear anymore crap about the stupid statue as long as I lived. He tried to argue, but I wouldn't listen, so he finally just left his business card on the bar with the phone number of the hotel he's staying at downtown. I picked it up and ripped it in his face."

"Nice. I would have done the same thing, so what's problem?"

"I got home that night and couldn't stop thinking about it, about everything: Elle, Dunning, Marcus, the Freedom Eagle, Lily, you and me. I mean, what did they die for? I would have been killed down in that basement if it weren't for Elle, and Dunning sacrificed himself for us. But what about his legacy and work? What if Ashworth is right and he can actually find it? They died saving our lives, maybe we owe it to them to try and exhaust every lead on the Freedom Eagle."

"First of all, their deaths were a tragedy, and no one will ever forget them. Their legacies are sealed," Benny said. "Second, it sounds like you have some stuff you haven't resolved, which is completely normal. I still think about Elle every hour of every day."

Kal chewed on the straw of his drink and stared off into the distance. "Maybe I'm not over it and I keep trying to fool myself into thinking I am. All I know is there is something deep down inside of me, bottled up, that I thought I had control of that keeps telling me I need to finish this for closure."

Benny took his time before answering. "Listen, I'm no psychologist. I actually took that class for fun and cheated off the girl next to me to pass. But what I do know is there are issues that occur in life that can eat a person up from the inside unless they're resolved. I'm not telling you that you do or don't need to go talk to Ashworth. What I am telling you is my philosophy on life is you can never be wrong for following your heart, and if it's saying finish this once and for all, then that's probably the answer you're looking for."

Kal was silent as he looked down at the floor and studied the pattern of small, dirty ceramic tiles, the grout filled with the remnants of a variety of mashed up McDonald's cuisine.

"I don't know if I can take all of that baggage resurfacing," he finally said.

"I know this sounds corny and straight out of a Disney movie, but we can do it together. I was serious when I said my life sucked right now. Honest to God, I was sitting in my car crying like a baby when you called this morning because I forgot to bring my wallet to get coffee. I'm a mess.

"Maybe I need closure as well? We'll just go to the hotel and see what he has to say. It can't hurt."

Kal smiled. "I guess Elle was sort of right about you. You're not a total asshole."

Benny laughed and picked up the last nugget, cramming it into his mouth. "What do they put in these things, crack?"

****

Kal stopped and held open the front door of the Four Seasons Hotel for an elderly couple returning from the parking lot. He and Benny had driven straight from the restaurant to find Ashworth and get some answers.

"I meant to ask you how you knew he was here if you ripped up his card?" Benny asked.

"I saw 'Four Seasons' written on the back when I threw it away. I figured we could just ask for him at the front desk since I don't which room he's in," Kal said. "This is the only Four Seasons in town."

"Actually, I know of a pay-by-the-hour hotel that hookers supposedly use called 'On All Fours.' Maybe you read it wrong?"

Kal just looked at Benny with bewilderment. "You're trying too hard on that one," he said, still adjusting to his sense of humor.

This particular hotel was one of the nicest in the city, located in the heart of downtown Atlanta. Kal had never actually been inside a five-star resort before and immediately felt subconscious wearing shorts and a t-shirt, as if there were a sign tattooed across his forehead flashing 'OUT OF PLACE'.

"Excuse me, ma'am. I'm trying to find the room number for one of your guests," Kal said to the front desk agent—a dark-haired girl in her late twenties.

"I'm sorry, sir. I can't give out guests' room numbers, but I can call them. What's the name?" she asked.

"Robert Ashworth."

"Hey," Benny said to her in a low, suave voice, trying to make eye contact as she looked up the name in her computer. "How's your day going?"

Kal elbowed him in the ribs.

"My day is fine, sir. But unfortunately Mr. Ashworth is no longer staying with us. He checked out this morning."

"No idea where he went?" Kal asked, hoping for a miracle.

"I'm sorry, sir."

He slumped his shoulders and turned away, slapping Benny on the back. "Well, that's that. We gave it a shot, but I guess it was not meant to be. Sorry for dragging you into this. Let me make it up to you with a cold one."

"I think I love you," mouthed Benny to the desk agent as he turned to follow.

"Were you seriously hitting on her?" Kal asked when they made it back to his Ford F-150 in the parking lot.

"Just having a little fun," Benny said. "I'll be honest, I haven't even thought of the opposite sex since . . . I've pretty much become the definition of celibate. But getting out of the house and doing all this has got my blood going."

The thought of Benny and Elle together in a physical manner crept into Kal's subconscious and reached all the way down to his stomach. It hurt like hell she was gone, and being around Benny wasn't necessarily helping things.

"So what's next, how are we gonna track this guy down?"

"There is no next. That's it—it's a wrap. We tried, it didn't work, and now I get over it and move on," Kal said, starting the truck up and adjusting the AC so it was on full blast.

"Are you kidding me? That's it?" Benny said shaking his head. "All the crap you just told me, about not being able to sleep at night, wanting to help Dunning's legacy, not giving up, yada, yada. And then you hit the first little roadblock and you're ready to toss in the towel? That's B.S."

"It's not like we didn't try. I don't want to drag this out further than necessary and forever search for answers. What the hell else should I do, drive up to Virginia and just show up unannounced in the middle of the night to Ashworth's house?"

Kal immediately clammed up, which made Benny crack a smile.

"I know the two of us haven't gotten along in the past, but this is the best I've felt in a long time and I'm not stopping now. I have nothing going on this week, and judging by what you've been up to, it doesn't sound like you're exactly booked solid. How far is it from here to UVA, anyway?"

"Eight hours," Kal said. "I happened to MapQuest it the other day."

Benny raised his fist in the air. "Pack your bags. We're going on a road trip like in *Dumb and Dumber*! I got dibs on Lloyd Christmas, you can be Harry Dunn. You know you want to do this!"

Kal sighed and laid his head back against the headrest. He started this and now realized Benny was right. He had to finish it even if it meant investing more of himself than he desired.

# CHAPTER 25

"Oh my God, that was bad," yelled Kal, rolling down his window for the umpteenth time. "What do you eat to make it smell rotten?"

Benny was having a hard time breathing from laughing so hard, doubled over and smacking his fist against his seat in an attempt to catch his breath. He had gotten comfortable enough to release his toxic fumes the whole ride from Atlanta, and eight hours later after a diet of beef jerky, fast food and a single orange, they were just as potent and funny to him as the first one he let go.

"Stop, stop!" Benny managed to squeak out. "I'm going to piss my pants!"

Kal grunted, annoyed but semi-entertained, "Go ahead, it smells like you already did something else in them."

The truth was neither man smelled decent. They had been driving since the morning, only stopping for gas and food, and were just now pulling into the beautiful town of Charlottesville, home of the University of Virginia. Located in the foothills of the Blue Ridge Mountains, Charlottesville was a quintessential college town rich with American history—Thomas Jefferson's mountain home overlooking the city,

Monticello, its most famous attraction. Kal loved this area, with rolling hills and lush greenery. He had little wonder as to why Jefferson picked it for his château.

"What now?" Benny asked as they drove down the main avenue.

"Well, since it's 7 p.m., we have no idea where this guy is other than his campus office, I'm tired and you need a shower, I say we find a hotel room and start early in the morning."

"Cool. Maybe we can get a bite to eat and check out the local flavor? I hear they have a pretty nice downtown area with a bunch of restaurants and bars."

Kal thought better of it for a moment, but for some reason the notion of a nice meal and a nightcap sounded really good—plus it would probably help him sleep better.

"Okay, but just a couple. We need to find this guy and take care of business tomorrow. I want to be fresh."

****

"And then this mother effer right here, says to my girlfriend at the time, 'Follow my lead,' and cold-cocks the guy with a pipe!" Benny said, pounding the rest of his beer and shouting to the bartender. "Another round of shots for me and my friends!"

"No more," Kal weakly resisted, struggling to keep his bearings on his stool. He wasn't positive, but he was pretty sure Benny was telling the story of he and Elle's escape from the Cannonball House to a group of college kids, and it was getting him riled up. He didn't like rehashing those events, even with close friends, and now Benny was showboating for an entire bar at a place called Miller's. What he initially intended as dinner and a drink at a local pub had several hours later degenerated into a full blown bar crawl, and he was on the verge of slipping past the point of no return.

"So what are you guys doing up here? Are you giving a speech or something?" asked a co-ed.

"Nope, we're trying to meet up with some guy on official business. What was his name, Kal? Dr. Ashyface?"

"Ashworth," Kal said groggily, looking up from his drink. The room was starting to spin a little, so he discreetly poured the shot of vodka Benny ordered onto the floor, out of sight. "Why don't you leave these people alone. They don't want to hear your stupid stories."

"Yeah they do," Benny replied, turning back to his new audience. "Don't mind him, he's still working out some issues. Anyway, this Ashworth guy is a big fat ass, works with the history department."

"I believe the correct term is overweight," boomed a man's voice from across the bar, interrupting Benny's cackle.

"Excuse me?" he said, turning to look at the rotund, bearded man who was sitting all by himself, nursing a beer and watching the TV.

"Fat ass? That's not really P.C. these days. Now big-boned, that's somewhat more acceptable."

"Um, alright," Benny replied, rolling his eyes and continuing his story. "Oh-kay, where was I?"

Kal studied the man, crossing his eyes to focus his inebriated vision in the dimly-lit bar. It took a few seconds, but when the light from the closest neon beer sign reflected off the man's face, he nearly choked.

"Benny," he said softly, gently nudging him in the side.

"Hold on a sec, Kal. I'm almost to the best part of the story."

"Benny," Kal said with more force. "Shut up, it's him. It's Robert Ashworth, he's here."

"What? Are you serious? Where?"

Kal pointed to the man who just interrupted Benny and was now smiling and waving at them.

"The big-boned guy."

Benny looked over and smiled.

"Well, that sucks," he said through gritted teeth.

****

The Cadillac Escalade slowly pulled down the darkened lane toward the massive brick home, which was illuminated like a single, lonely Christmas tree in the night.

"Wow, beautiful house, Mr. Ashworth," Kal said from the passenger seat, sipping on a bottled water and trying as hard as possible to not slur his words. "It looks like a classic."

"It's Doctor, Dr. Ashworth with a Ph.D, and yes, it was actually built only 10 years ago. I wanted it to reflect an older era, but have all the modern amenities," he said with an awkward wink. Kal wasn't sure if he was trying to be funny or serious.

The Georgian-style residence sat on 25-plus acres of beautiful farmland outside of downtown Charlottesville. It took the group 30 minutes driving country roads to reach the house, with Benny drunkenly apologizing from the back seat most of the way. "Again, sir, I am so sorry about the bar back there. That is not me, I don't do that type of thing."

"Oh, it's alright. I've been called much worse in my lifetime," Ashworth said, followed by a high-pitched laugh. "Fat ass actually used to be one of my ex-wife's pet names for me. You boys just so happened to partaking in libations at a place that I like to consider my home away from home. The drinks are cheap, and as you experienced, the scenery not bad. Besides my office, I hardly spend more time anywhere else."

It had been somewhat awkward for Kal back at Miller's to explain why he and Benny were in town. He never expected to run into Ashworth within hours of arriving and the fact he was drunk made it even worse in his opinion. The man was gracious, however, and seemed to be genuinely happy Kal changed his mind and was in Virginia, insisting he and Benny leave their vehicle behind and visit his estate to talk.

The doublewide garage doors raised as the truck pulled closer, revealing an ostentatious showroom housing several classic cars, including a 1957 two-door, hardtop Chevrolet Bel Air and a cherry red '66 Lamborghini 400GT, as well as an all-black Dodge Viper GT.

"Whoa," Benny said.

"Yes, this is one of my passions—collecting cars. I have quite a few in storage in addition to these," Ashworth said, followed again by the laugh. Kal noticed during the ride he did it quite often, almost after every sentence. He also blinked incessantly for large periods of time, as if he had a tic of some sort.

"That, right there, is my favorite," he said of the Lamborghini as he walked through the garage and into the house, ushering Kal and Benny inside. "I love to get it out on these roads in the evening and really open it up. These machines are incredible, possessing both delicate beauty and raw power—a real testament to the ingenuity and spirit of the men that built them. I also love going mano-a-mano against other collectors at auctions, staring down straight into their souls, then ripping their hearts out by outbidding at the final possible second. It's a rush, different from the one I get finding Civil War artifacts, which of course, you have experienced. That is how I initially came to meet our dear friend, T.A. Dunning."

Ashworth stopped briefly in the kitchen to grab a couple more waters from the fridge and a bag of Hershey's miniature chocolates. "Can I get you two some coffee?"

"Water is fine," Benny said, "Do you mind if I use your bathroom, though?"

"Not at all. It's down that hall, third door on the left. Kal and I will be out in the living room."

Benny high-stepped it to relieve himself and Kal followed Ashworth into a common area like none he had ever seen—a small museum wing was a more appropriate description. Flags from all 50 states, as well as two massive American and Confederate streamers hung from the 30-foot vaulted ceilings, and pictures and paintings of Lincoln, Jefferson Davis, and many others—collectibles that put those in Dunning's study to shame—covered almost every inch of wall space. A vintage Confederate cannon sat next to a couch, and several muskets and swords were housed in specially constructed cabinets towering over a lone table in the back.

"This is the epicenter of my collection, Kal," Ashworth said, proudly looking around the room and stuffing a chocolate in his mouth. "It's taken me years to find some of these pieces. That top revolver over there belonged to Stonewall Jackson and this cannon here is a Confederate 10-lb Parrott rifle, found at Gettysburg and fully restored—don't ask me how I acquired it. This is how T.A. and I became acquainted. The circle of Civil War buffs has not exactly expanded these days."

It struck Kal as odd that Dunning would work with someone like Ashworth—a collector, not a researcher. He recalled Dunning expressing disdain for those he felt stole valuable pieces of history that could teach younger generations solely for ego and greed. And Robert Ashworth definitely had enough loot pirated in this room alone to make any university jealous.

*Perhaps finding the Freedom Eagle was too tempting for the professor, and he temporarily abandoned his morals for the thrill of the hunt?*

"So how are you affiliated with the University?" Kal asked, casually examining some of the pieces in the cabinets.

"Let's just say I scratch their back and they scratch mine from time to time. You won't find my name on any official faculty roster, but I have all the access I need to the school's facilities and research, as well as a small office. I made a fortune in the Internet boom, got out early and focused attention on my passions. It's amazing how money will provide you access and privilege these days. You start a few scholarships, sponsor some grants, and it's as if you were one of the university's founding fathers."

"I'll be honest," Kal said. "I'm not interested in that type of research anymore. I lost some zeal after everything happened."

"Really?" Ashworth said, raising one eyebrow in surprise and opening another candy. "Then why, may I ask, did you come up to Virginia to see me?"

"That's a really good question. I have been asking myself it since we left Atlanta," Kal answered, pausing to compose himself through the cloud of alcohol. "I guess to put it simply, Dr. Dunning would have pushed me to keep going, to pursue the quest. He would have wanted to find the Eagle without a doubt. The least we could do was hear you out."

Ashworth nodded in understanding and smiled. "Good, because I think I can find it. First, though, you have to tell me how you figured out Sherman's code."

# CHAPTER 26

**B**enny plopped down on the couch next to Kal, whose right leg was elevated on an ottoman, and gave a quizzical look as Ashworth rifled through his desk, muttering to himself. Kal shrugged back—he had no idea what was going on. One minute he was explaining in detail how the group unlocked the code back in Atlanta, and the next the quirky man was talking to himself and throwing things around.

"Ah yes, here they are. I hid them so well I almost forgot where," he finally proclaimed. "I can't believe the code was that easy, right in front of our faces the whole time. And you cracked it under duress and fear of physical reprisal. Simply amazing. Anyhow, these are more letters, telegraphs, and correspondence from Sherman I've since broken down using your technique. I believe these letters prove you were on the right track and the Freedom Eagle does in fact exist, and was at one time hidden at what is now referred to as the Cannonball House of Macon."

Kal didn't like being referred to as a code-breaker, because in fact he wasn't. It was the perfect storm that led to the discovery—access to telegraphs and letters by Sherman, belief in the existence of the Freedom Eagle, and luck. He was more in shock over Ashworth's last statement regarding the Cannonball House.

"This telegraph was sent in November of 1864," Ashworth said, selecting one of the papers. "After using your code, or the Dunning Method, as some of our colleagues have begun to call it, you get the message 'EAGLE MOVE FROM MACON SEARCH SECURE PLACEMENT.' Here's one from a few days later that Sherman sent to a major in St. Louis stationed at the Jefferson Barracks: 'EAGLE DESTINATION SAFE HELVETICA VIA LAND.' And there are several more I possess that mention Helvetia."

Ashworth stopped and looked at the two men, both of whom had blank stares.

"Don't you see? Sherman is telling us where he moved it!"

"No offense, Dr. Ashworth, but we've been down this path before," Kal said, trying to be as tactful as possible while focusing his thoughts. "We thought we knew where the Eagle was, but turned out to be wrong. Horribly wrong. So wrong it cost two good people their lives. I honestly believe the statue is lost—that's why no one has ever found it. But I came here with an open mind out of respect to T.A. and Elle, hoping maybe there was new indisputable evidence you found that would overwhelm me. I want you to be right, I honestly do. But I can't go on another wild goose chase. I did it last time because I had a gun to my head. This time I have a choice, and if that's all you have to sell me on, I'm afraid I made a mistake in coming."

"But don't you see?" Ashworth said. "Sherman is telling us where he took it. Helvetia!"

"Helvetia?" Kal asked, vaguely identifying the word. "Isn't that somewhere in Europe? There is no way he took it overseas. Plus, if that's the case, he contradicts himself by saying it was traveling via land. Unless there was a giant bridge over the Atlantic back in the 1800s I'm not familiar with, I don't think it's possible."

"Okay, wait. I can explain everything if you fully hear me out. I'm not being very articulate right now, so bear with me."

Benny leaned into Kal and hit him on the shoulder. "Relax for a minute. Chill. Let him finish."

Kal eased back into the couch and rubbed his knee. The drive from Atlanta exacerbated the arthritis that developed in the joint over the last month. Plus, he was still slightly miffed at Benny for the scene back at the bar.

Ashworth took a big sigh and started over. "First off, have you ever seen this symbol before?" he asked, picking up a sketch of a bear holding a snake in its mouth.

"Yeah, we saw it a few times. Kal said it was at the Cannonball House in Macon," Benny said. "We figured it was Sherman's personal crest."

"Really? That's good, very good. Did you see where I put my Hershey's down? I have a terrible sweet tooth. Never mind. Let's see, how much do you really know about William Tecumseh Sherman?"

As simple as it was, the question perplexed Kal. "Do you mean about the Civil War?"

"No. How much do you know about Sherman's life before the war, what he did for a living, who he associated with, et cetera, et cetera?"

Benny clearly had no idea, but neither did Kal. "I honestly don't know a whole lot about him pre-war."

"Okay, good. Actually not good, but I'm about to fix that," he said, followed by the annoying laugh.

"Sherman was an Army man, through and through. He attended West Point at an early age and entered the service as a lieutenant in the artillery division, fighting against the Native Americans down in Florida. He headed west after that and while the rest of his army cronies were duking it out in the Mexican-American War, Sherman was stationed up north in San Francisco as an aide to the governor in the newly acquired California territory. Now remember, this became the cradle of the Gold Rush, and people flocked to gold fields in the California foothills by the thousands to get a piece. So after watching a tidal wave of people and money flow through the region, Sherman and the governor decided to open a supply shop in the hills to capitalize, as any good entrepreneurs would. This is where it gets interesting. It was during this period he befriended a Swiss explorer named John Sutter, who was one of the first pioneers of California and set up headquarters in an area that is today the city of Sacramento, which at that time was just a small supply stop for miners heading up the hills. Sutter was a wealthy man and also owned the mill outside of town in Coloma where the first piece of gold was initially discovered."

"I vaguely remember reading in high school about the guy who found the first nugget. Wasn't his name Marshall?" Kal asked.

"Yes, James Marshall—he was one of Sutter's workers. Anyway, Sutter conducted his day-to-day business out of his own fort in Sacramento," continued Ashworth. "But because he came from Swiss roots, guess what he called the area?"

"Helvetia . . . " Kal said, trailing off as he connected the dots Ashworth was setting up. "I just remembered what it means. It's Latin for Switzerland."

"New Helvetia, to be exact," Ashworth said, visibly excited his guest was finally showing some proclivity.

"Okay, so what?" chimed in Benny. "So Sherman says in one of his hidden messages he's sending the Eagle to Helvetia, and it just so happens he was friends with a man who owned a fort in California with the same name? It's good circumstantial evidence, but it doesn't prove anything."

"Oh, but wait, there's more. Much more. So Sherman spends more time in northern California trying to earn money during the rush, particularly the rural Sacramento area, which by this time had grown substantially and become a major transportation hub and the capital. He was later, in fact, hired by Sutter's son and heir, John Sutter, Jr., to design and survey the streets of Sacramento, which are still laid out the exact same way today."

"Wait, wait, wait," interrupted Kal. "Are you trying to tell me Civil War General William Sherman designed present-day Sacramento? Why did I never hear about this?"

"Yes, he was a part of a team of engineers that created the grid for the city. It's not a well-known fact, but it is true. He also was at one time the first superintendent of the Seminary of Learning of the State of Louisiana, which eventually became the university we know today as LSU."

"Amazing," Kal said, shaking his head. "This is why I love history, Benny."

"So to continue," Ashworth said, finding the candy bag and chomping down on a Mr. Goodbar. By now the corners of his mouth had a large mixture of chocolate and spit residue from talking so much. "Sherman later dabbled in banking and eventually became the vice president of California's first railroad, the Sacramento Valley line, which ran about 25 miles east from downtown to the town of Folsom. It's during this time he befriended Theodore Judah, the chief engineer of the small railroad. Judah was plugged into the high society of the West—he later became the driving force behind the first Transcontinental Railroad—and it was through him Sherman was introduced to and became friends with the Big Four, opening all kinds of doors he never imagined."

"The Big Four?" Benny asked.

"Leland Stanford, Charles Crocker, Mark Hopkins and Huntington," answered Kal. "I can't remember the last one's full name. They were Sacramento businessmen that founded the Central Pacific Railroad, which was the California-to-Utah portion of the Transcontinental Railroad."

"That's right, Kal. Four of the most influential men of the early West. Judah planned the Transcontinental Railroad and was able to convince them to invest in it before the Big Four forced him out and took the railroad and its spoils for themselves. That's another story for another time, though. The important point is a networking connection was cultivated between Sherman and these men of high society. He was now a part of their inner circle, and as a result came into contact with other influential titans of that time, including men like California's first millionaire banker, Sam Brannan, who originally convinced Sutter's son to build the city of Sacramento in its current location. All of these connections lead us back to this symbol."

Ashworth again picked up the paper with the bear's head and snake and emphatically shook it.

"This symbol was not Sherman's personal crest or any other lone man's. It belonged to a group—a group whose sole intent was to better California and make it the jewel of Western civilization. This group was disenfranchised with the national politics that eventually caused the Civil War and desired their own land that took the best attributes of the East Coast and Europe, which they would then mold into their own society. California was to be their utopia. They collected fine artwork and historical documents and sublimely recruited doctors, engineers, lawyers and businessmen they felt could be leaders in their new state, as well as build a massive reserve of wealth."

"Are you serious?" Benny asked. "It sounds made up."

"Trust me, son. It's as real as anything I've ever hunted or chased before. Much of the artwork you see in museums in San Francisco, Los Angeles, Sacramento, and Seattle—up and down the West Coast—came from these men. Crocker's family has a large museum in their name in Sacramento to this day. The group never attached an official title to themselves, although through research I have found several references to 'Die Verein'. Sutter spoke German and apparently referred to the group by this moniker, which roughly translated means 'The Association.' This bear holding a snake in its mouth was the lone identifier they used, like the stamp you found on some of Sherman's letters. I've also found multiple examples of it with the words PARIO PARADIUS underneath the bear's head. Do you know what that means?"

They both shook their heads. Kal deduced the Helvetia right; he wasn't going to push his luck with his Latin skills.

"Roughly translated it means 'birth' and 'heaven,' the birth of heaven . . . the creation of paradise . . . the creation of California. When the war broke out in the East, this group became obsessed with saving and preserving historical pieces they worried would be destroyed in the fighting, and began secretly procuring and shipping items back to New Helvetia, back to Sacramento for safekeeping."

"How come no one has heard about this or exposed the group before?" Benny bluntly asked.

"Because they weren't formally organized and didn't operate publicly. These men all acted like double agents, living their normal lives but subversively working to better the cause. When I was a child I always heard whispers and rumors of them from my grandfather, whose great, great granddaddy was a gold miner. And much like you heard the rumors of the Eagle from Dunning, it wasn't until I started unlocking these letters and more from other men of the time using your method did it became apparent this group was in fact authentic. My research found as the years passed and more and more were indoctrinated into their mission, The Verein felt the obligation to legitimize and go mainstream to keep their ideals for California alive through future generations, so they formed a sub organization: the Native Sons of the Golden West."

Ashworth walked around to the back of his desk, pulled out a colorful, modern pamphlet, and brought it over to the couch for Kal to read. "As you can see by their current mission statement here, the Native Sons were formed in 1875 and still exist to this day. They were nativists, bordering on racists originally, that wanted to keep California pure. The individual that created the group—now stop me if you've heard this before—was an entrepreneur from the East Coast who came to California to make money from the Gold Rush and ended up settling at Sutter's Fort. He later became Sacramento's first mayor and was highly influential in civic duties and shaping the direction of the town. My theory is over time the Native Sons of the Golden West became the accepted political wing of The Verein, almost like Sinn Fein is to the IRA in Ireland. When the original members of The Verein began to die off from old age, the Native Sons of the Golden West were all that was left and became the stewards of that past. They are still a functioning organization today."

"My head hurts," Benny said. "I haven't had a history lesson since my freshman year."

"So were they a version of Freemasons? Or based on religious principles? Because that's what it sounds like," Kal asked.

"I guess you could say this group loosely resembled Freemasons, but they were nowhere near as organized. In fact, several people that I believe were in The Verein were also Freemasons. Where Freemasonry was a lifestyle and brotherhood rich in tradition and history, this was more of a group whose origins were based on money, wealth, and status. They were a conglomerate of the elite."

He stopped for a brief second and smiled.

"I know it's a lot to process, but believe me," Ashworth said.

"We are on the precipice of unlocking one of the greatest secret societies of this country. One that no one knows existed. Take the current State Seal of California, for instance. It's a picturesque scene with the Roman Goddess Minerva, who is the Goddess of Wisdom, sitting at the entrance to the San Francisco Bay with ships in the harbor and miners working the field behind her. In front of her is a bear eating a grape vine. This is not the original piece, though. The original was created in 1849 and redesigned in the 1930s."

Ashworth held up a sheet with two logos on it—one was California's current State Seal in full color, the other a black and white copy of the original design. "The one on the left is a copy of the original California Seal I was able to track down. What's different between the two?"

"Holy crap," Benny said. "It looks like the bear has a snake in its mouth . . . "

"Yes! The California Legislature changed it in 1937 to a grape vine to represent the wine production in the state, but as you can see in the original, the bear is clearly holding the snake in its mouth—which just so happens to be the brand of The Verein we've all now identified. Look at the state flag of California. It's no coincidence the bear is most prominent."

"Let me guess," Benny said, pointing up to the California flag on Ashworth's ceiling, which had a large brown bear in the center, a single star to the upper left corner and a solid red bar along the bottom. "The star was at one point a snake in the bear's mouth and the state changed it?"

"Um, no. The star was always a star. I like your thinking, though," said Ashworth with a chuckle. "But, the bear is key."

"Let's say you're right about all this. Say Sherman did move the Eagle to California as part of this 'movement.' What happened to it then? Where would it be now and who has it?" Kal asked.

"Over time, the ideals, secrets and the old methodology of The Verein and then the Native Sons of the Golden West eroded and died off to the point they are not the same organization that was founded in the late 1800's. No one in the current version of the Native Sons has any idea of how or why they were truly created, or any inkling of the actions their forefathers took to shape California and preserve their past. They are a group of history buffs now—a fun little club. I believe the answer lies at Sutter's Fort, which is where those original forefathers of the movement initially stored items like the Freedom Eagle after smuggling them across the country."

Kal shook his head—he still wasn't totally buying it. "That was 160 years ago, I'm pretty sure that fort is long, long gone with whatever's left buried under a parking lot, which is the same problem the Cannonball House presented."

"Ah, yes. One would think."

Ashworth went to one of his book shelves and pulled out an encyclopedia, thumbing through pages until he found what he was looking for: an image of a massive white rectangular fortress surrounded by trees. Two guard towers stood at each end of the citadel protecting an enveloped courtyard and a plain-white, three-story house. More intriguing to Kal was the modern office building and a street lined with parked cars outside the fort.

"Sutter's Fort still stands today as it did in 1850, smack dab in the middle of downtown Sacramento."

Benny stood up and grabbed the book. "Just like the Alamo in San Antonio."

"It's a living historical landmark that takes up most of two city blocks. And there's an even more interesting fact . . . the only original section remaining is the main house you see here," he said, pointing to the building in the middle of the courtyard. "This was the hub. Everything from medicine to business transactions took place here. Even Sutter, himself, lived there. This is where the Eagle would have been housed. Sutter suffered financial woes after the discovery of gold—he was manipulated by prospectors and forced to sell the fort for $7,000 to a man named Alden Bayly, who turned around and immediately resold it to a woman named Isadora P. Supria. Here's the funny part. I can't find any reference to an Alden Bayly throughout historical documents or a Ms. Supria. It's as if they never existed. There is no record of them before or after that time."

"So?"

"So two people made what at that time was a major land purchase in the heart of the capitol city and then let it sit for 30 years, unattended and ignored—one of them a single, unmarried woman? It didn't make sense until a few weeks ago when I was staring at Ms. Supria's name and it hit me. It's an anagram."

Ashworth grabbed a piece of paper and jotted her name down in large, bold letters. "Do you see it?"

Isadora P. Supria

Kal was still too intoxicated to work on puzzles or codes. "No idea."

Ashworth wrote two more words underneath and held it up.

PARIO PARADIUS

"It should sound familiar because I just mentioned it. It's the Latin I found on The Verein's stamp under the bear meaning Birth and Heaven. Isadora P. Supria is an anagram for Pario and Paradius. I did the same thing with Alden Bayly and eventually came up with Dylan LeBay. Noteworthy because a person with that name just happened to be the Big Four's main land acquisitionist at the time."

Benny turned to Kal. "Remember the letter Dunning used to break the code? It was addressed to a Major he never heard of by the name of LeBay."

"Exactly!" said Ashworth, pausing for dramatics. "Do you understand the pieces? These two were shill buyers, fronting for The Verein. But wait, it gets better. So guess who came into ownership of Sutter's Fort after these two? That would be, none other than—drum roll, please—the Native Sons of the Golden West. They made an official purchase then restored the fort back to its original condition in the 1890's. In this case, truth is stranger than fiction."

Benny chimed in, "They bought it back because they were saving their past and preserving their heritage, which might have included the Freedom Eagle."

"Exactly, the whole time the fort was under the ownership of

The Verein, they were moving artifacts in and out, including the Eagle. It doesn't take a genius to see the connections."

Kal sat quietly, not sure what to make of the whole thing. It reminded him of the night Dunning invited him to dinner—the night that started the initial circus, when he first learned of his professor's intention to find the Eagle. Ashworth made a compelling argument like Dunning had that fateful evening, but this time Kal's gut was telling him to run away and leave the whole mess alone.

Or was it the shots of alcohol?

"So you just expect the Eagle to be sitting there in that building somewhere, untouched all this time?"

"It's a one-in-a-million shot," chuckled Ashworth. "I'd settle for a clue the fort might offer as to its whereabouts."

"Let me ask you this, why do you need our help? Why can't you do this on your own or hire someone with more experience?"

"Because I lost a friend as well in the blast, Kal. He always said you were one of his greatest students, his protégé and the future of his field. What better way for me to honor his life than by finding this artifact with the man he felt would succeed him?"

The last sentence warmed Kal's heart. Dunning was never overly effusive in regard to his potential, but to hear that he spoke positively of Kal to colleagues was an ego boost.

"Besides, in light of your prior involvement, who has more experience regarding the Eagle? Other than myself and Dunning, you are the most qualified. The final chapter of the Freedom Eagle hasn't been written yet, we can do it together," Ashworth pleaded.

Kal's head was beginning to throb as the buzz waned. "What do we need to do?"

"We go to Sacramento as soon as possible and dig around. See what we can find. Tomorrow, preferably."

Kal laughed and shook his head. "Tomorrow? Just head out there on a whim like that? No way. We just got into town and I only packed one change of clothes. Besides, we can't go out to California, I don't have the money for a plane ticket."

"Listen, it's late," Ashworth said, glancing at his watch. "All of the details can be taken care of in the morning. Why don't you two stay the night and sleep on it. I have plenty of room and will drive you back to your hotel in the morning whether you agree or not. Okay?"

"I'm exhausted. A nice bed and some sleep sounds really good," Benny said. "Let's get some rest before we answer."

Kal shrugged his shoulders and sighed. "Okay, we'll stay. But I'm not going to California. I can't fly off, I have a life. I'm sorry."

"I understand, Kal," Ashworth said. "But please, just think about it. Ponder the opportunities this presents. Think about why you love history, and if yielding to your fear will prevent that passion from culminating into something special."

And with that the sales pitch concluded and their host showed them to their rooms for the night. Unfortunately for Kal, despite the booze sleep did not come easy.

# CHAPTER 27

A ray of sun peeked through the drawn shade in Benny's room, which was sparsely decorated sans beige walls and a giant teak frame that enveloped the king mattress he lay on. Ashworth had done a lot of work to dress up the downstairs of his massive house, but apparently the upstairs was a work in progress. As he groggily rubbed his eyes, totally confused as to where he was, Benny realized someone else was sitting on the bed.

It was Kal, fully dressed and staring at him.

"Hey," he whispered. "You ready to leave?"

"What the hell? What time is it? I think I'm still drunk, let me sleep."

"It's 7 a.m., get up. We gotta go."

"How? We don't have a car. Ashworth said he was going to drive us. Is he even awake?"

"I called a cab, it's on its way. I want to get back to the hotel asap so we can get on the road to Atlanta."

Benny sat up in the bed and grabbed his bottle of water off the nightstand, chugging half. "Just like that? We're not going to talk about California?"

"Nothing to discuss," Kal curtly replied. "I'm not going to the West Coast on another wild goose chase. I have to get back to work, back to my life. Now get your clothes on and let's roll."

"I'm going."

"I know, hurry up."

"No, you don't understand," insisted Benny. "I'm going with him, with Ashworth to Sacramento to find the Eagle."

Kal was speechless, and Benny knew he caught him off guard.

"I know things have been tough for you since the bombing. But you're not the only one it affected. Everything that happened that day happened to all of us. My life changed too, and right now, it's pretty much shit. My girlfriend died, I'm living with my parents, and I still have nightmares about the whole damn thing. I have nothing going on right now, except this. This is an opportunity from God, or whoever is up there, to get out of my rut and do something for myself."

"What are you talking about? Are you even religious?" Kal asked.

"You know what I mean. Just because I wasn't as close with Dunning doesn't mean I wasn't affected by his death. I'm doing this man, and you should as well . . . you know it."

In the back of his mind Benny knew he could talk Kal into going—he could already see him softening to the idea as he got off the bed and walked over to the window, pulling the shade open to peer outside.

"You know she loved me, right?"

"What are you talking about?" Benny asked.

"The day she died, in the car driving back from Macon. Elle said she was still in love with me. She was going to leave you."

"You're full of shit."

"Am I? All the time we spent together, you think there wasn't something still going on?"

"Just shut up, man. I know you're lying and I don't care how much bigger you are than me," said Benny, jumping out of the bed and clenching his fists.

"Bah," said Kal, dismissing him with a wave of his hand. The cab he requested was pulling off the main road onto Ashworth's driveway. Kal headed out of the room and stopped to look back at Benny. "Have fun going at it alone. You can't change the past or what happened."

****

"Ah, good morning, fine sir," Ashworth said, already awake and cooking scrambled eggs on the stove as Kal made his way into the kitchen. "Did you sleep well?"

"Pretty good, thank you for letting us stay," Kal said.

"It was my pleasure," Ashworth responded, robotically moving the eggs around in the pan before immediately broaching the million-dollar question. "So, were you able to come to any kind of decision regarding my proposal?"

"Count me in," said Benny, bounding down the stairs to join the conversation.

"Excellent! You men won't regret this. I have the plane tickets already. First class to Sacramento, leaving this afternoon from Dulles. Don't worry about expenses, everything you can think of will be taken care of, courtesy of myself. This will be an experience of a lifetime for both of you, and I am thrilled and honored you have decided to participate. We are going to make history!"

Kal didn't bat an eyelash.

"I'm not going, it'll be just him."

"Don't worry about clothes, we'll get you some brand new ones in Sacra- . . . wait, what?" Ashworth asked, finally registering what Kal said. "You're not going?"

"I'm heading back to Atlanta—my cab is outside right now to take me to our hotel. Thanks for your hospitality and the offer, but I have to pass. I'm officially retired from treasure hunts. Besides, you're in more than capable hands with Benny. He was with us every step of the way and knows just as much as me."

Ashworth, in an obvious state of shock, put the spatula down on the counter and took a moment to compose himself.

"I have to be honest, and this is no disrespect to you, son," he said, nodding to Benny. "But this offer was contingent on your involvement, Kal. I'm sure he would be a great help, but I'm looking for the knowledge you alone have through working with Dr. Dunning. I'm not sure this would work without you."

Kal could see Benny's pride take a direct hit realizing what Ashworth was delicately trying to intimate, that he was just a toss-in to the deal, and Kal immediately felt horrible. He lied upstairs about Elle because he was angry with Benny for deciding to continue on this silly quest, and his temper had gotten the better of him. The truth was having spent the last few days around the guy actually opened his eyes as to why she liked him so much. He was kind of fun.

"Robert, you'd make a huge mistake in not taking Benny. He is without a doubt the savviest person I know, and if you want the truth, he was the one who first identified and cracked Sherman's code. Not I, not Dunning, but Benny. You can forget about me going out to California, so your best bet is to hope he isn't offended and still feels like working with you."

Ashworth sized Benny up and down. "Well, if that's the case, then I have no choice. I guess it's just the two of us, kid. Can you be ready to leave within the hour?"

"You bet. Let me just go run up and grab my shoes and wallet and I'll be ready to go," he said, jogging toward the stairs, stopping briefly at the first step. "You won't regret this, I promise."

Kal walked over to the still-stunned Ashworth and offered his hand. "Thank you for the opportunity. I honestly do appreciate what you are trying to do, and I don't want you to think I'm not grateful. I hope you understand it's not you, it's something I need to deal with. You'll be more than happy with Benny."

Ashworth just nodded as Kal walked away and let himself out through a side door to the front drive where the cab was idling, knowing full well their host was not exactly pleased with what transpired.

"Downtown Charlottesville, please," he said to the driver, settling into the back seat. "Red Roof Inn."

The yellow and white Crown Victoria barely pulled away from

the house when the driver suddenly hit the brakes. "Looks like that guy wants to talk to you."

It was Ashworth, standing by the front door trying to get the driver's attention. He motioned for Kal to roll his window down as he meandered over to them.

"There is something I think you should know before you leave," he said with a crooked grin. "I've changed my mind. Unless you come with us, I fully intend on leaving your friend here and heading to the airport myself. My offer was for you, not him. I'm not giving an extended vacation to one of your friends. I need someone who is experienced and knows what he is doing. I need you. So unless you want to be the one explaining why he isn't headed to California, you'll be on that plane with us. I'm sorry I have to insist on this, but it's for the good of the project. It's your involvement or nothing."

It was Kal's turn to be stunned.

"I'm leaving in 15 minutes, so you better decide quickly. I need your help, Kal. I need you to help me find the Eagle."

He leaned his head back on the headrest, looked up at the ceiling of the car and thought to himself for a few seconds, feeling the conflict rage inside.

*This guy is trying to strong-arm me.*

"You know what?" he finally uttered. "Thanks for everything, really. But go fuck yourself."

He rolled his window back up and motioned to the driver. "Let's get the hell out of here," he said, not even looking back to see Ashworth's reaction.

\*\*\*\*

"Alright I'm ready to go. I think I got everything I need—my wallet, ID, and phone. Kal can take my stuff at the hotel back with him to Atlanta. You said we'd be able to get some new clothes out there, right?"

Ashworth barely grunted a response as he picked a small duffle bag off the kitchen counter and headed to the garage. It was obvious to Benny the man was still stinging over Kal's rejection.

*No matter. I'll just have to show him just like I did Dunning that I can be a real asset. Besides, I'm heading to California. This is gonna be fun!*

"There is something I need to tell you before we leave you're probably not going to like," Ashworth finally said in the garage as he opened the rear door to the heavily tinted SUV and tossed the bag in before heading around to the driver's side.

A sinking feeling hit Benny as he tugged on the locked passenger door. *He changed his mind. He's going alone.*

"It's really not about you, please understand," continued Ashworth, using all of his might to pull his considerable girth up into the truck. Once in, he grabbed a handful of chocolates from the glove box and rolled the passenger window down to finish what he had to say to Benny, who stood silently with his hands in his pockets, ready for the bad news.

"The thing is, and I'm sorry about this . . . you're going to have to share a room with Kal at the hotel in Sacramento. It's the only accommodation they had left. I reserved the last king-sized bed. I'm sorry," he said as Kal leaned forward from the back seat, peaking his head through the window.

"You didn't really think I would leave your sorry-ass to do this all alone, did you?"

Benny cracked a semi-smile, relieved but still angry about their exchange in the bedroom earlier that morning. "You came back. I thought you were too busy with your real life to go on another wild goose chase?"

"I was wrong. You were right."

Benny nodded, content with the simple apology. "I'm just glad Mr. Ashworth decided not to leave me."

"Nonsense," Ashworth said, looking back at Kal with a smirk. "You're an integral part of the team. I wouldn't dream of going without you. Having him decide to come as well is just the icing on the cake."

Kal didn't bother to acknowledge the man, instead leaning back into his seat. Benny hopped inside and looked back, realizing that despite his new friend's earlier objections, this was Kal's own chance to break out of the rut his life had fallen into.

# CHAPTER 28

Kal's knees were killing him—not just the bad one, but the good one as well.

The more he tried to adjust, the worse they felt.

"Ladies and gentlemen, the captain has turned on the fasten-your-seatbelt sign as we make our final approach into Sacramento International Airport. Please turn off all electronic devices, place your bags underneath the seat in front of you, and return your seats to their normal, upright positions. Thank you and welcome to Sacramento."

He gave up his favorite window spot to Benny as an unspoken apology for his earlier behavior and was crammed in between him and a woman on the aisle who decided midflight the armrest they shared was unequivocally her property. For five hours he remained in the same upright position, only rising once to go to the bathroom and killing time by reading the entire SkyMall magazine twice. Never having experienced claustrophobia before, he understood for the first time how some people could panic when they were confined in a tight space.

*Thank God we'll be on the ground in a few minutes.*

The United Airlines Airbus 320 had just crossed over the Sierra

Nevada, passing idyllic Lake Tahoe and was now descending into the northern portion of the Central California Valley, where Sacramento lay at the foot of both the American and Sacramento Rivers. Flanked to the east by the Sierra Nevada and to the west by the California Coastal Range, the valley stretched for 400 miles down the middle of the state, providing some of the best agriculture in the world. It was at the confluence of those two rivers that John Sutter originally laid the roots for what eventually became the city of Sacramento and where Ashworth believed the Freedom Eagle still rested. From several thousand feet up, the Sacramento metropolitan area appeared to be an oasis of green surrounded by brown farmland.

Kal slowly unfolded himself as soon as the plane came to a complete stop at their gate. Even though he and Benny had to wait in the back for every row in front of them to dig out their carry-on luggage and slowly file off, getting to fully stretch felt glorious.

"You really owe me," he said to Benny, adjusting his knee brace. "That was brutal."

"Really? I slept like a baby, I can't believe we're here already," he said with a big yawn.

"Hey, I know I said it earlier, but I really want to apologize for that stuff about Elle. I was way out of line. None of it was true."

"We're fine," said Benny, waving his hand. "Let's just forget about it. We're here to find the Eagle and have fun."

Kal felt the truth begin to spill off his tongue in regards to Ashworth's blackmail, but stopped himself. He still wasn't completely sure why he turned the cab around and returned to the house, but protecting Benny had something to do with it, a notion that would have been laughable only a few days prior.

Kal's sole consolation prize of dropping everything and jaunting across the country on a whim was the lack of luggage to check, therefore nothing to wait for, a fact that made him smile for the first time all day as they made their way to the front of the plane.

"Hello, gentlemen. How was your flight?" asked the waiting Ashworth when they entered into the first class area. There was one seat available in the section when the group checked in, a fact the older man failed to mention when he initially made the offer, not hesitating to grab it for himself.

"Not bad. I slept the whole time," Benny said.

Kal didn't even bother to answer. He had barely uttered a word to the man since their exchange in the driveway back in Charlottesville, but his anger at getting blackmailed was subsiding now that he was in California. Still, he was in no disposition for small talk.

"As well did I. Let's head over to the rental car kiosk and pick up our transportation, I have a convertible Mustang waiting for us to enjoy this weather. Then we can head to our hotel to rest and get refreshed, perhaps pick up some supplies."

It felt weird to Kal seeing the clock read only four as they walked into the heavily air-conditioned terminal, considering they had left D.C. just after two p.m. He could tell the three-hour time difference was going to wreck havoc on his body—that and the fact the last two days had been a complete whirlwind of travel, starting with the car ride from Atlanta to Virginia, followed by the drive to D.C., and now the flight to California.

The group headed through the terminal and passed a food court where a giant digital clock showed the outside temperature as 99 degrees, eliciting a groan from Benny.

"I'm gonna melt."

"Don't worry, Benny," Ashworth said, holding up an AAA travel booklet with 'Northern California' printed on the front cover. "I've been reading up on the city. It's a dry heat, there is almost no humidity here. Once you're in the shade it cools off considerably. The nights are pleasant as well, when cool ocean air comes down from the coast through the delta of the Sacramento River and drops the temperature."

"99 degrees is 99 degrees. That's hot as balls no matter how you spin it."

Kal chortled loudly. The expression 'hot as balls' always made him crack up, and it wasn't the first time Benny used it.

"If you'll excuse me gentleman, I need to make a quick pit stop before I burst," Ashworth said, pulling his cell phone out of his pocket and scrolling through it as he scurried off to the bathroom, leaving Kal and Benny alone.

"You hungry?" Benny asked. "The pretzels on the plane were crap and Cinnabon over there is calling me."

Kal barely grunted a response—he was focused on something that caught his attention in the book store next to the food court.

"Alright, you can have some of mine if you change your mind." shrugged Benny, peeling off to purchase a gut-busting cinnamon roll.

Kal walked briskly toward the store, Capitol Marketplace, unsure of whether his eyesight was playing tricks on him. He thought he spotted a familiar face, one that made his heart stop.

*Probably just a coincidence.*

Ever since the Atlanta explosion he felt somewhat haunted by those unfortunate souls who perished, often spotting familiar features in a crowd only to be wrong. At least a half dozen times he chased down someone he swore was Professor Dunning, consequently apologizing for an embarrassing case of mistaken identity.

This felt different to Kal, though. Much more real. And it was a different face he saw this time that sent fear down his spine.

He walked through the bookstore slowly, scanning the exits. But the only person inside besides himself and the cashier was a young man reading through magazines—the person he spotted under a ball cap was gone.

*Probably never even existed.*

"What are you looking for?" asked Ashworth, startling Kal.

"Oh, nothing," he responded. "Thought I saw someone I knew."

"Do you have family or friends out here?"

"Nope," he said curtly, picking up and flipping through a book.

"Listen, Kal. I'm sorry for having to do what I did. But please look at it from my perspective. I need someone who knows what they are doing. I want to find this thing, and you're my best shot. You friend is a fine fellow, but he's not you. He doesn't have the experience of working with Dr. Dunning, and that's what I need. Consider it a compliment."

Kal put the magazine down and decided to address the issue head-on.

"There is one thing you need to know about me. I'm loyal to my friends and family to a fault. If you cross them, you cross me, and I didn't turn that cab around for you or the Eagle. I'll put this behind me but make no mistake, I won't ever forget it."

"Fair enough. As long as we can work together on a professional level."

Kal nodded in agreement, realizing he publicly acknowledged Benny as a friend for the first time. Ashworth held out his hand to shake, which Kal squeezed hard as Benny rejoined them, half of a cinnamon roll shoved in his mouth.

"Mmm mfhghhg mhhhm," he muttered, trying to say something.

"That good?" Kal asked.

Benny smiled—frosting smeared on both sides of his face.

"I ruv Califurnia ar-weady."

"You know they have Cinnabon everywhere, right?"

"Tastes better here."

\*\*\*\*

Kal pumped the engine of the Mustang heading south on Interstate 5 from the airport into Sacramento, passing several tractor-trailers and leaving them in his dust.

"Yeah," yelled Benny from the back. "Gun it!"

"This upcoming part of the freeway will take us over the beautiful American River, which flows straight from there," Ashworth said, holding up his booklet and pointing toward the impressive Sierra Nevada. Within seconds the car raced over the raised freeway where a sizable river flowed underneath, filled with boaters and swimmers.

"Look over to the right past that bridge, you can see where it merges into the Sacramento River—which is the largest river totally confined within California—and then heads past downtown. You can actually see the difference in the clarity of water as they mix. This was one of the reasons settlers came to this area. The two rivers surround it, and in fact, the city is basically built on a flat piece of land that was a flood plain. The downtown flooded frequently in the winter seasons during the 1850s. Nowadays there is a very complex earthen levee system running alongside these rivers up and down the state protecting the entire region from flood waters."

Kal navigated the car though traffic and toward the J Street off-ramp, taking them into the heart of downtown.

"What's that over to the right?" Benny asked, pointing to a two-by-five block area isolated from the rest of the city by the freeway. Built along the Sacramento River, it appeared to be a replica of an old West town.

"That must be Old Sacramento," Ashworth said. "It's a reconstructed version of what the city probably looked like in the 19th Century. Officials preserved the area as a historical landmark and renovated most of the buildings, moving stores and restaurants in."

The rest of downtown Sacramento resided on the opposite side of the freeway, comprised of a modest skyline with a handful of 30-story high-rises, as well as the glistening-white California State Capitol building—a smaller replica of the U.S. Capitol in Washington, D.C.

"Boys, I hope you are soaking all this in. We are basically at one of the epicenters of America's expansion into California and the West. This city is teeming with historical sites from the Gold Rush to the Transcontinental Railroad to the Pony Express. They all started here."

"Where to now?" Kal asked.

"Just stay on 'J'. This is the main street through downtown and will take us right to the hotel. Remember, this was all laid out by Sherman in the 1850s. Like most cities, you have one row of streets lettered alphabetically, while those crisscrossing are numbered sequentially, making it an easy grid to figure your way around. We're on 'J' and 5th now, so we just need to go five more blocks."

Kal still found it hard to conceive the Civil War general was responsible for designing and surveying a city 3,000 miles from where he was famous for destroying another one—he just couldn't wrap his head around the irony. He had a permanent mental image of Sherman on horseback, leading his men into battle, not as an opportunistic 49er profiting from the California Gold Rush.

The Citizen was the newest boutique hotel in town, housed in an old 1920s insurance high rise across the street from City Hall and Cesar Chavez Park. Kal felt like he had been transported to another time and era upon stepping inside with Benny after valeting the rental. The marble elevator lobby could have doubled for the set of a black and white movie with arching doorways and a resplendent fresco covering the vaulted ceiling. The registration check-in was equally spectacular, channeling the motif of a vintage library with wall-to-wall issues of West's National Reporter series rising to the sides and behind. This is the area Ashworth came from with two room cards, one for himself and the other for Kal and Benny.

"You guys are on the seventh floor, I have a suite on the 12th. I suggest we freshen up and relax tonight before going strong tomorrow, beginning at Sutter's Fort. What do you think?"

It sounded delectable to Kal. All the travel and sudden heat exposure was catching up to him and his eyelids weighed heavy. He wanted to buy some new clothes but was so fatigued any thought of spending time in a department store made him cringe. He followed Benny to their room in a zombie trance, hardly aware of the elevator ride or the fact their room offered a great view of the mountains in the distance, topped by thunderclouds rising into the vast expanses of atmosphere like a healthy helping of whip cream on a sundae. He didn't even make it to one of the beds, collapsing onto the lone recliner and instantly falling into a deep, snore-filled sleep.

****

Kal couldn't shake the sensation of being underwater. He was aware he was in the middle of a dream, but the wetness felt real enough to actually shake him from one of the most incredible naps.

Touching the chair cushion he realized two things: 1) he felt water because he drooled a massive puddle, soaking his face and the recliner, and 2) he had no idea where he was. He groggily lay in his own saliva for a few moments collecting his thoughts, finally ascertaining he was in a room with beds. *Was it the hotel in Charlottesville? Ashworth's house? No, I'm in friggen California!* He repeated it several times before it finally sunk in, then rolled to his side and stretched his back—the air conditioning in the room was pumping in cold ventilation, sending goosebumps down his arms.

"Benny?" he said, pulling himself out of the chair to go to the bathroom, the only light provided by a small lamp on the nightstand. As he groggily passed one of the beds he noticed a neatly stacked pile of brand-new clothes with a handwritten note on top.

Kal,
Had these clothes dropped off by the local Macy's. Didn't know your size exactly, so hopefully they fit. Benny and I are down the street at Ella for dinner. Feel free to join us,

Robert

*Thank God. Another day in these clothes and I'm going to have to peel them off.*

The khaki shorts and polo shirt Ashworth picked out fit perfectly, but he was especially grateful for the new set of boxers and socks as he stepped outside of the hotel feeling refreshed. The night temperature was at least 30 degrees cooler with a light breeze swaying the tree branches gently as he walked the short distance to the restaurant.

According to the concierge, Ella was one of the premier eateries in an up-and-coming dining scene, and Kal immediately felt out of place upon stepping inside. Benny and Ashworth did not seem to mind the atmosphere as much as they chowed down on their steaks and drank from what appeared to be a second bottle of wine at a table near the kitchen.

"Kal, glad you made it in time. Looks like the clothes fit," Ashworth said loudly as Kal sat down in one of the open seats. It was obvious he had imbibed plenty as he shakily motioned to the waiter. "Can I order another portion of those Tri-tip steaks for this young man? I'm guessing medium-well, and another one for myself, too, medium-rare. You have to try this cut of steak. I've never had it before. Apparently it's a California thing. Absolutely delicious."

"I don't know why Dunning worked with this guy," whispered Benny to Kal while their host chatted up the server. "He's basically a legitimized thief buying artifacts for profit. You should have heard some of the bunk he was telling me."

Ashworth reached into his back pocket and pulled out a piece of paper with some scribbled handwriting as the waiter set up Kal's place setting.

"So let's talk shop here. I found out a ton of local elementary schools take field trips to Sutter's Fort, where they spend a day living inside the walls as settlers, including spending the night camping outdoors in the courtyard. It's some sort of learning program through the government. Lucky for us, there's a group of sixth-graders scheduled to stay at the fort tomorrow night from St. Ignatius Elementary in San Francisco. I managed to reach out to one of their deacons and convince him, with the help of a rather large donation of course, that you two 'former alumni' would be a perfect fit to act as chaperones for their field trip."

Kal groaned. The thought of spending the entire day with a bunch of pre-pubescent teens was not overly appealing.

"If you analyze it, it's the perfect cover for what we need to accomplish. It's the only way we can gain access to the original portion of the fort at night. When everyone falls asleep, you two will be able to investigate unmolested. You'll already be inside the main walls and can search the building under the cover of darkness."

"What if the house is locked up?" Kal asked.

"The three of us are going to make a trip over there tomorrow as soon as the fort opens and case the place. If there is a complex lock on the main building we'll have to figure something out before you need to check in later in the afternoon with the school."

"So what are we looking for, specifically?" Benny asked.

"What were you looking for back in Macon?"

"We weren't really sure. We ended up finding the bear symbol carved above the cellar door and we knew we were on the right track," answered Kal.

"Okay then, look for anything like that. Any clue that might suggest the Eagle is or was there at some point. Remember, the fort was the way station for The Verein and all the booty brought into California. Maybe we get lucky and all of it is still buried underneath the floorboards, undiscovered for 160 years."

Kal ripped off a piece of bread from the basket and slathered butter on it, shaking his head. "Judging how things have gone in the past with this, it's not going to be that easy."

"No, you're right. It's probably not. But we can still hope. There is one more thing. Did I mention you two have to wear clothing from that time period when you show up tomorrow? Everyone who participates in the program has to dress authentically, meaning we're going to a costume store so we can fit you."

"Oh, no," Benny said, dropping his fork onto his plate. "I'm not dressing up like an idiot so a bunch of kids can ridicule me."

Kal and Ashworth looked at each other and smirked.

# CHAPTER 29

**B**enny cussed up a storm in the bathroom of the hotel as he pulled up his faux deerskin pants with fringe trim.

"It's the only thing they rented in your size that kind of looked like it was from that era," laughed Kal.

"I look like friggen' Davy Crockett!"

"At least you don't have a coonskin cap, that would really put it over the top."

"Oh, yeah? Look what I found in the bottom of the bag," Benny said, walking out with the exact item Kal mentioned. "Why couldn't I have gotten something like yours?"

"Luck? We gotta go."

Kal managed to find a rather simple ensemble at a local costume shop perfect for Sutter's Fort. It resembled a farmer's outfit of that era with a simple long-sleeved shirt, pants that fit over his knee brace, high-ankle boots, and a long scarf hanging down from the neck. A wide-brimmed, sun hat completed the look.

The three had spent their early morning scouting the fortress like tourists, walking the grounds and taking pictures. Kal was immediately struck by the neighborhood surrounding the landmark, flush with stunning Victorian homes and shaded by canopies of huge elm trees. The fort itself looked untouched by time, its white walls standing over 15 feet with sections of masonry exposed under flaked paint. It was a severe contrast to its next-door neighbor, an expansive hospital aptly named Sutter General.

Two massive wood doors formed the entrance to the parallelogram, and once inside, tourists could stroll around the open courtyard or check out the various rooms built into and along the entire base of the citadel wall. Several tour guides dressed in similar fashion to Kal were set up in 'camps' in the courtyard, performing nominal 1850s tasks such as chopping wood or selling animal felts. Guests could sit down and chat or ask questions, which the group avoided like the plague, instead scouting the main building for over an hour, examining every entrance and exit for weak spots vulnerable to break-in.

"That gut might be the first problem. Maybe Davy Crockett was a more voluptuous man, like yourself," Kal said as they walked out of their room fully costumed and headed for Ashworth's suite. They were to meet the school in an hour and he wanted to go over details one last time.

"Sorry for no shirt, it was hot in here," he said, answering the door topless. Kal feigned to Benny like he was going be sick from the sight of Ashworth's pale, mole-ridden skin as he stepped inside, surprised at the transformation of the space. All of the pictures from their morning visit were blown up and taped to the wall, scribbled post-it notes adorning most.

"Here it all is: our target, the main house of Sutter's Fort," he said, tapping the wall. "From analyzing all of this, I'm thinking we're going to have to find access going down into that sealed first floor/basement, which won't be easy. In terms of security cameras, we're golden. They only have them outside the fort to make sure no one gets in. You'll already be within the walls, so you just have to find a way inside the building."

Kal carefully studied the pictures of the three-story house. The entire first floor was shuttered and locked down with every window covered by an iron bar or boarded and bricked over. Visitors were provided access via the second story using a pair of staircases on the east and west sides, and even though the floor was free to explore, several of its rooms were caged off for display. The third story appeared to be an attic with a lone staircase restricted by a mesh gate.

"So you and the kids are going to participate in a bunch of interactive, hands-on exercises with the fort staff, like churning butter and making crafts. At bedtime, they'll split everyone up and have groups trade off keeping guard all night, just like they would have back in the 1800s. This is going to be your opportunity. I figure you'll have about an hour to disappear and get into the building to root around."

"What about the padlock on the first-floor door?" Kal asked.

Ashworth pointed to his bed where a small, black tool lay. "It's a pick gun—don't ask me how I got it. I have a few dummy locks for you to practice on that look similar to the ones they have on the doors there. It's easy and takes a few seconds to use. The bigger issue is where to look once you've managed to get inside."

He stood up and ran his fingers over the pictures, stopping occasionally to read his own writing. "I highly doubt there is anything upstairs, so I wouldn't even bother. The bottom floor should be your target area. What do you think?"

"Well, they have that floor locked down for a reason," Kal said. "It could be storage, or it could be something else. I'm just worried about getting in there. The only entrance is not only padlocked, but possibly rusted shut. Our cover is blown if we have to make a lot of noise to open it."

"Agreed. There has to be an alternative entrance to the bottom floor from the second level. If you can't get in through the main door, you'll have to be creative and find another way in. A lot of these old forts had hidden passageways between floors. I don't see anything here that jumps out at me, but it doesn't mean one isn't there."

"Are you sure this is the only option? I didn't really plan on getting arrested out here."

"It's all we got at this point," Ashworth replied.

Benny was already playing with the keyhole on one of the locks. "Got it!" he said, proudly holding it up.

"Wow," Kal remarked. "It looks like we have ourselves a natural thief."

****

Kal stared mindlessly into the crystalline sky and admired the sun peeking through the trees rooted next to Sutter's Fort. The block possessed a diversified amount of species, from palms to oak to redwoods—which is what Ashworth parked next to on the west side of the building, away from the main entrance and across the street from a massive Catholic church.

"The sleeping bags and pillows are in the trunk. Keep your phones on in case I need to get a hold of you. I'll be parked here all night."

"Come on, Davy,. Let's get your coonskin cap and mosey on outta here," Kal said, gingerly hopping out of the back of the convertible and grabbing his sleeping bag.

"Screw you," Benny fired back, slowly easing out of the passenger seat, two large sweat stains already taking shape under his pits. Kal could feel his own perspiration encompassing his knee brace and starting a race down his leg. The heat index was heading upward as the two made their way across the park, past a small pond and to the front entrance of Sutter's Fort, where the sixth graders from St. Ignatius were all gathered single-file, along with several chaperones—none of whom were wearing costumes.

"You two young men must be our late additions to the group, Mr. Boyce and Mr. Rebelski," asked an older man in his sixties attempting to take attendance of the vocal youngsters. He was dressed in black from head to toe, including the classic Roman collar, the definitive giveaway for a man of the cloth. "I'm Deacon Barry, the teacher of this class. Our headmaster called and informed us you would be joining us on this adventure. It's a pleasure to have you. Your getups are quite exciting."

"I'm sorry," Kal said, glancing over at a Benny. "We were instructed to dress in era-appropriate attire. I guess we were told wrong."

"I think normally that is the case, but we had the rules relaxed a bit for our group because of the heat. Just jeans and a school T-shirt. In my case I'm afraid my uniform is non-negotiable with the big boss upstairs. So, you two are former Bulldogs?"

They both nodded in unison.

"How many years did you two attend the school? I don't recognize your last names," he said, closely examining Kal. "You do look familiar, though."

"K through 6th," he offered, hoping the deacon hadn't recognized him from the Atlanta incident.

"Just one year," Benny said at the exact same moment, leading to an awkward silence between the three men.

"I forgot Benny here was only at St. Alliaceous for one year. It's been so long for both of us," Kal finally offered.

"You mean St. Ignatius," said the deacon.

"What's that?"

"St. Ignatius. You said St. Alliaceous."

Kal looked at Benny and shook his head in disagreement.

"No, I'm pretty sure I said St. Ignatius. How would I forget my own school?"

"Yeah, he said Ignatius," Benny chimed in, confusing the older man even more.

"Yes, well, they say the hearing is the first to go, then the memory," chuckled the deacon. "It's very unusual for former students to join like this at the last minute, but we're glad to have you. The students will get a kick out of the outfits, especially yours."

Benny's face turned an even darker shade of red as the man pointed and slapped him on the back. "We're going to separate you two if that's okay and team you up with another chaperone and then break you up with your group of kids."

"Actually, sir . . . "

"I know you two would probably like to stay together, but I always say the best way to meet new people is to get outside your comfort zone. Benjamin, you will be with the orange group over there, and Kalei, you're with the green. Let's go have some fun!"

Before either could object the deacon escorted them inside the massive gates with his arms around their shoulders. It had only been five minutes and they were already experiencing the first crimp in their plans.

****

"Benny, wake up," whispered Kal. "Wake up!"

Kal knew that Benny was struggling to stay alert earlier in the evening due to all the time spent in the sun playing with the kids. They managed to communicate when their groups passed each other moving from task to task during the day and then again at dinner time, agreeing to meet up at midnight when the green group was supposed to be awake and 'guarding' the fort whilst everyone else slept. The plan was for Benny to slip out of his sleeping bag unnoticed while Kal took a bathroom break, rendezvousing on the unattended side of the main house.

But Benny zonked out hard, and now Kal was forced to discretely wake him.

"Wha-...what's up? I'm awake, I'm awake," he finally mumbled, slightly lifting his head, illuminating a thick strand of drool connecting the corner of his mouth to his pillow.

"Nasty," Kal said, pulling back in disgust. "Wipe that off and meet me in five minutes at the spot we talked about, and bring the bag with the tools. I'm gonna go tell them I'm getting sick."

"Okay. Five minutes," Benny responded, plopping his head back down.

Kal got up and quietly walked away from the sleeping area. The heat took its toll on everyone during the afternoon, so much so that water breaks became mandatory every 20 minutes. But as soon as the sun disappeared over the horizon and the weather cooled, the pack of tired campers hit deep sleep instantly, exactly what Kal and Benny hoped.

"Hey, guys," Kal announced to the group, which included another chaperone, Deacon Barry, and one of the park rangers, whose job was to stay the night and presumably prevent the criminal activity he and Benny were about to undertake. "I've got to hit the head, I don't think dinner is agreeing with my stomach. I might be in those Port-a-Potties for awhile."

"I have some Imodium, if you think it'll help," the Deacon offered.

"No, I think I'll be alright. Just need to let it out," Kal said, making a flatulent noise with his mouth, causing the kids to giggle.

*Poop humor never goes out of style.*

Kal walked away from the fire and toward the darkened center of the courtyard where the main house stood, partially aglow from the dancing light of the bonfire. He glanced to the sleeping area but could not tell if Benny still was in his bag. The Port-a-Potties were clear on the other side of the fort—necessary because the main bathroom was in the process of renovation, but a bonus since it provided him the perfect excuse to enter the uninhabited section where the door to the lower level was located. He just needed Benny to meet him with the flashlights and tools.

Because there was some light cast from the moon, he was able to slowly make his way over the bumpy ground without tripping as his eyes adjusted. *Like a ninja*, he thought, carefully creeping around the main house and disappearing out of sight. Just as he assumed he was in the clear, two arms extended out of the darkened shadows and shook him.

"Boo," Benny said with a laugh.

"What the hell! When did you get over here?" Kal asked through gritted teeth, part pissed Benny was joking around and part impressed at how well he scared him.

"Sorry, I couldn't resist. I snuck over here while you were telling everyone you had the runs."

"Nice, don't do it again. We've got to do this fast. I figure we have about 20 minutes before they start getting worried and check on me."

Benny put his bag onto the ground and pulled out the pick gun, a small bolt cutter, a crow bar, and two flashlights, one of which he handed to Kal.

"Hold the light on the lock for me," he said, examining it for a few seconds to find the make and model. "Sweet, this is just like one of the ones I worked on back in the room. We're good."

Kal looked around the deserted half of the courtyard, the voices from the campfire on the other side of the building echoing off the walls of the old fort and creating the illusion someone was approaching.

"Hurry up," he said nervously as Benny broke the lock and began pushing the door open with the crow bar.

"Dammit," Benny whispered. The door was not budging despite putting all of his weight into it. Not even the slightest creak. "See if you can try."

Kal grabbed the bar and took a turn, using all of his might with no result.

"Okay, what now? We go upstairs?"

"Going to have to, even though I don't want to," Kal said. The second floor of the building had a simple entrance—a lone padlock—but also several large windows throughout that made it harder to stay inconspicuous. Plus, there were no guarantees that a passageway down to the first floor existed.

"We'll have to turn our lights out once we get in, or at least cover them. We can shine our phones if we absolutely can't see anything."

Benny nodded and slowly followed Kal up the rickety wood stairs to a small landing where the door was located, careful not to creak the old boards. This was the only area of the building open to tourists during the day, and because they visited earlier, they were familiar with the layout. The lock was the exact same model as the version below, but this time attached to a gate-like hinge welded to the door and frame. Benny disposed of it even quicker than the first and they were inside with the door shut behind them within seconds.

Kal turned his phone on and shined it around the barren room, empty sans the wood floor, white walls and ceiling—this once was the dining hall for the fort. Off to the right was a smaller room that originally served as Sutter's office and had been restored to its original state, complete with an old desk, a small dusty bed and a large armoire filled with old rifles and knickknacks. The doorway was blocked with a thick wire screen that allowed visitors to see in but at the same time keep them from entering. Luckily, there was enough moonlight streaming in through the lone window to negate the need for flashlights.

"Let's start in there," Kal said, a knot forming in his stomach. "Ashworth said a lot of these old forts hid small passageways from floor to floor. Hopefully we won't have to go into the other rooms to find one." Altogether there were two other areas on the second floor set up in similar fashion to Sutter's office—one was the old infirmary and the other a textile producing area—they faced out onto the campers and bonfire, hence Kal's reluctance to venture into them unnecessarily.

Benny whipped out the lock cutter, easily sliced the simple padlock on the wire, and carefully pulled it open. "Try not to move anything if you don't have to," whispered Kal, just as Benny accidentally knocked a book off Sutter's desk and onto the wood floor with the back of his duffle bag.

"I'm sorry," he mouthed to Kal, who just shook his head and poised stiff like a hunting dog, his ears cocked. When enough time passed to alleviate his concern, he picked up the book and put it back on the desk.

"Are you trying to get us caught?"

"Sorry."

"Look over there behind the cabinet, I'm gonna check the bed."

Kal got on all fours and lifted the comforter off the bedding to see underneath, but found nothing except dust bunnies on top of an old tapestry throw rug, the sight of which nearly made him sneeze. His allergies had gone haywire since coming to Sacramento, forcing him to buy a package of over-priced Claritin at the hotel store just to get through the day without spraying mucous everywhere. "This is the allergy capital of the world," the kid behind the counter told him, and he didn't doubt it for one second after suffering for two days. Now, he put himself in a room covered in dust, the exact circumstances that seemed to set the sneezing off.

Not catching a glimpse of any passageway, he lifted himself back up off the floor to look elsewhere when the light from his phone passed over a raised bump under the rug. He grabbed the flashlight from his waistband and focused on the anomaly, pulling the carpet back from the corner to reveal a softball-sized brass ring attached to a section of the floor that appeared cut into.

"Benny, I think I got something over here. It looks like a small door or something under the bed."

"Sweet. Is it locked?"

"Doesn't look like it. The only problem is this bed is bolted down to the floor and there is only about a foot or so of space underneath it. Let me see if I can even pull the door open all the way."

Half of Kal disappeared under the bed, and within seconds the entire wadded-up throw rug came shooting out, followed by grunting and banging on the wood floor. Benny tiptoed out of the office and back into the empty dining hall. A small doorway led to the other half of the floor containing the other rooms and the staircase to the third story, from which Benny could see outside to where everyone was still gathered, none of whom appeared to be any wiser to what they were doing.

"Well, it opens," Kal said, sliding back out from under the bed and brushing himself off, just as Benny reentered. "The issue is that it lifts up only about halfway before hitting the bottom of the bed. It looks like they put it there and bolted it down on purpose to hide the trap door and keep it from opening all the way. I think I can fit in, but I'm not sure."

"There's only one way to find out, right?"

"Yep. I'm also not sure, though, if . . ." he said, trying to place his next words delicately.

"Listen," interrupted Benny. "If you think you can barely fit down there, there is no way in hell I am going to be able to. You go first and check it out, I'll stay up here and make sure no one comes looking for us."

Kal agreed and proceeded to disappear back under the bed with his flashlight when he suddenly realized something.

"Hey, hand me the video camera Ashworth packed for us. I can use the night vision down here instead of just the flashlight. I'll probably be able to see more clearly, too."

Benny grabbed the smallish Sony Handycam Mini DV recorder and slid it under the bed to Kal, who fussed with it in the cramped space until he managed to adjust it to night mode. He flipped open the small LCD side screen and positioned the camera above the opening, revealing a clear drop down to the first floor—no obstructions to sprain an ankle on. Even with the greenish glow of the night vision providing a clear image, he figured it was still going to be a challenge to move around once inside.

"If I'm not back in 10 minutes, call the authorities," he joked before sliding the top half of his body into the hole. Hanging upside down with blood rushing to his head and his legs the only anchors keeping him from crashing the eight feet or so to the ground, Kal swiveled the camera around and realized he was in a small shaft leading to the rest of the first story. He could feel the pain build in his knee the longer it supported all of his weight and grabbed the nearest support beam to clumsily begin dropping down the tunnel, letting gravity do most of the work. The rest of his body slowly slipped through the door above, which consequently slammed down on his brace, sending shooting pains throughout his body. There were times since the injury when he would hit it just perfectly, causing a near blackout-inducing experience, and this was one of them. Inverted 180 degrees upside down with all of his weight supported by the beam his arms were wrapped around, Kal slowly bent his waist and knees and let his legs fall over the top of his upper body to the ground until he was righted on the floor.

*That would have made a gymnast proud, but it's going to be a bitch getting back through.*

He brushed his hands off and gingerly rubbed his knee before focusing the camera forward. Dust and dirt from the floorboards above spilled onto his head as he slowly limped his way along the wall into a small room similar to the office above, minus the furniture. The ground below him was solid dirt pockmarked ever so often by a piece of broken furniture or discarded trash, very reminiscent of the Cannonball House cellar in Macon with the same musty smell, but less crowded.

*It must be a universal rule at these historical buildings that the basement serves as a place to store all the crap.*

Kal picked up a piece of wood that seemed to be the remains of an old chair, realized it wasn't even antique, and flung it back to the floor. The slow comprehension that no Civil War treasure was present, yet again, began to dawn on him as he felt his away along the wall and into one of the larger rooms. It was full of rows of stacked, metal tables blocking the old door he and Benny originally tried to get into.

*No wonder we couldn't open it.*

Kal had seen pictures of these tables in some of the promotional photos for the fort—they were used for banquets out in the courtyard during large parties. This meant employees had regular access to this lower floor, which in turn meant this area wasn't a secret, unmolested time capsule. Any clue would have been documented a long time ago, if any ever existed.

The fact Ashworth never presented them with bonafide proof The Verein used this building for storing their loot began to dawn on Kal, and he felt foolish for putting himself in jeopardy of being arrested for trespassing on restricted state property.

"Kal, Kal!"

It was Benny calling him, faintly at first, then progressively louder. Kal could tell from the urgency in his voice something was wrong and quickly made his way back toward the door, almost tripping twice.

"What is it?" he yelled up.

"Deacon Barry is coming," Benny said, lying partially under the bed with the door propped open so Kal could hear him. "He just got up from the fire and started heading this way. We have to get out of here!"

"Dammit," muttered Kal, grabbing the same beam he lowered himself on to shimmy back up. Luckily, some of the bricks in the wall were cracked and broken, providing small footholds for additional support. He ignored the pain in his knee and within seconds was hanging from the trap door opening, hindered by the physics of contorting his body through the space. Because the door under the bed did not open more than halfway, Kal had to pull his upper body up while squeezing and dragging his legs through the small opening that barely let him through on the way down. It was a concert of five different body movements at once.

By the second attempt he knew he was in real trouble when the small door banged down on his head and nearly toppled him to the ground.

"I think I'm stuck," he yelled to Benny, who was under the bed using one arm to assist with no luck. "Get out of here. Stall!"

\*\*\*\*

Benny raced through the outside door, ran onto the deck and nearly leapt the entire flight of stairs down to the ground. Running alongside the building to try and beat the deacon before he could reach their side of the fort, Benny turned the corner and ran smack dab into the older man, nearly knocking him off his feet.

"Good heavens, Benjamin! What is going on? Where is Kalei?"

Benny sucked air, trying to catch his breath.

"He's still sick in the bathroom. I've been checking on him, making sure he's okay. You can probably go back to the fire, he'll be fine."

"Are you sure? I think I should go see him," Deacon Barry insisted, trying to look over Benny's shoulder toward the portable bathrooms.

"No, no, he's gonna be fine. Just needed some diarrhea medicine. Luckily I always pack a load of it. Ha, get it? Load . . . " Benny laughed nervously.

"I don't feel comfortable with this. I'm going to check on him, I'm responsible for everyone's safety while we're here," said the deacon, stepping aside Benny and swiftly walking across the yard toward the temporary bathrooms. Benny trailed on his heels as they passed several display covered wagons, pleading for privacy while glancing back at the main building for any sign Kal managed to get out.

"You know what? Last I checked he actually fell asleep on the toilet, so he might not acknowledge you right away. He might be too embarrassed."

"I understand the compassion for your friend, Benjamin, but I have dealt with a sick child or two in my day. I'd like to think I know what I'm doing."

Benny realized there was no stopping him and resigned himself to the fact Deacon Barry was about to discover Kal was not actually in the lavatory. His mind raced ahead, searching for an excuse to rationally explain breaking into a closed section of the fort and why Kal was currently wedged in a trap door under a bed in one of the displays. Whatever lie he was about to tell, he knew they were headed for trouble.

The deacon reached the iconic blue lavatories and called Kal's name out with no response. He called again and looked back at Benny, who just shrugged his shoulders. Deacon Barry approached the first door and raised his hand to knock, but before he could make contact the door of the second bathroom swung open and Kal stepped out with a smirk on his face.

"You do not want to go in there!"

Benny's eyes were wide as saucers.

"Are you okay, Kal?" asked the deacon. "We were getting worried about you."

"I'm feeling better now, but my stomach is really messed up. I'm not sure if it was the dinner or what. I think it might be best if I call it a night and head home. What do you think Benny?"

Speechless, Benny just nodded his head in agreement.

"Are you sure? I'd love for you to stay and finish, and the kids will be disappointed, but if you think it's best I'm sure we can arrange to have you head home early."

"Yeah, I think that's probably a good idea. Just in case it might be a 24-hour bug, I don't want the rest of the children to catch it. And since Benny is my ride," Kal said, clutching his stomach for added effect.

"Well let's pack you up before you get hit with another round."

Deacon Barry gently patted Kal on the shoulder and headed to the fire. Benny followed with an elbow to his arm as they slowly walked together behind him.

"What the hell?" he whispered.

Kal smiled like a Cheshire cat.

"I found out what was blocking the lower door. There were a bunch of tables wedged up against it. Once you left I realized there was no way I was going to get up through the trap door so I dropped back down and moved some of the tables out of the way, enough to squeeze through and get out. I ran over to the bathroom right before you two walked over."

"Christ, you nearly gave me a heart attack! Did you find anything down there?"

"I know, sorry," answered Kal, before shaking his head in disgust. "There was nothing—Ashworth was wrong about the Eagle. And now we need to get out of here, quickly, before someone finds out those locks are busted."

"What about the bag with all our stuff?"

"We'll have to leave it. I still have the flashlight and camera on me. Text Ashworth, make sure he's ready to pick us up. This was a waste of time."

# CHAPTER 30

The girl sat on the arm of Kal's couch back in his childhood bedroom, flipping through his high school yearbook.

"I'll bet you were the big stud on campus," she teased, gently putting her hair up in a manner that was cute, yet extremely seductive.

"I wish. I cared about baseball, and that was it," he said, reclining in his desk chair, studying her. "I was socially inept." As she scanned the photos, she inadvertently touched her faint-pink lips with her nails, moving them along the nape of her neck to the top of her collarbone, Kal watching her every move like a hawk. The first few buttons of her white dress shirt were undone, revealing the top curve of her right breast—not too big, not too small, just perfect.

"Oh, you look so cute in this photo," she said, lifting off the bed to reveal she was wearing nothing below but panties, the skinny strings that held up the sides barely visible below the shirt.

As she drew close she dropped the yearbook into his lap and passionately kissed him, then pulled back and slowly unbuttoned the rest of her shirt and let her hair fall across his face.

"Let's do it in your bed," she whispered.

Kal instinctively believed it to be Elle, but for some reason could not get her face to focus, no matter how hard he tried.

She smiled and licked his ear. "Show me your Freedom Eagle."

"What?" Kal asked, taken aback. "What did you just say?"

"Show me your L'Aigle de la Liberté! I know you have it hidden down there, and I want it," she yelled, her head suddenly morphing into a bear. "Feed me!"

Kal screamed and woke up in his darkened hotel room, the mid-morning sunlight attempting to peak through the closed curtains.

He angrily checked the clock, pissed his brain wouldn't let him go another five minutes without slapping him back to reality. Everything that happened the previous evening came flooding back; he had been dead to the world for at least 10 hours, falling asleep the second his head hit the pillow after returning from Sutter's Fort, and now in addition to being extremely unsatisfied sexually, he was ravenous with hunger. Benny had been sleeping in the bed next to him at one point, but was now gone.

Even though his body was semi well-rested for the first time in days, a sense of depression and disappointment overwhelmed him because, once again, they hit a dead end in trying to find the Freedom Eagle. Hardly a word was spoken during the late-night ride back to The Citizen, with Ashworth in total disbelief they came up empty-handed. The only sound he uttered was the occasional, "Huh," over and over in an attempt to convince his brain of the impossible—his brilliant theory was false.

Kal got off the bed and inspected his knee. He knew part of the rehab process involved the painful breaking of scar tissue in the joint, he just wasn't prepared for how awful it felt. A quick self-diagnosis told him he hadn't done any more structural damage to the ligaments, so he threw on a pair of shorts and shoes, fixed his hair and headed out of the room to grab something to eat. He felt like shit—the entire trip was a waste of time, he was more than 3,000 miles from home and for the first time truly felt homesick for Atlanta. He had allowed himself to re-open the emotional wounds caused by the deaths of Dr. Dunning and Elle in the hope finding the Freedom Eagle would bring closure to the whole ordeal and allow him to move on with his life, but instead, all he accomplished was picking a scab.

A housekeeping cart blocked the hallway a few doors down from his own, and as Kal attempted to navigate around it the housekeeper rushed from the empty room she was cleaning to wave him down.

"Are you the Mr. Boyce in room 714?" she asked.

"Yes, but we don't need turndown service. Thanks."

"Yessir, but there was something else. Your friend was just here looking for you."

He turned around and smiled, imagining Benny forgetting his key.

"White guy? Kinda oafy?"

"Yes, I think he was white. Really tall and skinny. He had a cap and sunglasses on and asked for you by your last name. I couldn't really see his face, though."

*I've never heard Benny described as tall and skinny, not by a long shot.*

"Really? He never said his name?"

"Nope. Just he was your friend and wanted to know if you were in your room. I told him I didn't know and he left really quick."

"Okay, thanks."

Perplexed, Kal got on the elevator intending to head to the lobby but instead decided to ride up to Ashworth's room with the hopes of tracking Benny down.

*It had to be him. No one else knows I'm in Sacramento. Why the hell didn't he just come into the room and get me?*

He disembarked on the 12th floor and walked down the hallway mentally checking off potential candidates the housekeeper could have been referring to, but was distracted by the amount of noise coming from Ashworth's room. It was as if there was a party going on. He knocked on the door and was shocked when Ashworth answered with a huge grin and a meat-filled tortilla in his hand.

"Hey, there's sleeping beauty," he said with a laugh. "We've been waiting for you. Are you hungry?"

Kal followed him into the room in confusion and was quickly assaulted by a wonderful mixture of smells. Benny sat in a chair near the window chowing down on a plate of meat, rice and beans, so engrossed in his food he barely raised a hand to acknowledge him.

"This is some bona-fide Mexican food, my friend. The kind you can only get out here in California," Ashworth said, pointing to the desk with several metal containers resting on it. "I found a little hole-in-the-wall just down the street. We have carnitas, carne asada, chili verde, some special kind of grilled chicken, homemade tortillas, refried beans, and some delicious rice. It's out of this world. Go get some."

Kal immediately put the previous night out of mind and dove in, letting the juice from the pork roll down his chin as he stuffed his face, realizing he had never tasted anything so succulent before. But he was still confused as to why the portly man was in such a good mood, considering the circumstances.

"So I was really disappointed about last night, and decided to do what I do best when I'm upset . . . eat. I went down to the car to find my sunglasses and stumbled across this," he said, holding up the video camera Kal used the night before. "You must have left it in the back seat. Anyway, while I was waiting for the food in the restaurant I got bored and decided to see if you filmed anything—which you did. After nearly throwing up from motion sickness when you were swinging around upside down, something caught my attention. It wasn't until I came back to the room and blew the picture up on the TV that I realized you didn't return empty-handed at all. In fact, you may have broken this entire thing wide open."

Kal put down his fork and finished chewing.

"What are you talking about?"

Ashworth plugged the camcorder into the flatscreen and fast-forwarded a few seconds before stopping and freezing the video.

"You were standing in what I believe was the middle of the downstairs, right by the door blocked by the tables. You turned the camera toward the exit and then pointed it up to the ceiling for just a brief second, in which you caught this."

Ashworth moved the video forward a few frames and paused it again.

"Do you see it?"

All Kal could recognize was the underside of the floorboards. He started to ask what he was supposed to be looking for when a word in the wood materialized.

*Verein*

It was very faint, about an inch in length, but definitely visible. And there were more words, so subtle they almost intertwined with the grain of the wood. The whole thing opened like a puzzle in front of Kal's eyes—once he knew what to look for they appeared faster and faster until the entire paragraph revealed itself.

*Esta estructura marca el lugar de nacimiento de la Verein,*
*y donde la gran República de California*
*fue creada en la visión de Dios.*

*Nuestro homenaje a la tierra y la gente reside*
*en la ventana por encima de los árboles y pistas*
*que protegen el rey del ferrocarril hasta la eternidad*

"What the hell is that?" Benny asked.

"It's Spanish," answered Kal. "Look underneath it. That look familiar to you?"

Under the writing was the figure they had grown very accustomed to—a bear holding a snake. More proof, along with the word 'Verein', that Ashworth was right all along.

"How did I not see that when I was down there?" Kal asked. "I was looking all over."

"For one, it was very dark. Two, it was above you. And three, I don't think it's carved into the wood. It looks almost burned in by flame, most likely a very long time ago. The night vision on the camera is probably the only way you would have been able to spot it—thank God you took it down there with you. This has to be a clue left behind by the original Native Sons." Ashworth said.

"Have you translated it?"

"No, I don't know a lick of Spanish. I did write it all down on this piece of paper, perhaps we can find someone to interpret?" he said, popping two mini Mr. Goodbars into his mouth simultaneously, the genesis of his happiness now understandable.

"Here, give it to me," Benny said, grabbing the paper. "Where is your laptop? No need to find anyone, there is a website called Babelfish that can translate all kinds of languages. I used it a bunch in class a couple of years ago."

"Well, isn't that clever," Ashworth quipped.

Benny opened the computer and began typing the paragraph into the website, munching on a tortilla as he worked.

"I swear, every time we think this Eagle is lost for good it gives us just a taste to keep coming back for more," Kal said, amazed at the turn of events. "It's like a bad drug dealer."

"We're going to find it, Kal," Ashworth said. "I can feel it in my bones. I was right about The Verein and I'm going to be right about the Eagle. Have faith."

Benny jotted down the translation from the website on the same piece of paper and studied it, a quizzical expression overtaking his face.

"These things aren't always 100 percent correct," he said. "But I think we can get the gist of what it means. It looks like a riddle or something."

"Read it," Kal said.

Benny took a deep breath and slowly recited:

*This structure marks the place of birth of The Verein,*
*and where the great Republic of California*
*was created in God's vision.*

*Our tribute to the land and the people lies*
*in the window above trees and tracks*
*that protect the King of Rail for eternity*

"Amazing," Ashworth said, excitedly unwrapping another candy. "I was right. Sutter's Fort is where they brought their bounty for the new utopia."

"I thought you were sure of it," Benny said.

"I knew something had to be there, all the evidence pointed to it. But with these things you can never be 100 percent certain. Let's say it was more of a solid theory. That first paragraph proves, though, The Verein did indeed use Sutter's Fort as the gateway. It's where Sherman sent the Eagle and where it was stored. They then most likely were forced to move it when the fort fell into disrepair. The second paragraph appears to be some sort of clue the Native Sons left behind, but was lost over time. It literally faded out, left to speculation and old ghost stories, buried under the floor. We would have missed it, too, if it weren't for luck and this wonderful piece of technology."

Kal leaned back in his chair fixated on the frozen image on the TV screen.

"I'm gonna need more greasy meat."

\*\*\*\*

"Who the hell is King of the Rail?" Benny asked, getting down to business.

Ashworth drank directly out of the nice bottle of champagne delivered via room service. It was sheer luck that enabled Kal to catch the cryptic message the Native Sons left when they rebuilt the fort—the only real record of the work done by their forefathers, The Verein. The message almost vanished forever, but now Kal, Benny, and Ashworth had discovered the biggest clue to unlocking the mystery of the Freedom Eagle.

"They are talking about railroads, right? It has to be one of those Big Four guys," he continued, thinking out loud. "They founded the Transcontinental."

"You're probably on the right track, no pun intended," Ashworth said. "Either Crocker, Stanford, Huntington, or Hopkins could be considered the king of the railroads out here in the West. They all had a hand in its development. Look at the message again, starting with the second paragraph. 'Our tribute to the land and people' probably refers to the artifacts they were bringing in to the state. Some of this stuff eventually found its way into museums and private collections, but other more controversial items, like the Eagle, were kept hidden and could have been abandoned or forgotten."

"The next sentence doesn't make sense. How could all of those artifacts be 'in a window above trees and tracks' protecting the King of Rail?"

"I'm guessing it refers to the location, like a building or safe near some trees and train tracks. The part that confuses me is 'protecting the King.' Since none of these guys are alive, unless they developed some super powers, the only place they can be guarded at is their gravesite."

"Good point," Kal said.

"So let's assume it could be talking about their final resting place. When did these guys die and where are they buried?"

Benny tapped the idle computer and looked up the info on Wikipedia.

"Hopkins died in 1887, Crocker in '88, Stanford in '93, and Huntington was the last in 1900. Stanford is buried in a family mausoleum down in Palo Alto at the University, Huntington went back east and is buried in NYC, Crocker is buried in Oakland, and finally, the great Hopkins is buried here in Sacramento at the city cemetery."

"Okay, so three are in this relative area, even though Stanford and Crocker are down in the Bay Area," Ashworth said. "If it indeed is a burial plot, it would have to possess some of the characteristics mentioned . . . something constantly above the trees and tracks watching down over the grave. Correct me if you think it should be interpreted differently. Do we have any pictures of the cemetery plots?"

"Let me work my magic," Benny said. Within a few minutes he had pictures of all three California grave sites on the screen. "Stanford is out—he's in a giant mausoleum. No trees or tracks close. Looks like the same goes for Crocker, too. And as far as Hopkins, his tomb has some trees nearby, but it doesn't fit the description accurately."

"Hmm," pondered Ashworth. "Maybe we should take a drive

over to the city cemetery and see for ourselves. Perhaps we're missing something?"

Kal was deep in thought while the other two talked, trying to recall a story regarding the first railroad tycoons, something Ashworth told them back at his mansion in Virginia.

"Hold on a second!" he said, snapping his fingers. "The first time we met you talked about a man heavily involved in the creation of the Transcontinental who was pushed out before it finished. He was most responsible for getting it off the ground, not the Big Four. What was his name? Judas?"

"Judah. Theodore Judah."

"Yep, that was it. If he really was the driving force behind the completion of the railroad despite getting forced out by the big guys, wouldn't some consider him the King of Rail, especially the actual men who worked on the line? He was the one who toiled with the laborers surveying the route."

"That's a great point. Benny, look up Theodore Judah. See if you can find if he is buried out here or anything else that seems pertinent."

Benny typed 'Theodore Judah' into the Google searchbar and scanned the first few web pages, finally clicking on a biography of the engineer.

"It looks like he died at the age of 37 just as construction of the Transcontinental Railroad started. He developed Yellow Fever while heading to the East Coast and passed away in NYC. He is credited with surveying the best possible route for the railroad over the Sierra Nevada, as well as involving the Big Four in the financing before they squeezed him out. He is buried in Massachusetts."

"Okay, is there anything out here linked to him?"

"Let's see, there is an elementary school in Sacramento named after him. He has a memorial dedicated to him in Folsom, and another one in . . . "

Benny stopped speaking and examined the computer screen closely.

"Check this out," he finally said. "He has a giant memorial here in Old Sacramento."

Benny turned the computer around so the others could see the nearly 15-foot-tall granite edifice, which appeared to be composed of several large boulders fused together, the largest perched on a foundation of smaller rocks. A bronzed, half-circle marker engraved with Judah's accomplishments sat at the base near the sidewalk, accompanied by a bust of Judah resting on a large railroad tie halfway up the main rock. This entire section was also composed of bronze, the metal tarnished by a layer of aqua-green film—a classic sign of patination from exposure.

After studying the scene for a few moments, Kal's gaze strayed to the upper portion of the monument where a panorama of a forest and train bridge connecting two Sierra mountainsides rose behind Judah's head, all of it sculpted into the main rock as a scenic backdrop.

"The trees and the tracks that watch over the King of Rail," Kal said, his voice trailing off. "There it is."

"Holy shit," was all Ashworth could manage to utter, a half-eaten, chocolate bar melting in his hand.

# CHAPTER 31

The Mustang peeled away from the valet stand and headed directly for Old Sacramento.

"It all makes perfect sense," Ashworth said, sitting in the passenger seat as Kal drove. "Judah's monument was created by the men and women of the Southern Pacific Railroad. But do you remember who I said takes responsibility for maintaining and protecting all of the historical markers and plaques in California? It's the Native Sons of the Golden West. They hid another clue in one of their memorials!"

The three men had rushed out of their hotel room to the lobby as quickly as possible, only stopping to grab the camera and let Ashworth use the men's room. Old Sac, as the locals called it, was only 10 blocks away and within minutes they were pulling into one of the area's multi-level parking garages built under the freeway specifically for tourists.

"According to this map the monument is on the south side of Old Sacramento, a couple of blocks away," Kal said as they hopped out and started walking in the direction of one of the two main boulevards intersecting the entertainment district.

"There's the B.F. Hastings building," Ashworth pointed out, clearly enjoying the historical aspect of the area. "That was the final stop for the Pony Express."

Kal felt as if he stepped directly onto the set of an old western movie like Tombstone as they walked. The buildings were connected by raised, wooden walkways looming over the street by nearly a foot, and each block had the classic architecture of a Western saloon or bank. Only now they seemed to either house a candy store, souvenir shop or restaurant.

Despite this, he half expected to see Clint Eastwood as the outlaw Josie Wales come walking out from behind a pair of swinging doors with his guns drawn at any moment. It was truly a living snapshot of the Wild West, save the parking meters.

The Sacramento River flowed a few blocks to the west, where in the shadow of the iconic Tower Bridge the Delta King paddlewheel lay permanently anchored. Once a mighty passenger ferry along the Sacramento Delta and San Francisco Bay with its sister ship, the Delta Queen, it now was a permanent floating restaurant and hotel.

The area was packed with people on this toasty Friday afternoon either snapping pictures of the scenery, riding horse-drawn wagons, or interacting with one of the plentiful street performers.

"Is it normally this crowded?" Benny asked. "The streets aren't even paved. It's still all dirt."

"No, that's not right," Ashworth said. "I specifically read Old Sacramento is open to automobiles and there's parking available in front of shops. The pictures I saw showed pavement."

"Maybe it has something to do with that," Kal said, pointing to a giant banner hanging across the street that read:

## WELCOME TO GOLD RUSH DAYS

"Excuse me, sir," he said to a city worker who happened to be setting up a barricade near them. "We're from out of town. What's Gold Rush Days?"

"It's a festival that happens every Labor Day weekend," answered the man, reaching into his back pocket for a pamphlet. "They infill the streets and block out all the traffic so it looks like it did back in the old days. The city hires a bunch of actors for horse races, shootouts, the works. Started this morning—don't be surprised if you see a gunfight erupt between a bunch of cowboys occasionally in the middle of the street. It's part of the show."

If it weren't for the fact he was embroiled in an activity of some importance, Kal would have made a point to investigate the festival on his own free time. But duty called and he moved swiftly to catch up with the other two to fill them in.

"I think we're almost there," Ashworth said, after patiently picking his way through the crowded walkways. "It should be at the end of this street."

They passed the ultimate paradox—a Subway sandwich store operating out of the last historic building on the block—and strolled into a tiny park butted up against the freeway, where underneath a canopy of trees looking just as impressive in person as it did in pixels was the Theodore Judah Monument. All three men stood silent and studied the artwork, Judah's eyes blankly gazing back. The inscription on the half-circle marker at the bottom was almost unreadable due to the green corrosion, forcing Kal to brush some of the powder off to reveal the full dedication:

THAT THE WEST
MAY REMEMBER
THEODORE DEHONE JUDAH
PIONEER, CIVIC ENGINEER AND TIRELESS ADVOCATE
OF A GREAT TRANSCONTINENTAL RAILROAD
AMERICA'S FIRST

This monument was erected by the men and women
of the Southern Pacific Company, who, in 1930, were
carrying on the work he began in 1860. He convinced
four Sacramento merchants that his plan was practical
and enlisted their help. Ground was broken for the
railroad January 8, 1863.

Judah died November 2, 1863. The road was built
past the site of this monument. Over the lofty Sierra
– along the line of Judah's survey – to a junction with
the Union Pacific at Promontory, Utah, where on May
10, 1869, the "last spike" was driven.

The three men occupied the monument all to themselves, tucked
in isolation from any store or restaurant at the southern most portion of
Old Sacramento. Since all auto traffic had been cut off in the area the
regularity of anyone happening upon them was intermittent despite the
large crowds just a block away.

"Here he is, the King of Rail," Benny said as Ashworth took
pictures.

"Precisely."

Kal touched the metallic bust of Judah and circled the entire
memorial to inspect it. The large boulder that made up the main portion
was masterfully done and gave the scene behind Judah depth, while also
appropriately honoring his efforts in the Sierra. Kal studied the trestle
rising above the mountains and trees and was struck by a particular detail near the top of the rock.

"Guys look above the bridge, is that a hole?"

Up near the crown of the 15-foot boulder, undetectable in the
photos they saw online, appeared to be a small opening cut near the
peak of the mountain scene. It seemed out of place and was hardly
noticeable unless one was specifically searching for it.

"I think it's supposed to be a train tunnel cut into the mountain
looking down at Judah." Kal said. "It looks like . . . a window!"

"You're right!" Ashworth said. "When they built the railroad using Judah's mountain route they literally dynamited through the rock
inches at a time to create tunnels still used today. It was slow and gruel-
ing work because the granite was so dense. That's what the little hole is
meant to be, a train tunnel, and I'll bet it's the 'window' the Native Sons
were referring to."

Kal made sure the coast was clear and scaled the monument using the sculpture as a foothold. He effortlessly reached the small 3-by-2

inch opening without tweaking his knee and put his fingers inside to feel around.

"I can't see the end of it. It looks like the hole goes back quite a ways. Do either of you have a flashlight on you?"

Ashworth reached into his pocket and threw up a mini pen-light attached to his house keys. Kal fiddled with it for a few seconds before shining it into the small abyss.

"Man, it goes back really far. I think I can see the end, though," he said, craning his neck to get a good angle. "I see something! It looks like . . . it looks like a small metal hook near the back of the tunnel. Benny, throw me that stick over by the bench."

Benny grabbed the skinny twig and handed it up to Kal, who examined it closely before slowly working it into the shaft.

"Damn, it's too thin. I need something stronger to catch the hook, like metal. See if you guys can find anything."

Both Benny and Ashworth scrounged around the gutter and the nearby garbage can with no luck. "Would a crowbar work?" Benny asked.

"Yeah, actually that would be perfect—don't tell me you found one just lying in the can?"

"No, but there was an extra we left in the car trunk from last night. I can run and go get it."

"Perfect," Kal said, scrambling down off the monument. "We've waited this long, we can wait a couple more minutes. This thing isn't going anywhere. Run your ass off."

****

Benny put his head down and powered over the last few steps of the wooden walkway before reaching the park, crowbar in hand and totally out of breath.

"Here you go," he said, holding the black piece of metal in his outstretched arm while bent over at the waist. Had he not been so out of shape he would have immediately seen the rigid stances that Kal and Ashworth had assumed, their faces blank and eyes wide open.

"Take it, my arm's getting tired," he said, looking up at Kal after a few seconds without a response. But he wasn't answering, only nodding to his right, trying to point something out. Benny looked over and saw the previously vacant park bench now occupied by a man in sunglasses and a baseball cap. The slightly exposed handgun in the stranger's left hand wasn't very noticeable, only drawing his attention when the sun reflected off of it.

"Hello, Benny. It's been awhile," the man said, wiping his right eye with a handkerchief. Benny struggled to place him.

"Don't recognize me? How soon they forget, Kal."

The man pulled off the cap and sunglasses, revealing a hairline that ran like a jagged crack over the entire right portion of his scalp, the hair bald and matted in places. Even worse, the entire right side of the man's face appeared to be in the recovering stages of a severe burn with the bottom eyelid melted onto his cheek, leaving the opaque eyeball in a constant state of half-exposure seemingly on the verge of dropping out of the socket. The man again wiped the bottom of his eye with the piece of cloth to keep the fluid in the exposed tear duct from running down his face.

Benny forced himself to look at the other half of the man's features, as hard as it was, and felt a lump in his throat when his synapses finally put the pieces together. There was no mistaking the identity.

*Marcus.*

"Surprise, I'm not dead," he yelled, raising off the bench and walking to Benny with a small, but noticeable limp. "I see you're still as fleshy as ever, although you've found someone more pathetic than you in this old whale you're running around with. Well, come on. Say something to your old friend!"

"How . . . how are you—"

"Alive?" Marcus said, finishing the sentence. "First, why don't you be a good lad and put that crowbar down? Good boy, there you go. As you can see, I didn't come out of the experience totally unscathed. Like I was telling your friends, I now have a face only a mother could love, as well as this little souvenir."

Marcus slowly reached over with the gun and pulled his right sleeve up, revealing a prosthetic hand and arm reaching up past his elbow.

"You see, I was spared when that spade doctor of yours decided to play hero—the blast threw me about a hundred feet sideways into the parking lot behind some cars. When I came to I managed to steal a pickup, my face grotesquely burned and my arm shredded to hell. I escaped out of the immediate area before police closed it down, but because I couldn't walk into any old Atlanta hospital I had to turn to a friend, who, as you can see by his work, isn't quite up to snuff in the whole reconstruction aspect of medicine."

"But they found all the bodies."

"Actually, it's quite funny you mention it. Most of the men I employ have no traceable identities, including myself. It's one of the job qualities I most admire in a potential candidate. It so happens two of those men failed me when they let Kal escape, one of whom was killed. Weston was his name, I believe—never did find the other one. Anyhoo, the body was in the back of the van, waiting to be disposed of along with yours after the swap, when bada-bing, everything blows to high heaven. Since no one knows who I really am, it worked out perfectly. More than enough body parts to account for me."

"That was you at the airport I saw, wasn't it?" Kal asked. "And looking for me at the hotel?"

"I was on the same damn flight. But you were so wrapped up in yourselves I could have been serving cocktails and you wouldn't have been any wiser."

"What do you want, Marcus? Revenge?" he asked loudly, looking around for some kind of help: a passerby, a random car, anything. But they were totally alone.

"Don't even think about attempting something stupid like last time. I have nothing to lose this go around. I'm a ghost. The few people who knew of my existence now believe me to be dead."

"Seriously, what do you want Marcus? We're just here on vacation."

Marcus laughed hard. So hard he began coughing spastically.

"What do I want? What the hell do you think I want? The Eagle! And don't play stupid. I've been following you for the last week. I know you are back on the trail and are close, working with this piece of shit collector. Remember what I told you? I never, ever, fail to complete a job. The people who hired me will still pay top dollar for the Eagle once I retrieve it, enough to retire and forget about everything I lost that day. I should actually thank you for all the publicity you brought, it's damn near priceless now that it's gone mainstream. Got every fool treasure hunter in the South looking for it."

"There's no way we're helping you, Marcus. You'll have to just shoot us all right here. We don't know anything."

Marcus carefully reached into his pocket with his prosthetic hand and fumbled a cell phone, awkwardly flipping it to Benny. "Have you talked to your family in Buckhead, lately?" he asked. "Specifically your little sister? How old is she now, 12? If you remember from our past experiences, I have no qualm using children as collateral."

"There is no way you have my sister, she's with my dad. Some-one would have called me."

"No, you're right. I don't have her . . . yet. What I do have is her daily schedule down to the second. If you scroll through the photos on there you'll see I'm not lying. I have one of her leaving for school about a week ago. The next one shows her enjoying lunch with some friends at the mall. There's even a Hallmark moment—an action shot of her taking your family dog for a walk around the block. All I have to do is make one call and she is dead. Fucking dead! Do you hear me?"

Benny felt the heat from the sun on his head as a wave of panic rushed over him. He glanced at Kal, pleading for help through body language.

"Okay, okay. We'll show you. There is no need for anymore vio-lence," suddenly offered Ashworth.

"Ashworth, shut up! You don't know this man or what he's ca-pable of. Stay out of it," Kal said.

"We think we've traced the Eagle all the way to here, to this monument."

"To here?" Marcus asked, one eyebrow raised. "I've been won-dering why you three are running around California."

"It's a long story, too long to explain. I don't know you, so you'll just have to trust what I say is true. All I want is to find the Freedom

Eagle and spare everyone harm. There is something up in that small hole at the top of the monument. Benny went to get a crowbar to poke around in there. We're not sure what it is."

Kal shook his head in displeasure.

"I appreciate your candor," replied Marcus, turning the gun to Kal. "Now, if you would be so kind as to continue what you were doing, I'd be grateful."

Kal snatched the crowbar off the ground, gave Ashworth a dirty look and slowly made his way back up to the top of the statue. "I don't know if I'm going to be able to get up there, my knee has been killing me the last couple of days."

"You seemed just fine a few minutes ago when you scaled it. Please don't make this any tougher than it has to be. My patience these days is not what it used to be," Marcus said.

Kal continued to the top and once he secured his footing slowly worked the split end of the crowbar into the small tunnel, wiggling it around to try and catch the hook in the back. After several close calls he pulled it out and grunted with frustration.

"It's not catching. I almost got it a couple of times, but it just keeps slipping off the end. Do you see anything I can use as a lasso?"

Benny pointed in the direction of Marcus and the garbage can behind him. Lying next to it on the ground was a deflated helium balloon with the string still attached.

"Go ahead, get it," he said.

Benny ran to the can and retrieved the balloon, ripping off the remains of what had been an inflatable stagecoach.

"Here Kal," he said, handing it up. "It's string, it'll be stronger."

Kal made a small loop with the material, securing it to the end of the crowbar so it resembled a dogcatcher's pole and snare, then snaked the homemade contraption back into the tunnel. This time he caught the hook on the first try and slowly began pulling.

"I got it," he yelled down, his tongue sticking out of his mouth in complete concentration. "But it seems to be stuck."

"Quit being gentle," Marcus said. "Give it a good yank."

Kal locked his legs despite his precarious foothold and jerked with all his might, inducing a loud crack from inside the shaft that sent him tumbling off the monument into a heap onto the ground.

"You okay?" Benny asked, helping him to his feet.

"I'm fine, the string must have broken. Let's try it again."

"The string didn't break, Kal," Ashworth said. "Look, you pulled it out!"

The still-attached crowbar dangled from the hidden hook, which was now almost fully exposed from the tunnel entrance.

"Down there," Marcus said, pointing to the half-circle plaque at the base. The edge of the bronze piece slowly moved away from the monument about two inches, revealing a small, hollowed chamber. Vapor trails of dirt floated out, their first taste of freedom after decades of entrapment.

"It was a lock," said Ashworth. "You just unlocked and opened some sort of vault."

"We found it!" screamed Benny, trying to slap Kal on the back in congratulations.

Kal was stoic as he yanked the crowbar down, snapping the string off the hook. He wedged it between the rock and pried open the small door, slowly moving it away from the base until there was enough room to stick both of his arms in.

"There's a leather sack of some kind," he said as he blindly fumbled around inside, careful not to disturb anything fragile or, even worse, awaken a hungry spider. "Definitely not the Eagle. Not big enough."

Benny groaned loudly.

Kal finally squeezed the backpack-sized satchel through the hole after some pulling and closed the door, discretely making sure no one saw the defacing of the monument. The bag was very old, as evidenced by the faded and stiff leather, and appeared to be of the messenger variety with a single buckle keeping it sealed.

A young couple with a child in a stroller happened to pass by, causing the group, who had been shielding Kal, to nod and smile. The amount of people flooding into Old Sacramento was picking up—they were no longer guaranteed discretion.

"I'll take that, Kal," said the mercenary after the family walked out of earshot. "You've done good work here."

"You don't even know what this is, Marcus. It could be nothing."

"Whatever it is, someone went through a great deal of trouble to hide it and I'd be willing to wager it's an important piece of the puzzle to finding the Eagle. So I'll take my chances with it in my possession rather than yours, thank you. Now hand it over," he said, dabbing his cheek.

Kal pursed his lips and shook his head, exasperated by the circumstances. Then, without warning, he turned to the street and threw the bag at a group of young men in their late teens walking away from the Gold Rush festivities, yelling as it traveled mid-air, "There's free money in the bag, take it!"

"God dammit," screamed Marcus as the satchel landed in the unsuspecting grasp of one of the youth. He bounded off the wooden walkway onto the dirt toward the boys like a runaway locomotive, providing Kal an opportunity.

"Run," he yelled, pushing Benny and Ashworth. "Head into the crowd!"

The three men scattered toward the mass of people grouped a block away at one of Old Sacramento's busiest intersections watching an exhibition gunfight between two cowboys. Benny ran in the direction of the car, while Kal gingerly jumped down onto the street headed for the other side of the block with Ashworth close on his heels. As the bigger man landed, he tripped on a patch of uneven dirt and tumbled onto his chest, his momentum carrying him at least five feet into a cloud of dust.

"Benny, go ahead, we'll meet you back at the car," Kal yelled as he helped Ashworth to his feet and snuck a peak back at Marcus, who was in pursuit with the bag.

"We gotta move, he's coming."

Kal felt something whiz by his ear and then heard a pop as they ran. Seconds later something jumped off the dirt in front of their feet followed by another pop.

*He's shooting!*

Nary a person seemed to notice the noise from Marcus' handgun due to the louder shootout up the street, all oblivious to the real danger behind them. The two men ducked their heads and ran headlong into the crowd, jostling several folks as they picked their way through the sea of bodies, Kal struggling to find an escape route.

"Follow me," he said to Ashworth, cutting in and out of a candy store, then abruptly peeling off into one of the many sloping alleys in Old Sacramento that dipped and rose almost a full story.

"I have to stop, I have to stop, can't breathe," Ashworth said, looking very pale. "Was he actually shooting at us?"

"I don't know and I don't want to find out. We need to keep moving."

"I can't, I can't. Oh, no!" Ashworth said, pointing back to the street where Marcus slowly jogged by. He stopped at the entrance to the alley, just as Kal shoved Ashworth out of sight into an adjacent courtyard.

"Go hide behind the dumpster over there, I'll try and get him to come after me," Kal said, realizing he was offering himself as bait with only one good leg. He stepped out of the brick courtyard right into the sightline of Marcus, who charged toward him, only a few hundred yards away and closing. Kal jogged as fast as he could the other way, hampered by knee pain and the uneven cobblestone road, but made it up to the other side of the street relatively quickly. He glanced back for a brief moment, expecting Marcus to be right on his tail, but was instead shocked to see the gunman slow down and purposefully walk into the courtyard.

Kal cursed out loud, unsure of what to do next. He could hear Marcus kicking and overturning things, looking for Ashworth. It was only a matter of time before he found him—there weren't many hiding places for a man of his size. Kal briefly entertained the thought of returning to help but immediately recognized it as futile. He wasn't sure what Marcus would do, but getting himself caught was not an option, and so he headed back to the car to regroup.

****

Benny crouched low next to the Mustang, attempting to stay inconspicuous in the parking lot while still keeping a vigilant lookout for the others. He was kicking himself for not staying with Kal, but his adrenaline had been pumping and he hadn't thought clearly. Just as he talked himself into heading back out to the street, he heard his name cut through the overhead freeway traffic echoing through the garage. It was Kal, running to the car and yelling his name.

"You're okay! I was just about to head out and look for you. Where's Ashworth?"

Kal just shook his head. "He got him. Ashworth couldn't run anymore and hid in one of the alleys. I thought Marcus would chase me, but he went looking for him instead. There was nothing I could do."

"Damn, well let's go. We can figure out what to do later. You still have the keys?"

Kal pulled them out of his pocket and threw them to Benny, who unlocked the doors.

"Wait for me!" a voice boomed.

"Holy crap," Benny said, pointing to the street. "It's Ashworth, he got away!"

Kal whirled around in shock as he lumbered toward them, sweating profusely.

"What happened? How did you escape?"

"I don't know. He looked around for me in the courtyard for a few minutes and then his phone started ringing and he left suddenly."

"He just left, without looking behind the dumpster?"

"Yes! I don't know who he was talking to, but yes, I thought my goose was cooked for sure."

Benny stared at him in amazement—according to Kal there was no way Ashworth should be standing in front of them. They had caught another lucky break.

"Well, what now?" Benny asked. "We should probably get out of here asap."

"We can't go back to the hotel, he knows we're staying there. We need to regroup and figure out our next step now he has the bag from the monument. I don't really know what to do. This is a serious setback," Ashworth said.

"Well, that's not entirely the case," Kal said.

"You don't think it's a setback?"

"No, not that part. The part about him having the bag."

Benny could see from the smirk forming on Kal's face he was up to something. "What did you do?" he asked.

Kal smiled and started laughing. "Let's just say that Marcus has the bag that was in the monument, but not necessarily what was in the bag."

"What are you talking about?"

"When I reached into the vault, I quickly opened up the bag and pulled out the wood box inside and switched it with some rocks on the ground. So Marcus basically has a sack of rocks, while the box is still sitting in the vault. I figure we could probably wait and let the area clear out before we go back and get it."

"You . . . are . . . a genius!" Benny said.

"Brilliant," added Ashworth.

Kal made his hand into the shape of a gun and blew on the tip of his finger. "All in a day's work."

# CHAPTER 32

Ashworth and Benny sat in the car attempting to rehydrate with soft drinks, somewhat cooled by the shade from a phalanx of trees surrounding Crocker Park. The heat had become unbearable, different from anything either men felt before, as if the sun had directed all of its energy to their location. The park lay on the other side of the freeway across from Old Sacramento, in the shadow of the Crocker Art Museum, a converted 1860s Victorian that had been expanded over a century and a half and currently held the title of the oldest, continuously operating museum west of the Mississippi.

"How much longer is it going to take him?" asked Benny, craning his neck in all directions, the adrenaline long gone. "We're like sitting ducks out here."

"It hasn't been that much time. He'll be fine. Just keep a look out."

Benny suddenly spotted Kal in the side view mirror walking swiftly with a bunched shirt tucked under his arm. "Here he is, thank God."

"Any problems?" Ashworth asked as Kal hopped into the back seat, drenched from the walk.

"Nada. The place was still pretty crowded. I waited a while and scoped it out to make sure you-know-who wasn't lurking around. When I got up close to the monument I acted like I had to tie my shoelace and was able to pry the door back open and get this out pretty quickly. Benny, did you get a hold of your dad and sister?"

"Yup. They haven't even been home the last week—they're visiting family in Florida and won't be back until the end of the month. I didn't tell my dad anything we were doing, just that a TV station was looking to rehash the Atlanta stuff and to be careful of anyone following them. But I think we should probably call the police and let them know what's going on. This is too much, I'm freaking out."

"Whoa, hold on a sec. Let's think about that one," Ashworth said. "We are on the cusp of finding the Eagle, especially with Kal's little miracle here. If we involve the authorities right now, we run the risk of stopping our momentum dead in its tracks. Think about it—this guy Marcus has nothing. Your family is safe and, in my opinion, he appears to be working alone. He doesn't know where we are or what we have. We currently have total control of the situation."

"You don't know this man," Benny snapped back. "You just saw a glimpse of his psychotic-ness. He's a cold-blooded murderer."

"You're right, I don't. I do know we are on the precipice of unlocking one of the greatest Civil War mysteries. That thug can be taken care of when we're done. He poses no real obstacle to us at this point."

Benny looked to Kal for support.

"Why don't we do this," Kal offered, attempting to mediate, as well as satisfy his own increasing inner-desire to find the Eagle. "I still have the office number for the FBI agent in Atlanta we dealt with after the bombing. It's Labor Day weekend—we can call her work number and leave a message about what's going on. That'll give us a window to do what we need to before the law gets involved, and at the same time we cover our asses. Okay?"

Benny begrudgingly nodded and wiped his forehead, "Can we at least get out of here before Marcus shows up? I can't handle this."

"We're fine, he's long gone. Just give me a second and we can go."

Kal wiped his hands on the cloth interior of the car and slowly unwrapped the bundle to reveal a hand-carved cedar box. It was one of the finest pieces of craftsmanship he had ever laid his eyes upon, stained and polished so deep the wood grain resembled psychedelic waves of amber color, running one after another across the top of the lid. The all-too-familiar logo of The Verein sat in the upper right corner, lightly engraved and smoothed over so finely it almost appeared to be a natural mark in the timber.

He unlocked the small metal clasp holding the lid and opened it, revealing several folded pieces of very old and dried-out stationery stained yellow from time. Kal gently picked the papers up and slowly uncreased them, the black ink still as vibrant and legible as the day it was penned. He scanned the handwritten sheets, careful to place every page safely back in the box upon finishing. After several minutes he put down the last sheet and looked up at Ashworth and Benny with a crooked grin.

"Well, what is it?"

"It's the mother lode—everything is here, even their secrets. It's everything about The Verein. Robert, you were right. You were right about it all."

Ashworth reached over the seat and grabbed the letter, impatient to see for himself. He quickly read the first page, which was addressed to 'The People of California', and started laughing hysterically.

"Unbelievable! It's their manifesto, their Magna Carta, their Manifest Destiny—whatever you want to call it. All rolled into one and actually documented. This is probably the only written record which proves their existence," he said, pointing to the lone signature on the paper in his hand. "Look at the author."

Benny squinted. "Does that say Sam Clemens? Who is that?"

"Who is that?" Ashworth laughed. "His full name is Samuel Langhorne Clemens, but you would probably recognize him by his pen name: Mark Twain."

"That's not the only one," Kal said, holding up the last page of the document which contained nearly 50 signatures. "This is their entire roll call. Look at some of the names on this: all of the Big Four, Judah,

Sherman, and Sutter Jr. Here's Kit Carson, the famous frontiersmen. Sam Brannan and George Hearst, the mining baron. The author Bret Harte is here, too."

Ashworth could not contain himself anymore and begged for the paper to inspect it for himself. "Look at all these signatures, it's a veritable who's who of Western pioneers. Levi Strauss, the inventor of the blue jeans, as well as Lloyd Tevis, the founder of Wells Fargo Bank. Here's a big one—Darius Ogden Mills. He was California's richest man and owned the Bank of California. It looks like some of these names at the end of the list were signed later over time with different ink. There is even a woman on here, Julia Morgan, the famous architect. She wasn't born until the 1870s but still became a part of this group. This is amazing, just amazing."

"Does it say anything about the Eagle?" Benny asked, momentarily forgetting his paranoia.

Ashworth handed the signature sheet back to Kal and thumbed through the main sections of the letter.

"Let's see here. Twain talks about their common love of the land and people, about striving to create a state devoid of the corruption and conflict displayed back East and in the South. There's a lot of wordy prose regarding the origins of the group and their intentions to pass on to future generations of Californians. Okay, read this part," he said handing it to Kal

*Once arrived at a true and harmonious reconciliation as to the goals necessary to achieve our subversive casting of the State, the methodology and means to accomplish said goals were conceptualized and hastened into motion. From that point forward a conscious effort was attempted to pirate and hoard all things related to finer culture we could wrap our hands upon—the obvious being large sums of money, but fine works of art were included together with historical artifacts and other objects we felt would be invaluable over the course of history.*

*These artifacts were transported West from around the globe using our network of connections, occasionally via the beautiful port of San Francisco or over the breathtaking and majestic spires of the Sierra Nevada. Sacramento was the ultimate destination; within the confines of a parcel of land J.A. Sutter secured and developed many moons prior.*

*As the city itself grew, developed, and eventually became the capital of California, the need to find a suitable and secure athenaeum to store and gradually re-release the spoils of our efforts to the region became apparent to all involved, and an area known personally by Collis Huntington and Mark Hopkins was developed in the heart of the original city where it sits to this day. Eye-to-eye with the dual rills while hidden in plane site, some objects still waiting to be emancipated to the people of the Golden State when the proper time presents itself.*

"Wow," Kal said, dumbfounded.

"I get some of it," Benny said, as the others digested the contents of the letter. "They collected a bunch of valuable stuff and hid it to eventually endow to the people of California. But why hold on to them for so long?"

"Think about it," answered Kal. "Some of these items were not only considered stolen, but also highly controversial at that time. There was bad blood regarding the Civil War for decades after it ended—you and I know firsthand there is still a small group of people bitter about the outcome back in Georgia. If these men and women publicly acknowledged the fact they possessed something like the Eagle so soon after the war, it could have started a whole new firestorm. So they probably held on to it thinking they would one day be able to unveil it. If Ashworth is right, over time The Verein and then Native Sons evolved and changed . . . "

" . . . and the secrets died off with the last original members," Ashworth said, finishing Kal's thought. "This is the last piece of evidence those forefathers left for the future generations. This is the final clue. They even tell us where it is, eye-to-eye with the dual rills while hidden in plain sight in the heart of the original city. We need to get access to the Internet right now and research this."

"But we can't go back to the hotel where the laptop is, Marcus is probably waiting for us," Benny fretted.

"Where else can we access the Internet?"

"I think the main public library is not too far away," Kal said. "We could try there."

Ashworth handed the letters back to Kal, turned around in his seat and fired up the ignition on the car, revving the engine.

"Can you taste it, boys? I can!"

# CHAPTER 33

The three men parked on the upper level of the public garage next to the Carnegie Building, a nearly 100-year-old structure modernized to house the main branch of the Sacramento City Library. They wasted no time making their way inside and headed directly upstairs to the computer lab, aware the very-much-alive Marcus could be lurking.

"Okay, let's start simple with Collis Huntington and Mark Hopkins—the two people Clemens, or Twain, mentioned," Kal said, motioning Benny to hop on one of the open computers and start the login process.

He typed their names into the Google search bar and pulled up a Wikipedia entry. "It seems that besides their affiliation in the Big Four and founding the Central Pacific Railroad, the two operated a hardware store together called 'Huntington, Hopkins and Company' here in Sacramento. By the 1860s it grew into a pretty big brokerage supply company for northern California, importing items from the East."

"The perfect cover to smuggle home the black market artifacts they were snatching up," Ashworth said. "Where was the store located?"

"Is located," Benny corrected, talking as he read. "Just like Sutter's Fort, it's still around. It's on the opposite end of Old Sac from the Judah monument, next to that massive railroad museum we passed. It says here the hardware store was in a structure commonly referred to as the 'Big Four Building' back in the 1850s next to Leland Stanford's warehouse. The two buildings were interconnected."

"Interesting," said Ashworth. "So we have the Big Four operating a supply shop along with a warehouse in the original city of Sacramento. Coincidence with the kind of work The Verein was performing at the same time? No way. But I think we're going to run into the same problem as with Sutter; the building there now isn't the original, and if there were any valuables left behind, they would have been discovered by now."

"Yeah, you're right," Benny said, reading further from the website. "It looks like the buildings came into disrepair and were torn down and remodeled in the 1960s to resemble the originals. They are completely modern on the inside, housing offices for the California Railroad Museum and a gift shop."

"A dead end," sighed Kal, massaging the back of his neck. The cold air pumping in from the building's AC had dried all the dirt and sweat in his hair and on his body, creating a layer of grime. "But Twain says in the original city. So that has to mean somewhere in Old Sac, right?"

"One would think, but almost all of those buildings were also remodeled or restored. Maybe it isn't necessarily the original city he was talking about," Ashworth posed.

"Hold on a second," Kal interrupted, taking over the keyboard from Benny. "I remember seeing something in that pamphlet the city worker gave me about Sacramento."

He navigated around several official city websites before stopping on one in particular. "Behold—the original city of Sacramento."

Titled UNDERGROUND SACRAMENTO, the webpage was plastered with various pictures of what appeared to be an abandoned, subterranean city. Kal clicked through the site, revealing more incredible images of a hidden world long left in obscurity by civilization: old brick store fronts untouched for decades, decaying structures and artifacts from the 1800s strewn over the ground. In some pictures it appeared as if the people that inhabited the area dropped whatever they were doing and fled.

"What is that?" Benny asked.

"It's Sacramento. The real Old Sacramento," Kal said. "This is how the city was first built after Sherman and Sutter, Jr. originally laid it out."

Ashworth jumped in. "I remember hearing something about this. Remember when we drove into town and I pointed out the Sacramento and American Rivers? This city is basically built on a flood plain next to these rivers, and back then when rains came in the winter they flooded every year. The leaders decided the best option was to raise the streets, similar to what Atlanta accomplished. I didn't realize the Underground still existed, though."

Kal read on. "It says here in the 1860s and 70s the city built massive brick walls in between the street and sidewalks of Old Sac and then filled the street with dirt, raising the roads. If you were on the first floor of a building, you would walk outside onto the sidewalk and be facing this giant wall holding back the dirt and newly-raised road. Eventually the building owners either elevated their structure to meet the new street level or converted their second story into the first floor. It took awhile for the sidewalks overhead to get filled in, but when they were finished, a labyrinth of tunnels stretching for blocks were left behind preserving the original building façades. That's probably why those alleys in Old Sac dipped down nearly a full story—they were the original street level. It's exactly like the Underground in Atlanta."

"But they never fixed it up like back home," Benny said, looking intently at the pictures on the screen. "So this could be the original city Twain was talking about?"

"It makes sense," Ashworth said. "Remember Twain's line, 'eye-to-eye with the dual rills while hidden in plain sight'? If I correctly remember some of my own educational studies, I believe a rill is a body of water cutting a path into the land. A rill initially starts small, carves into the earth gradually allowing more water through, until it becomes a stream, then a creek, until finally—"

"It's a river," Benny said.

"Eye-to-eye with the dual rivers," Kal said. "The Sacramento and the American. Sacramento's Underground is at that same level, or eye-to-eye, with the two rivers that run next to the city. It has to mean they hid everything down there."

"In plain sight," added Benny. "Somewhere we can all see?"

"Benny, find everything you can on Underground Sacramento— where it goes, how we can get into it. Everything."

Kal reached into the plastic bag he clutched by his side holding the wood box and carefully pulled out the letter to read again.

"What are you doing?" asked an alarmed Ashworth, nervously glancing around the library to make sure no one was watching.

"Look at the last line Twain wrote," Kal answered, putting his finger by the section he wanted Ashworth to see. "It's been bothering me since I first read it. What do you notice about the sentence where he mentions the rills?"

Ashworth studied it for a moment. "Nothing jumps out at me. Although it appears, and I would never be confused with an English expert, that he spelled 'plane' and 'site' wrong in the context of the sentence. Shouldn't it be 'hidden in plain sight'?"

"Exactly! This was Mark-friggen-Twain. I don't think he just made mistakes like that. You were talking about Sacramento being built on a flood plane just now and it hit me. What if he's telling us exactly where it is? What if The Verein hid everything not in 'plain sight', as in for everyone to see, but literally on the 'site of the plane', with plane referring to a geometrical shape: the flood plane. Twain used the lesser-utilized spelling of the word to attract the reader's attention."

"Interesting theory," Ashworth said.

"Think about it. If that's what he is talking about, the hidden location would have been underground in an area no one frequented anymore, in an area that flooded all the time—the perfect place to put something where no one would go. Keeping the water out of an entire city was nearly impossible, but keeping it out of a small storage space down there would have been much easier."

"But technically, all of Sacramento would qualify as a flood zone," argued Ashworth.

"Yes, but all we need to know is where in the original city, or Underground Sac, flooding was the worst. I guarantee you if we can somehow find the spot where the river usually crested and initially flooded, we'll have a pretty good idea of where to look."

Ashworth ran his hand through his partially graying goatee and stared off, his mind feverishly at work. "If that's the case, we're going to need some geological maps of the area from that time period," he finally said, looking down at his watch. "And I know exactly the place to look. But I have to get there before they close."

He grabbed the keys to the car and headed toward the elevator. "I'll be back in 30 minutes. Keep looking for info on the Underground. We're going to need to know everything."

****

The elevator doors dinged and opened causing both Kal and Benny to startle and look up as an elderly woman disembarked and headed for the newspapers.

"I keep thinking Marcus is going to step off that thing," Benny said with a nervous laugh.

Kal smiled. "Me, too. I honestly pee a little each time that bell rings."

Benny placed a photocopy on the out-of-the-way table they had relocated to in an attempt to consolidate information. "Here's an interesting article I found from a local indie paper called the Sac News and Review. The Underground has mostly been sitting abandoned for the last 150 years," he said as Kal read. "There are stories about it being used at times over the last century as everything from a massive opiate den to a smuggling network for Chinese immigrants. Some people swear a large homeless population still lives down there to this day. Anyway, there used to be a clean shot from right around where our hotel is, all the way down to Old Sacramento—about 10 blocks."

"Used to?"

"Well, if you look on one of those pages I gave you, they've done a lot of construction with an outdoor mall and other high rises that have destroyed portions and cut off the tunnels. If we wanted to get to Old Sac now we would have to explore our way. There doesn't seem to be a straight path anymore."

"Isn't there anywhere in Old Sac where we can just drop into the tunnels?"

"There are limited tours in the spring and summer, but they don't really invade the main sections of the Underground. For all we know the starting point could be in the offices of the California Parks and Games Department—which would be bad. But I did see something with potential."

Benny pulled out another article with a map of all of the recorded sections of the Underground highlighted. "This is from a couple of years ago. There is an Italian restaurant on 7th and J Street called Gio's Trattoria where the owner found a gaping hole in the brick wall of his basement that led to a small tunnel connecting to the Underground. He said he checked it out and walked at least a block toward Old Sacramento before getting scared and turning around. He patched the opening up and hasn't been back since. If we could somehow get down there, that's only a handful of blocks from Old Sac, and if what he says about a long stretch of uninterrupted tunnels is true, we'd have our perfect insertion point."

Before Kal could answer, the elevators chimed and Ashworth came bursting through the doors, nearly giving both men a coronary. He strutted over to their area with several large, rolled-up maps in his arms.

"I just made it to the Sac Flood Control Agency before they closed. The lady at the front desk was the usual uptight government worker, but there is nothing these little babies can't help with," he said, putting the maps down and pulling a few Hershey's out of his pocket.

"Aren't they melted?" Kal asked.

"Doesn't make them any less tasty. You want one?" Ashworth asked, licking the partially liquefied chocolate off the wrapper, to which Kal declined. "I offered her a few, told her I was a high school teacher from a low income school who needed some info for a project, and whazam! Copies were in my possession in seconds. I've always found some charm combined with a little white lie can help you get what you want."

"Like priceless, stolen artifacts?" Benny asked.

Ashworth proceeded without even acknowledging the comment. He wiped his hands on the back of his pants and unrolled the two maps onto the table.

"Here's the first diagram of what Sacramento looked like in the 1860s. You can see the Hastings Building where the Pony Express was, the footprint for the Capitol building over here, et cetera. Now here is the map of where the flood waters used to rise," he said, laying the second topographical map over the first. "When it rained heavily, the water crept in off the Sacramento and American Rivers into a small overflow lake bordering the city called China Slough right near Old Sacramento, then flooded the whole downtown. This was always one of the first sections to get overrun."

Ashworth took a red pen and circled the area, then pulled the first map from underneath and laid it on top. "So now if we put the 1860's map of Old Sacramento over the topographical map of the flood zones, we see the most disturbed area would have been almost directly right here."

The red ink he used on the flood map was visible through the white paper of the 1860s map and encircled the area adjacent to the Big Four Building.

"You were right Kal—the flood plain entry point was next to Hopkins and Huntington's store and Crocker's warehouse. It's the 'plane site' Twain was talking about. If we look at a map of the area from the AAA guide, the current location would be underneath, right next to the railroad museum."

Kal paused for a second and studied the smaller, up-to-date map more closely.

"Something grab your attention?" Ashworth asked with a smirk.

"Is it just me, or do you find it weird every inch of Old Sacramento has been developed and built upon, with the exception of the block you just circled—the one right next to the Big Four Building and the museum? It's just an empty grass field with a couple of small buildings on one corner."

"Good boy! That's the first thing I noticed while I was at the Water Department, so I asked the clerk about it. Turns out there was an amendment added to the city's original charter late in the 1800s stating this area cannot be developed or impeded upon under the guise of an archaeological site—it's been left unmolested for nearly 150 years and used as a gathering place for festivals. A developer tried to sue the city 40 years ago to get access but was denied, and since that time no one else has shown interest."

"Perhaps the building moratorium was inserted way-back-when because The Verein and the Native Sons had something valuable underneath the land that couldn't be disturbed?"

"Which would mean we've hit the jackpot. We've got the flood plain and this empty lot intersecting each other. It can't be a coincidence."

Benny and Kal fist-bumped as Ashworth smiled.

"So what else did you find on the Underground?"

Kal looked at the clock on the wall, which read almost 5:30 p.m.

"We can probably explain it better over Italian food. I think we found a pretty good place."

# CHAPTER 34

"**F**lashlights?"

"Check."

"Bottled water?"

"Yep!"

"Spelunking tools?"

"What the hell is spelunking?" Benny asked.

"It means cave exploring," answered Kal with a laugh. "You've never heard of it?"

"Whatever Daniel Webber. I don't have the vocabulary you do."

"It's Webster. But good try."

"Don't have it. But I did get rope, a couple small shovels, and some other stuff. Not sure if they are specifically designed for 'spelunking,' though," he said, sarcastically making air quotes. "They should be fine for what we need. Everything is in your new backpack."

They were headed back to pick up Ashworth after stopping at the nearby department store for supplies. The older man had insisted on staying at the library to identify a more direct path through the Underground, as well as set up their visit to the basement of Gio's.

"He better be ready to go," Benny said, still a bit jumpy. "I don't know why he attempted to find another route. I told him I printed everything we needed."

"You've seen how he is. He thinks he's a genius—probably wanted to prove you failed to find a crucial fact."

"Yeah, you're right," Benny said. "There he is, out front."

Kal maneuvered the Mustang alongside the curb next to the entrance of the library and Benny got out and folded his seat, allowing Ashworth to occupy the entire back row.

"Did I miss anything?" Benny asked.

"What?" Ashworth replied in confusion. "Miss anything? Oh, about the Underground? No, you found everything—good job. The manager at Gio's is waiting for us. I told him we were a group of reporters from out of town who wanted to do a follow up story on the hole in his basement. He was more than happy for the exposure. What did you get at the store?"

"Everything you wrote down, plus a change of clothes. It's all in one pack."

"Good, now give me my credit card back. When we get to the restaurant, let me do the talking. I have this all planned out," he said, looking anxiously at his watch. "Let's go."

Within minutes they navigated their way through the confusing one-way streets of Sacramento to Gio's, finding a lone parking space out front. "Sweet, it's past six," Kal said, looking up at the street sign as he pulled his gear out of the trunk. "We don't have to pay for parking."

Benny just shook his head. "Really? We're about to descend into the depths of an unknown underworld and you're worried about paying for parking? Besides, it's a holiday weekend, genius."

"I was just mentioning it. It's a good sign," Kal said with a chuckle as he followed the other two inside.

The décor of Gio's Trattoria appeared to be untouched from the day the restaurant first opened. Dimly lit pictures of Sinatra and the rest of the Rat Pack littered the walls as accordion music softly echoed through the narrow restaurant. Most of downtown Sacramento was made up of either large office buildings occupying a whole city block or narrow, row structures like this one, with a business on the first floor and residences above. These smaller buildings were some of the city's originals and had the basement access to the Underground they were now seeking.

"Welcome, you must be Mr. Wadsworth," said the restaurant owner, a slight man who appeared to be 40ish. Only he was trying to shake Benny's hand. "I'm Dino. We spoke on the phone."

Benny didn't even say a word, simply pointing to Ashworth while still holding the man's hand.

"Oh, excuse me, I'm so sorry."

"No problem, and it's Ashworth. Dr. Ashworth," he said, again gazing at his watch. "We're sort of pressed for time here. Is it possible to go look at the basement now?"

"Of course, of course. Follow me," Dino said, leading them toward the back of the restaurant while providing a quick guided tour. "My father Giovanni opened this place in the '40s. It used to be the only Italian joint in downtown Sacramento. Three of the Rat Pack ate here— Dean, Sammy, Peter Lawford. Not Frank, though, unfortunately. That would have made my father's existence, may he rest in peace."

"So about the basement," Ashworth segued.

"Yes, yes, it's right through here, down these steps."

Dino took them past the freezer, opened an old door falling off its hinges, and carefully navigated them down a narrow set of stairs into the small and cramped basement. A single light bulb dangled from the ceiling, illuminating old food boxes and several pieces of broken-down cooking equipment come to permanently reside in the musty underbelly of the building.

"How old is this place?" Benny asked.

"My father once told me it was here since he was a boy in the 1910s, but it was built before that. I imagine it might be one of the city's originals. Over here is where I found the hole, back behind these boxes. Let me move some of them out of the way. I did the repair work myself with some new brick."

Kal sidled up to Ashworth and whispered in his ear, "How are we going to get some alone time? This guy isn't going to leave us by ourselves."

"Just wait," answered Ashworth, again looking at his watch.

"What the—" cried out Dino, standing in front of his previously repaired wall, which was now crumbled. "What happened? It's broken again. I was down here a few weeks ago and it was fine."

The bricks looked as if they were smashed or kicked in, allowing Benny to shine his flashlight into the gaping darkness, revealing a small passageway.

"I can't let the city find out about this. They'll fine me and make me hire a legit contractor to fix it for real."

"Dino!" yelled a voice suddenly from the top of the stairs. "Phone call for you."

"Tell 'em I'm busy," he screamed back. "I've got an interview with some reporters going on and now the wall is broken again."

"It's the hospital. They say they got one of your family members and they need to talk to you right now!"

"Oh, Lord," said Dino, quickly heading for the stairs. "I have to take this call, guys. You going to be okay down here for a bit without me?"

"Fine, fine," Ashworth insisted.

"Just make sure you don't go into the hole. It's dangerous down there. I don't need some hurt reporters I have to pay insurance for."

"No problem. Go ahead and check on your family. We'll just wait here."

Ashworth watched their host disappear up the stairs before scrambling for the opening in the wall. "Hurry up, we only have a few minutes before he comes back."

"What did you do?" Kal asked.

"Nothing too bad. I just paid some kid at the library $50 to call the restaurant at exactly 6:25 and say Dino's cousin had been taken to the hospital. That's why we needed to get down here so fast. It's the only chance we'll have to be alone. I figure we've got a few minutes before he comes back."

"Wow," Benny said, squeezing into the passageway. "That's ingenious, but totally slimy."

"Thank you," Ashworth said, taking a mocking bow then motioning for Kal to go next.

"But how did you have someone knock down the wall before we got here?"

"I didn't."

"What?" Kal said, stopping himself halfway through the entrance. "I thought you did this."

"Nope. I planned on doing it myself, that's why I had Benny buy a small sledgehammer at the store. But we lucked out. The wall must have collapsed on its own. I saw some of Dino's entrees, I doubt his work with mortar and brick are up to snuff. Now go!"

Kal plunged in headfirst, nearly bumping into Benny inside the small four-by-four brick tunnel, followed by Ashworth, who nearly got himself stuck in the entrance. Both men were forced to turn around and pull on his arms to squeeze him all the way through.

"Thanks gents. Let's get moving before he comes back."

Kal took the lead of the single file line and slowly made his way through the short passageway, bent at the knees and crouched over at the waist. His heart rate had only recently returned to a normal level following the chase with Marcus, but began fluttering again at the prospect of delving into the unknown.

*I am so sick of crawling around in basements and the dark looking for this thing.*

"Looks like the chamber is only a couple of feet away," he yelled back to the others. He followed the cobweb and bug-infested passageway as it sloped down for a bit and then abruptly ended, dropping off into the main section of the Underground. Kal carefully lowered himself out of the tunnel, which was elevated about three feet off the floor, and onto what was once an original dirt street of Sacramento, momentarily taking it all in with his flashlight.

Above him lay a roof of concrete constituting the current, modern sidewalk alongside J Street, supported by rows of beams added early in the 20th Century for support. Small streams of daylight poked through pin-sized cracks in the cement, finding their way into the darkness and illuminating sections of the Underground every so often like a glowing exit ramp in a darkened movie theater.

The façade of the building he stood in front of was built entirely of brick with the window archways still in good shape—some of the wooden frames still holding their 100-year-old glass panes, the area behind the archways sealed off by lumber and masonry to form the current basement of Gio's. Yet it retained enough of its original design for Kal to visualize how it could have been the first floor of the business at one point, despite modern plumbing running all over the place.

The sight oddly reminded him of the Pirates of the Caribbean attraction at Disneyland—the dark and dank jail scene in particular. He visited the iconic theme park as a wee lad with his parents, and the buccaneer tour was his favorite by far.

*You put a couple of drunk pirates in a cell trying to get a key from some mutt down here and you could charge hundreds.*

Looking east toward midtown and Sutter's Fort, the tunnel appeared to stop after only half a block—probably cutoff when a new office building was put in. But in the other direction, to Old Sacramento, the passageway was unimpeded for as far as the light could shine.

"This is so cool," Benny said. "It kind of feels like we're in an old hallway."

"We are, basically. We're in one long hallway that used to be the original sidewalk," explained Ashworth, motioning for them to follow as he made way through the dark to old town. "This wall on the right is a rampart holding back the dirt infill that raised the road where the cars are driving now. On our left are the original first floors of the town, and the current sidewalk is overhead. If we were in 1860 right now we'd be strolling down the streets of Sacramento which Tecumseh Sherman helped survey for John Sutter, Jr."

"And we might be underwater," added Kal.

"Back then, yes. There would be a good chance of that."

The group slowly hiked their way through the dark, hampered by small obstacles such as garbage and the uneven and constantly changing ground slope. Crude man-made passageways, most likely hand dug by traffickers or the homeless over the course of decades, cut through the rampart walls and in-filled cross streets intersecting J Street, creating a network of even smaller tunnels leading from block to block. It was nerve-wracking to crawl on all fours through the unsupported space, which shook and dropped dirt every time a car drove overhead, but it was the only way to cross to the next block, each of which projected a different feel. Some buildings still had their original architecture intact with areas behind the façade untouched by time, almost as if society above completely forgot or was oblivious to the domain below, while other buildings were altered and modernized, leaving only a bland and soulless cement wall to protect the basement.

The thing Kal found most eerie was the evidence of recent human activity, his flashlight occasionally passing over a broken beer bottle or food wrapper buried in the ground. Benny found a truly unique piece of American history when he discovered an empty can of New Coke—notable in that someone actually drank the foul-tasting substance. In one particularly well-traveled area they passed an old, abandoned campsite created by a long-gone transient, complete with a small fire pit.

"You guys think anyone is still down here?" Benny asked.

"That would be freaky," Kal said. "Can you imagine a deranged homeless guy jumping out at us right now? Or some kind of new mole-man species?"

"I'd piss myself."

Ashworth stopped ahead under what looked like a small skylight in the sidewalk above. "See those glass squares in the cement above?" he asked. "The city put them in a long time ago so light could stream down, sort of a piece of working art. I noticed them under my feet when I was out getting food earlier and just now realized what they were. You can tell the sun is going down, though. Hardly any light is coming through."

"Can we rest for a second and get a drink of water?" Benny asked. "I'm drained."

"Good idea," Ashworth said, pulling one of his maps out. "I'll figure out exactly where we are."

Kal set his pack down to get the supplies and noticed they were standing in front of a particularly old building still in solid condition. He imagined with a little paint and some elbow grease it could fit right in with the other restaurants in Old Sacramento.

"Check this out," he said to the others, shining his light through the front window and several cobweb-filled rooms. "It's still got stuff in it. Look at that old wooden bench over there."

He put his pack down, grabbed a bottle of water and headed through the front doorway, taking a big chug.

"Wait for me," Benny said. "Don't leave me alone with Ashworth."

"Keep your voice down, he can hear you."

"I don't care. The guy is so weird. I mean, why is he wearing a scarf down here? It's not even that cold."

The evidence of frequent flooding over decades was apparent once they stepped inside. The dirt floor rose within a few feet of the ceiling in certain areas, suggesting after the water came rushing in it left behind layers of mud and silt, enveloping everything. Kal was reminded of the television images of Hurricane Katrina and how similar this looked to the insides of homes after the flood waters receded from New Orleans.

"Hey, Benny," Kal said, assuming he was still behind him. "Look at this room. You can see the original cabinetry and wallpaper. This is amazing."

But there was no response.

"Benny? Where'd you go?" he yelled, making a complete 360 degree turn.

Kal retraced his path, heading all the way back out to the subterranean sidewalk where Ashworth was still seated on the ground, studying the map.

"Did Benny come through here?" he asked, poking his head out of the front door.

"I did not see him. Please tell me he did not get lost?"

"He couldn't have, he was right behind me," Kal said, heading back into the structure.

"Goddamn it Benny, stop messing around." he yelled. "We have to get going. I'm going punch you in the balls if you try and jump at me!"

Kal halted in one of the vacant rooms to listen for his heavy-footed sidekick, certain he was trying to scare him, just like at Sutter's Fort.

"Run!" Benny suddenly screamed, bounding from around the

corner. He hauled ass past Kal and headed toward the front. "It's Marcus, he's right behind me!"

Kal's adrenaline immediately kicked in, combined with sheer terror, and he mindlessly turned to follow, tripping on a piece of door frame and falling face first into the dirt. Panic and pain from his knee coursed through his body as he imagined the deformed man pumping a bullet into his back while he lay helpless on the ground. He scratched and clawed as fast as he could on his hands and knees through the abandoned building in the direction of the main tunnel, churning up a cloud of dust and rocks before finally propelling himself out into the open, where he stumbled and fell again trying to get up to run.

Only Benny didn't appear to be in any hurry to escape anymore, leaning against the doorway and laughing his ass off.

"Oh, wow. You should have seen your face just now, it was friggen priceless. I totally got you!"

Kal slowly got up to his knees with his head down and calmly brushed his hands off, realizing he was right all along.

Benny was just screwing with him.

"I swear I am going to kick your ass. You are not going to see it coming, but it will be the ultimate beat down."

Benny could barely breathe or speak, he was laughing so hard.

"It'll be . . . it'll be worth it," he finally mumbled, rearing back and cackling.

Kal gingerly got up and picked his flashlight off the ground.

"Ha, ha," he sarcastically laughed. "Get it out, get it all out." He adjusted his knee brace and flexed the joint a few times, making sure all the parts were still working.

"Let's get Ashworth and go. Where is he?"

Benny composed himself and pointed his light toward the spot Ashworth had been sitting. "He was over there last time I saw him."

Only now he wasn't. No one was there.

"Don't tell me he's playing this game now," Kal said.

"Oh, he's not playing any games—he's right here with me," said a familiar voice standing no more than 20 yards behind them in the dark.

They whirled in that direction, spotlighting Ashworth. He was standing alone, upright and stiff, the silhouette of a handgun pointed at his head barely visible.

"You see," said the voice. "Benny was right without even knowing. I *was* behind you the entire time." Marcus stepped out of the shadows and smiled, unable to hide his burned and mangled face even in the dark recesses.

"You didn't think I'd just go away, did you?"

Kal's stomach dropped.

"This is our destiny, Kal. We were meant to find the Eagle together. I understand and accept that now, I just wish you would," he said nudging Ashworth to move to them. "I forgive you for trying to run away from me earlier, but it still pains me greatly. I know you know where it is, and you are going to lead me to it."

Marcus abruptly stopped Ashworth by hitting him in the shoulder with the gun when they were within a few feet of the younger men.

"I need to feel comfortable we can work together on this, because I'm not going anywhere. I'm here to stay. Can we, Kal? Can we work together?" Marcus said with a strange speech cadence, his mannerisms jerky and spastic.

"You can trust me Marcus. I swear."

"Yes, you've sworn your allegiance to me a few times already, haven't you? I'm sorry, I'm going to need something a bit more substantial this time."

Marcus suddenly turned the gun from Ashworth toward them and fired, hitting Benny in the midsection.

"No!" screamed Kal as Benny doubled over and fell to the ground.

"I have to know you're not going to run again. I think that should do the trick. At least I know he won't be able to."

Kal and Ashworth immediately dropped to tend to Benny, who initially writhed around for a few seconds but now lay still, loudly moaning. Kal grabbed some of the spare clothes out of his nearby backpack and ripped Benny's blood-soaked shirt to begin applying pressure to the wound. He was still conscious but each breath was labored—the amount of blood gushing already slowing.

"I can't believe he shot me," he finally yelled.

"He'll be fine for the next few hours," Marcus said, towering above them with an ugly smirk. "It was a clean shot through his side, probably didn't nick any organs. As long as we keep moving to wherever you were headed and take care of business, you'll have plenty of time to get him to a hospital afterward."

"We need to get him to a hospital right now!" screamed Kal.

"Now, Kalei. We know that's not going to happen. You have two choices here: either leave him and hope he doesn't die or bring him along. It's your decision, but time is ticking to find the Eagle. And we're leaving in the next minute."

"I'm not going to leave him here alone," Kal insisted to Ashworth. "Ben, do you think you can walk?"

Benny grimaced and pushed himself up a little bit as the blood drained from his face, leaving him noticeably pale, even in the dark.

"I think so," he said raising an arm for Kal to pull him up—the other holding his side. Both Kal and Ashworth slowly helped Benny to his feet and propped him up, throwing his arms over their shoulders.

"Fuck!" he screamed at the top of his lungs in a combination of pain and frustration. Kal grabbed the last spare sweatshirt from the bag and wrapped it tightly around Benny's waist and the wound to keep constant pressure.

"You sure you're okay?"

Benny nodded. "Just keep moving, don't stop," he said.

"Alright Marcus, let's go."

"You lead the way, my friend."

# CHAPTER 35

The blood and dirt on Kal's hands was thick, the sticky combination creating a nasty sensation that would have nearly driven him bonkers under more ordinary circumstances. Of more concern at the moment, however, was the welfare of Benny, who was laboring to walk even with two men holding him up. His left leg was almost useless and dragged along the ground as they steadily navigated to Old Sacramento. The only medical training Kal ever received took place during his freshman year in high school when he joined the Junior Lifeguards, and oddly enough, his studies skipped the section on gunshot wounds.

"Look at us, Ben. One pair of good legs now between the two," Kal said, eliciting a small, forced laugh.

They only managed to progress a few blocks in the 30 minutes since the shooting, carefully maneuvering through the maze of tunnels and stopping frequently despite protests from their captor. Kal measured the possible outcomes as they slowly walked, contemplating the best way to find Benny medical attention, but found his mind wandering—specifically questioning how Marcus inexplicably found them.

*Was he following us the whole time?*

*I should have known when I saw the wall kicked in back at the restaurant that something was wrong.*

*We were so careful after he tracked us down in Old Sac.*

*Did he somehow spot one of us at the store and shadow us?*

The manner in which Marcus hunted them down was now moot. The current reality was they were in similar circumstances to the situation in Atlanta that resulted in so many nightmares over the past year. Only Benny was now the one seriously injured instead of Dunning and the odds of escaping unscathed seemed even worse.

*The Freedom Eagle is an object of death. No wonder it was never found, The Verein probably kept it hidden on purpose once they realized its powers.*

"I need to stop. I need a break, some water," mumbled Benny, cutting into Kal's concentration.

"Let's put him down here," he said to Ashworth, the two coordinating to gently lower the injured man against a brick wall. Kal pulled out a bottle of water and let him slowly drink from it as Marcus followed Ashworth to scout their path ahead.

"Just leave me here Kal, I'm slowing you down," Benny said, his breathing getting shallow. He coughed some of the water back up, a trickle of it spilling onto his chin—rose-colored instead of translucent.

"No way. We're almost there. Once we get this statue and give it to Marcus, we're going to get you to a hospital and you'll be fine."

"You know he isn't going to let us just go, Kal."

"You don't need to worry about it. Remember how I got us out of that jam back in Atlanta? I'm gonna do the same here."

"You mean the clusterfudge Elle and Dunning bailed our asses out of?" Benny asked, his eyes closed.

*At least he's still making jokes.*

"I'm not leaving you under any circumstances. And if you try and tell me again I'm going to have Marcus shoot you in the other side to even the wounds out," he said, getting another pained chuckle.

"Looks like bad news," Ashworth said, returning with Marcus close behind. He pulled out the map and laid it on the ground for everyone to see.

"I'm pretty sure we're right here," he said, pointing to a spot around 3rd and J Street. "That huge mall on K is over to our left. That's why we've probably seen less and less of the original buildings as we've made our way—I know they did a lot of construction and demolition of the original roads when they built the stores in the late '90s. The major problem is there is a dead end at the end of this block."

"What do you mean a dead end?" Kal asked.

"Meaning end of the line, everything has been concreted in. I'm not sure if it's the basement of an office building or what blocking the tunnel. But we can't move forward, the street is to the right and another wall to the left. We have to backtrack and try and find another route around."

"We can't go back, Robert," Kal said, looking over his shoulder at Benny, before tightening in to speak in a hushed tone. "We're wasting time if we head back. He's not going to make it."

"We don't have a choice, Kal. We can either go find another way or give up, and I don't think your friend with the gun is going to allow the second option."

"We could always blow through it," interjected Marcus.

"What are you talking about?"

He opened the right side of his jacket to reveal several bricks of C-4 explosives. "Boom."

"No, absolutely not," Ashworth vehemently protested. "We have no idea what is behind that wall. It could be a business filled with people or a load-bearing structure that'll drop the entire place onto our heads. Either way we'll have cops crawling all over us if we detonate it."

Benny perked up, slowly picked himself off the ground and stood on his own. "We're not giving up and we're not blowing anything up. We keep going. I can do it. And I think I know another route that doesn't involve an explosion."

"Benny, take it easy. What are you talking about?"

"When I was messing with you back in that building I accidentally stumbled into what looked like another passageway in the rear. I think it was an old alleyway or something. I poked my head in and it looked like it ran for awhile toward Old Sac. I meant to go back and check it out, but this asshole had to go and shoot me."

Kal exchanged glances with Ashworth, who shrugged his shoulders. "It's as good an option as any. It could be an underground alley running down the middle of all these blocks that was never destroyed. We're only a few streets from where we need to be and we've got no other option."

Kal nodded and moved to put his arm around Benny to help him walk, but he was having no part of it. "I'm okay. I can do it myself." Kal could tell from the look on his face he wasn't trying to be a jerk in dismissing him—Benny just wanted to show the others his toughness.

****

Ashworth carefully inspected the small entryway into the narrow tunnel, testing the strength of the stone walls and poking at the ceiling to make sure it wasn't on the brink of collapse.

"There's a couple inches of running water down here headed west toward the Sacramento River—it's probably an old sewer or water runoff system," he yelled to the others, stepping down into the sunken underpass and splashing water all over his shoes. Giant rats scattered in all directions when he cast his light further down the tunnel, startling him. "It looks like it runs for quite a distance. There isn't a ton of space and the smell isn't pleasant, but it might just get us there."

Kal looked back at Benny, who was swaying against an empty doorframe with his eyes closed and both hands clasped to his bloody side. "How are you doing?"

"Fine, fine. Is it going to work?"

"Yep, you saved our asses by finding this. We'll be to the Eagle in no time."

True to his word, Benny meticulously hoofed it all the way back to the location unassisted but now appeared to be paying the price as he struggled to stay on his feet.

"I know you're fine, but why don't you let me help you get down into the tunnel. If you think you can go on your own, then let go of me. Otherwise you can just use me as a crutch to save your energy."

Benny begrudgingly accepted the offer and let Kal hoist him on his shoulder. "Guess what? We get to go into another dark and cramped space. Sort of a like a cave within a cave."

Benny barely grunted back. He was getting steadily worse despite the earlier bravery.

"After you," Marcus said, waving his prosthetic arm. Kal obliged by slowly dropping through the broken wall into the tunnel and turning back to help Benny, who followed inside and grimaced loudly upon landing, sending an echo shooting through the narrow space. Kal was immediately overcome by the smell and noticed how different this passageway was—he had to bend over and navigate like a hunchback to keep from hitting his head, which, combined with having Benny on his shoulders, put an enormous amount of strain on his spine.

"Everyone ready?" asked Ashworth, who was on point. "Let's go."

The group made their way through the shaft at a snail's pace, occasionally stopping so Ashworth could stab away thick nets of spider webbing. Kal deduced from the crumbling construction the spillway had to be at least a century old, if not more. The crude fabrication of stone and brick was breaking apart in sections, yet still managed to stay upright and undisturbed from the world above.

"Wow, look at this," Ashworth said, interrupting the rhythmic beat of their feet pounding through the water. "It's ripping right through the tunnel in front of us." His light hit a large section of steel beam entering through the top right corner of the spillway and continuing on through the lower left-hand side, exiting at the bottom and slicing their already narrow pathway in half.

"What do you think it's from?" asked Marcus.

"I'm not sure," Ashworth answered, kneeling down to study the map under his flashlight. "We should be getting pretty close to old town. I think we're somewhere around 3rd or 2nd Street. It could be a support beam or a piece of infrastructure. Not sure if there's enough room for us to get by, though."

"I think I know what it is," Kal said, touching the exposed metal. "If we're around 3rd, we should be right next to the freeway. The engineers who built it were forced to pile drive these girders deep into the ground to structurally support the raised roadway, and ended up cutting through this tunnel without knowing it was here."

Ashworth shined his light up and nodded. "You could be right. It looks like construction-grade steel. If that's the case, then we're only a few blocks from where we need to be."

"Are all of us going to be able to get through?"

"Only one way to find out. I'm the heaviest, so if I can fit, than everyone else should be fine." Ashworth dropped flat into the mucky water and immediately began contorting his body to get around the beam, his movements resembling a floundering snake attempting to slither back into its den after digesting a meal twice its size. Kal watched with amazement as the large man wiggled and shimmied his way through the opening—first his head disappeared, then his shoulders, then his gut until he was completely on the other side.

"Not too bad," he yelled. "You guys should be fine."

"That was amazing," Benny said weakly, having witnessed the entire scene while leaning against the wall in front of Marcus. "The only time I've seen him move faster was when he dropped one of his candy bars under his seat on the plane."

"Do you think you can get through?"

"I can do it. Just help me down."

Kal gently lowered Benny onto his back and helped him gradually slide his way under the beam, while Ashworth assisted from the other side until he was completely through.

"See you on the other side," Kal said to Marcus as he followed suit, dropping into the small stream of water and gliding under with relative ease. For an instant he contemplated taking advantage of the mercenary while the one-handed man was tied up underneath the beam, but before he could act was interrupted by Ashworth tapping him on the shoulder.

"Looks like we're not the first ones here," he said, pointing his light five yards ahead to what remained of a human skeleton, its tattered clothes still hanging from the torso, the lower half nowhere to be found.

"Poor sucker."

"Has to be a homeless person who either lived down here or got lost and died," Ashworth said, walking over to pick through the clothing for some kind of identification. "Look at the t-shirt—it's a Body Glove. That brand used to be popular in the late '80s and early '90s."

"You think this guy has been here for two decades?" Kal asked.

"Possibly. Who would even know to look in this area?"

"Let's please keep moving, this isn't an archeological dig," interrupted Marcus, pulling himself up with his one good arm, his face covered in muddy water. "Good ole' Benny here may find himself in a similar resting spot if we don't pick up the pace."

"Screw you," Benny retorted weakly. Kal could tell speaking was becoming overly tedious.

"Okay, we're going," Ashworth said, slowly moving away from the remains with a longing look. "I'd love to check that out further."

"It'll be fine, buddy. We're getting close," Kal said as he lifted Benny's arm over his shoulder and followed, the muck and grime from the miserably cold water rubbing between his shirt and skin. Benny tried whispering something in response but ended up coughing up blood as they trudged ahead, the tunnel starting to slope slightly downward.

"Take it easy, Ben. You don't need to speak. Save your energy."

Benny again attempted to say something that Kal couldn't understand.

"What is it? Do you need to stop?"

Benny shook his head and looked directly at Kal.

"Don't let me die down here," he whispered. "Don't leave me, please."

"You know I won't, don't even talk like that. You'll be fine."

But the truth was Kal was terrified—more so than back in Georgia when Dunning sacrificed himself, more than when he saw his mangled leg after the explosion, and more than the passing of his mother when he worried for the well-being of his father. He could literally see and feel the life draining from a person he could not have cared less for nine months earlier, and was consumed by immense sadness. He wasn't going to let another person die; not this time.

"Remember our argument back at Ashworth's house?" he asked as they walked.

"Yeah."

"Well, the truth is she was in love with you." Kal said, hoping the words would take his mind off the pain.

Benny weakly shook his head side to side. "You're just saying that."

"No, it's the truth, she told me on the drive back from Macon, but I didn't believe it. I tried to kiss her, thinking there was still something there . . . but there wasn't. At the time I couldn't understand what she saw in you, so I was jealous—probably still am—that's why I said those things."

Benny was silent as they trudged through the darkness, causing Kal to wonder if he fully heard him.

"You think she really felt that way?" he finally whispered.

"Yep."

Benny went quiet again, before responding, "She was a heck of a kisser, wasn't she?"

Kal smiled and picked up the pace. "That she was, my friend."

Ashworth suddenly slowed to a stop ahead, "Dammit."

"What? What is it?"

"It looks like we've hit another dead end. The tunnel just stops."

"What are you talking about?" Marcus said, rushing in. "It can't just stop!"

Ashworth knocked on the giant slab of stone completely blocking the tunnel and preventing them from going any farther.

"What would you call that?"

Kal laid Benny down and inspected it for himself. "Marcus is right. This doesn't make sense. Where is the water going? It's flowing in this direction, it has to go somewhere."

Ashworth turned on his more powerful portable lantern and held it down to the ground—there was no apparent hole or drain siphoning the water off, it seemed to just slowly taper and disappear into the floor of rocks, sand and slate.

"It's going farther down somewhere," Kal said. "That doesn't help us at all. How close are we to the Railroad Museum?"

"Hard to say," Ashworth said, tapping and inspecting the walls around them. "I'm no geologist. We could be right next to it. The problem is it looks like we've gotten further into the bedrock. It's not going to be as simple as digging out through these walls to get back into the Old Sac Underground. We have no idea how far we'd have to go, these walls could be several feet of pure granite."

Kal looked back at Benny and made his mind up.

"We could blow it up."

"No," Ashworth said. "I told you. It's too dangerous."

"We can't go back, it'll take too long to find another route. We're close, I know it."

"Enough!" yelled Marcus. "I'm going to make the decision easy for both of you, because neither of you have a say. We're going forward, even if it means bringing this whole blasted tunnel down."

He opened his jacket and dropped two bricks of C-4 onto the ground, then pulled out a small remote detonator.

"If you don't like it, just go suck on one of those little Hershey bars you're always shoving in your mouth," he said to a disapproving Ashworth, before turning his attention to Kal. "Go put this at the base of that rock at the end of the tunnel. Unwrap it and mash 'em together like silly putty, then stick the detonator in the middle. I'll hit the switch when you are clear. We all need to retreat behind that freeway girder to keep from getting sucked back in by the blast or hit in the head with debris."

Kal nodded in understanding and began to work while the others headed back down the tunnel to the safety of the beam, leaving him all alone in the dark. The off-white material felt like clay as he carefully combined the two squares and rolled them into a cylinder, unaware the material was basically harmless without the detonator. The residue coated his hands and the potent chemical odor stung his nose as he hastily finished up and made his way back to safety.

"I think it's ready to go," he said, sliding underneath the giant pillar, nearly knocking Benny over. Marcus had positioned his friend's back alongside the beam to help shield from the brunt of any potential shockwave while he and Ashworth comfortably kneeled behind.

*Probably figured he's going to die anyway.*

Kal huddled next to Benny, who was at least partially protected by the metal, and gave him a sip of water. "Go ahead and blow it, I'm gonna stay here with Benny."

"Fine, your choice. Might want to plug your ears, though," Marcus said as he pulled the trigger, resulting in a deafening explosion. Rocks and dirt hurtled through the tunnel like tiny SCUD missiles, followed by an enormous cloud of smoke and dust that moved down the shaft and enveloped them like a black monster.

Kal managed to get his hands over Benny's ears and turn his head into his shoulder to cover one of his own, but the exposed eardrum immediately felt as if it was lacerated by a hot poker, ringing painfully as his shoulders were simultaneously pelted by flying debris. The dense cloud almost completely blacked out the flashlights and filled his lungs and nostrils, causing him to cough and hack in an attempt to heave the residue from his throat. Finally, after several minutes of choking off the oxygen, the cloud slowly settled and dissipated.

"Everyone okay?" Kal asked, shining his light onto Ashworth and Marcus. Both men were caked in a chalky dust that covered their hair, skin, and clothes, immediately reminding him of pictures from his dad's National Geographic detailing the South African Xhosa tribe. Kal thought it cool at the time that the male members covered their faces and bodies in grey paint after going through a secret rite of passage sending them into manhood and wanted to somehow incorporate it into his high school baseball team's pre-game ritual. It was a short time later that he discovered the secret ceremony actually involved adult circumcision, causing the idea to lose its luster.

Marcus' leaky eye was already leaving a tear trail down his dusted cheek, and realizing that he, too, was covered in similar fashion, Kal brushed his face and hair and checked on Benny to make sure he wasn't covered in the gunk.

"I'm okay," he mumbled, semi-conscious. "Did we find it yet?"

"We're close, real close. We need to see what's behind the rock we just blew up."

"Was that what that was? It sounded like one of your farts," Benny said, slowly grinning—the outline of his lips covered in wet dust. "Yours usually smell worse, though."

Kal chuckled. "Hang tight. I'm gonna check it out."

He crawled back under the beam and headed down the tunnel toward the blast site, covering his mouth with his shirt to keep out the acidic air, which became thicker and harder to see through the closer he moved to the genesis of the explosion. He felt his way along the wall hoping for the best, but his heart sank when his flashlight smashed into the rock face that had been the target of the C-4—it was still standing, relatively undisturbed. He shined the light along the base of the wall and found a small crater dug into the floor, and realized it would take 20 times the amount of explosives they used to get through.

"Did it work?" Ashworth asked, emerging through the haze holding Benny with Marcus close behind.

"No, barely scratched it."

"Impossible!" Marcus said, kneeling to inspect the crater for himself. "It should have at least blown—"

Before he could finish his sentence the floor beneath them rumbled and shifted, then dissolved as if flushed down a toilet, plunging the group down a dark chasm. Kal bounced and rolled head-over-heels, his stomach clanging around his insides as his outside banged into rocks, boulders and the others who were tumbling with him. Just as he began to believe they might be falling all the way into the recesses of hell, his descent was interrupted by the cool, but welcomed, sensation of water enveloping his entire body.

Kal struggled to make sense of what was up or down in the pitch black liquid, his head fogged from blows during the fall. He began to thrash and panic, his clothes clinging heavily to his skin and his air supply running out when a hand suddenly shot through the water and grabbed his shirt collar, pulling him upward and out onto solid ground. Dazed, confused and exhausted, the last thing he saw before passing out was the silhouette of a large man pulling Benny alongside him.

# CHAPTER 36

Kal awoke on his belly to the sound of two voices arguing in the darkness, only part of the conversation audible enough to make out.

He rolled over and looked up at the 15-foot high earthen ceiling, several man-made support trestles spanning its length. His head was throbbing, most likely from the large knot on his forehead he gently massaged with his fingers, but his vision was finally focusing. He tried to flex his knee and immediately realized everything was not copacetic. The pain was beyond the normal ache he'd been recently experiencing—the joint felt loose, and he realized he likely tore the ligaments again.

He raised his head and looked around. They appeared to be in some kind of large cavern. Benny lay next to him, unconscious and sopping wet as well, but breathing. He spotted Ashworth and Marcus 50 yards away. The lantern Ashworth held bobbed up and down as they argued with one another, sending their shadows dancing all over the limestone walls.

Kal ascertained he and Benny were lying on the shore of a small subterranean pond. He could slightly make out the hole they fell through in the ceiling a hundred feet away and the steep slope they tumbled into the pool of water.

*That tunnel must have been built to channel the water down into this small lake. That's why the water appeared to fade away—it filtered down through the ground. The explosion probably loosened the floor just enough for all of our weight to punch an opening through it.*

"Kal," yelled Ashworth, rushing over to check on him. "Are you alright? You bumped your head pretty good."

"I think I'm okay," he said, tightening his brace as far as it would go without cutting the circulation before groggily standing up. "Were you the one who pulled me out of the water?"

"I guess I managed to get the soft landing and then fish you and Benny out once I got my bearings. He's been unconscious the whole time, but seems to be stable and is breathing well."

Kal felt Benny's forehead and checked the wound. "Thanks. Luckily that water wasn't too cold. Let me have your coat and scarf, I want to bundle him up as best I can."

Ashworth hesitated for moment, reluctant to give up not the jacket but the piece of cloth around his neck, before finally acquiescing.

"What's he doing?" Kal asked motioning to Marcus, who was studying something on the wall with the lantern.

Ashworth smiled. "Come see, I think you are going to be interested."

Kal bundled Benny up as tightly as he could before limping behind Ashworth and for the first time got a good feel for the dimensions of the chamber they were in. Roughly half a football field in diameter, it appeared to be at least partially man-made with mortared walls and stone holding back sections of dirt. The wood beams supporting the ceiling were extremely old and in poor condition, likely due to the cumulative stress from above.

"This is the place, isn't it?" Kal asked. "This is what The Verein was hiding under that grass field. We're underneath it right now, right?"

"Yes, Kal. This is it," answered Marcus, turning to face him but still keeping his light pointed at the wall. The hat that covered his burned head was lost in the tumble as well as his prosthetic arm, leaving him in his natural monstrous state.

"Behold."

In front of them stood two large iron doors in excess of 10 feet while a large, bronzed bear's head with a snake in its mouth rested overhead, keeping watch. "Behind these closed doors is where the Freedom Eagle has been resting for a century and a half, waiting to be emancipated. The Verein and Native Sons of the Golden West built this place to store the bounty Mark Twain described in his letter. And I found it. Finally, everything I worked for has come to fruition."

Marcus got down on one knee and bowed his head briefly, overcome by the moment.

"I can't believe we found it," Ashworth said.

Marcus looked up and glared. "We? WE? I should shoot you dead right here."

"Marcus, please. All I was saying—" Ashworth said, glancing over at Kal.

"You fucked this situation to high hell to begin with," continued Marcus. "If you hadn't involved that monkey Dunning in the first place, I'd still have my hand and face! You're nothing but a thief with a bankroll."

"What's he talking about?" Kal asked Ashworth, thoroughly confused.

"N-nothing."

"Nothing? Why don't you tell him the truth, for once. Tell him about our little business arrangement!"

Kal again asked, this time more forcefully. "What is he talking about, Robert?"

"I-I don't know what he's talking about," Ashworth stammered. His eyes were twitching full speed, faster than the night they first met.

Marcus put the light on the ground and raised the gun, cocking the hammer. "Tell him. Tell him, or I swear to God, I will kill you!"

Kal's stomach dropped as he realized what was happening. His mind began to slowly lift from the fog and put the pieces of the puzzle together. He became angry that everything had been as plain as day in front of his face but he never stopped to link it all together: Ashworth always disappearing around the hotel and at the airport, Marcus knowing their exact location time after time, Ashworth's insistence on staying alone at the library and his inexplicable escape from Marcus in Old Sac when he was cornered.

*These two men did not meet for the first time at Judah's monument. They knew each other and were working in tandem from the start of this trip, perhaps even before, back in Atlanta.*

"It was never supposed to happen the way it did," pleaded Ashworth. He appeared on the verge of tears. "Please believe me when I say no one was ever supposed to get hurt."

"No, no, no," Kal said, shaking his head in disbelief as the blood pumped down his forearms and into his fists. "Don't even say it!"

It was too much to handle. Kal realized he had been kidding himself the whole time. Marcus had no intention of letting them go. He controlled everything from the start, watching over them like a puppet master, and Kal played right into the game by never questioning Ashworth's intentions.

For the first time he allowed the realization to creep into the inner recesses of his mind that he might die. But instead of causing him to panic or become hysterical, a calm blanket of peacefulness and clarity spread over his spirit. He was tired and overwhelmed by the situation. He didn't care about the Eagle anymore, about Dunning, about anything. He was giving up.

"You're not going to let us go, are you?"

"He *is* going to let us go. We found what we were looking for," Ashworth said. "He has no reason to harm us."

"Of course, I gave you my word," Marcus said with a smirk.

Kal just shook his head and started walking back to Benny. "He's not going to let us go, Robert. You're fooling yourself if you think otherwise. I'm done. You made a deal with the devil."

"You're wrong, Kal. We're all going to be okay. Be happy, we found the Freedom Eagle!"

"Let him be," Marcus said, reaching into his coat. "Here, take these last two bricks of C-4 and wedge them in between the doors. Those things are extremely solid, but it should be enough to blow open the lock and get us inside. You need to turn on this trigger device and let it charge for a second until this little light turns green. Understand? I'll blow it once you are clear. It's my last one, so don't screw it up."

"Yes," mumbled Ashworth, looking over his shoulder at Kal one more time as he walked away, saddened the young man was not enjoying the moment. He had developed a fondness for both Kal and Benny and now considered them friends, of which he did not have many in the world. He felt bad he deceived them, but was confident in the end it was for the best. After all, they were on the cusp of making history.

Ashworth looked up at the immense bear's head ominously staring down at him as he unwrapped the explosives and mashed them into a ball, slapping it onto the giant handle just below the key hole like a big hunk of Play-Doh. He carefully turned the electronic detonator on and placed the business end into the soft clay, waiting for the green light to come on.

Clear on the other side of the chamber, away from the double doors, Marcus walked over to the water's edge where Kal was sitting with Benny.

"You shouldn't be so trusting," he said as Kal re-checked Benny's wound. "None of this would have happened if you followed my instructions back in Atlanta."

"Pound sand."

"That's the spirit! You know, this is our discovery, not his," he said pointing to Ashworth. "He's not on our level, he's just garbage. He's trash, no better than all the impure races that have destroyed this country. He's the lowest common denominator, in it for the money and fame. Me and you are different—we understand the cultural meaning of a piece like this."

Kal never looked up to acknowledge him.

"The detonator is ready but the light is not coming on, what do you want me to do?" yelled Ashworth from across the chamber, his voice bouncing off the walls.

Marcus smiled to himself and softly said, "The light only comes on when I pull the trigger, fucking moron."

Just as Ashworth reached to adjust the detonator, the LED lit up green.

He cupped his hand over his mouth to yell. "There it goes, it's workin—"

The initial heat from the blast immediately scorched Ashworth's skin and melted his eyelids shut and the hair on his head, face and arms in a nano-second, the following shockwave breaking all of his ribs and several other bones while catapulting his body a hundred feet through the air. Though unconscious, his death came only after his neck attempted to slow the rest of his body, snapping as he slammed headfirst into one of the unforgiving limestone walls. His body finally landed into the pool of water that only a short time prior acted as a safety net when tumbling from above. It would end up becoming his final resting spot, the light from a pin-sized LED the final image his brain processed.

Kal threw himself on top of Benny as soon as the explosion occurred, stunned because there was no warning before Marcus activated the C-4, and also because he didn't think Ashworth cleared the blast zone. He shielded his friend from flying debris and immediately got up off the ground to look for Ashworth, but could only see smoke.

"Where's Ashworth?" he screamed at Marcus, who remained crouched on one knee with a crooked smile, the trigger still in his hand. "Where the hell is Ashworth?"

"I believe I saw a piece of him land over there in the bath," he said, pointing to the water. "Some of him went the other way over by that wall. I wouldn't bother trying to help him. I'm pretty sure he's dead."

Kal ran to the edge of the pool and quickly scanned it with the intent of jumping in, but the second he saw the state of the smoldering body, he knew there was no chance Ashworth survived.

"He was useless, Kal. He meant nothing to us. Now come on, let's go. Let's get our trophy."

Kal slowly turned to face Marcus. "No, I'm done. I'm not moving an inch. I'm nothing like you—you're a cold-blooded murderer. I'd rather die right here than help you find that tainted thing. You killed him for nothing, just like you killed the others!"

"Please do not take that tone with me. I did not kill your friends, they chose their fates."

"Screw you, I'm done!"

Marcus' face turned red. "You're done? You are done? I'll tell you when you're done." He strode over to the semi-conscious Benny and ripped off the jacket.

"You may not care what I do to you, Kal," he said, sticking the barrel of his pistol into Benny's open wound, eliciting a primeval howl and awakening him fully. "But if you don't pick your friend up and start moving, I won't just shoot him in the head. I'll make him feel an incredible amount of pain before he dies and have you watch the carnage. Now get your ass over here and pick up the light and your friend."

"Leave him alone!" Kal said, amazed at how quickly Marcus knew the pressure points to use. He helped Benny up, grabbed the lantern—the only remaining light source they had—and headed toward the blown out vault with Marcus' gun pointed at his back.

Before he could make it five feet, two of the humongous wooden support beams overhead groaned and snapped in two, collapsing only yards in front of them in a blast of dirt. It was followed seconds later by a large chunk of the ceiling dropping into the pool near Ashworth's body.

"We need to escape," Kal yelled as yet another section of the roof broke and burst to the ground on their right. "I think the explosion weakened the support in here, we need to find a way out before the whole roof collapses!"

"No, we keep moving!" Marcus responded above the din, shoving Kal in the back with the gun. "Move!"

Kal tried to maneuver as fast as he could to the doors, but was forced to stop and regain his balance every time the ground rumbled from the impact of a falling ceiling chunk. The eerie, distressed noises emanating from above were increasing in volume and frequency.

As they approached what was left of the vault doors, Kal had to sidestep the once mighty bear's head, which lay broken into pieces in the smoldering blast crater. The twin sentinel gateway that previously stood guard for decades was blown back on its hinges and twisted inward like aluminum can tops, leaving a hole big enough to drive a car through. The same chemical odor that permeated the air in the tunnel after the first C-4 blast lay thick here, as well, forcing Kal to cover his mouth with his arm.

Using the lantern to knife through the darkness ahead, he took a deep breath and slowly entered the unknown, slowly illuminating a smaller, more intimate offshoot of the main chamber roughly the size of a large meat locker. Chills ran down his spine immediately. For some reason he knew this was it.

"I'm going to sit you down against that wall over there so I can look around," he said softly to Benny. "Okay?"

The room offered a temporary respite from the chaos outside and seemed to be more structurally safe than the bigger chamber. It was plain and unassuming on the inside and filled with two rows of multi-leveled wooden shelving units reaching over eight-feet tall, reminiscent of those in a grocery store—some rotted and partially collapsed.

*There has to be at least twenty in all, ten per row.* But Kal noticed immediately that many, if not all, appeared empty.

Marcus was giddy as he stepped inside. "This has to be where everything was stored, right? Do you see anything?"

"The racks look empty," said Kal, taking a closer examination. "But look at the little metal tags along the front of them. This one says, '#12331, T.Hill, *The Last Spike*'. That's gotta be Thomas Hill, the famous painter. His most well-known work was a portrait of the final spike of the Transcontinental Railroad being driven into the ground. Ashworth owned a reprint in his home."

"Where is it now, though? It's not here."

"I think I read in one of those Sacramento pamphlets that it's in the California Railroad Museum—the building we are probably right next to. Most of the stuff in here was eventually returned to the people of California by the Native Sons and The Verein. Start looking for anything that says Freedom Eagle."

The two men began listing off the tags out loud, no small feat due to their tiny size and the lack of light being produced from the single lantern.

"I've got George Caleb Bingham's *Boatmen on the Missouri* on a tag over here. That's a pretty famous painting, and I'm not positive, but I think it's currently at the de Young museum in San Francisco."

"This one says *Bronco Buster* by Remington and this one *General Andrew Jackson* by W. Rush," Marcus added.

"Wow," Kal said, pausing for a moment to take it in. "I've seen both of those sculptures in history books—they are both extremely famous. There had to be hundreds of similar artwork in here at one time."

"I don't care, keep looking for the Eagle'" snapped Marcus, his voice frayed from the crescendo of noise escalating in the main chamber outside the vault.

The two men meticulously worked their way down every aisle, Kal cataloguing each notable piece in his head for future reference. Pieces of art by Whistler, Catlin, and Homer had been there, as well as sculptures by Thomas Crawford, whose body of work included the *Statue of Freedom* piece above the Capitol dome in Washington, D.C. Kal was astonished to see that originals from famous American poets Dickinson, Emerson, and Poe also sat in the vault at one time. But when they reached the final shelf, not only was it clear every single piece of treasure formerly housed in the room was now long gone, there was not a single shred of evidence the Freedom Eagle ever was there either.

"It's not here," Kal said.

"Start over, we must have missed it."

"Even if we missed it, it's not here anymore. There is nothing left—"

"It has to be here. Keep looking," insisted Marcus, menacingly pointing the gun. Kal once again began listing off the markers and retraced his path in the other direction, slowly taking his time to make sure he didn't skip anything. When he reached the front near the double doors and Benny, he began to laugh.

*It really is finally over.*

The object that dominated his life for so long was once again lost to the universe.

*If it even existed at all.*

Whatever the case, the last shred of his being that yearned to discover the Eagle for scholarly reasons, or to memorialize Dunning, or whatever, was officially extinguished. He honestly and truly did not care anymore and limped over to get Benny and find a way out before they were killed.

Marcus was becoming unglued, demanding and pleading at the

same time. "What are you laughing at? What the hell are you laughing at? We're not done! Come on, keep looking. It's here!"

Kal just kept chuckling and helped his friend to his feet, empowered by his indifference.

"You don't get it, Marcus," he said. "It was never meant to be found. I finally figured it out. The Freedom Eagle is like one of those high fastballs I used to see in baseball all the time—I chased it all day because the ball looked so big and juicy when the pitcher let it go, even though I knew what the final outcome would be. I'd constantly tell myself to leave it alone, but I couldn't do it. And just when I thought I was finally on the brink of doing the impossible and making solid contact, I realized as I swung and missed once again it was an optical illusion. My eyes and mind were playing tricks on me, because the ball was going too fast and was too high for me to ever catch up to it. I eventually learned my lesson, though. I learned to let it go. And that's what I'm doing now. I'm done chasing, man. I'm taking my friend out of here."

Marcus fired a shot that flew by his head and imbedded in the wall behind them.

"No, you're not! I'll kill you before you leave. The Eagle is here, we can find it."

"Just let us go," Kal said. "It's over. It's not here and it never was. If we're all going to die down here anyway, what does it matter if it's from your gun or the roof collapsing? At least give me a shot to leave. I've done everything you asked of me, it's not my fault the Eagle is gone."

Marcus lowered his weapon for a brief second and appeared to be contemplating the plea.

*Perhaps he does have some humanity left.*

That thought was immediately erased when Marcus jerked the gun back, aiming directly at Kal's head. "No. This isn't finished until I say so."

He shrugged his shoulders and closed his eyes, ready for the end to mercifully come. His body was in pain and he was exhausted. *Go ahead, do it.* His mind darted all over the place before finally locking on an image of his mom, and the thought of being able to see her again comforted him. He imagined her patiently waiting for him, surrounded by family and friends, as well as what he honestly took to be angels bathed in white light.

*White light . . .*

*Light . . .*

*Light!*

Kal opened his eyes and looked around the room, smiled, then plunged the vault into complete darkness. He blindly dragged himself and Benny to the middle of the chamber as quickly as possible, feeling his way and using his memory to move in between the rows of racks to hide as Marcus shouted and cursed in anger.

In the chaos of the explosion that killed Ashworth and the search for the Eagle, Kal forgot he was holding the only light source—something far more valuable than Marcus' weapon. Without the light, they were all equally blind and the gun no longer dictated terms.

"Kalei!" screamed Marcus, firing a random shot toward the spot the two last stood, the muzzle flash brightening the vault for a mere millisecond. He fired again, trying to use the small window of light to scan the room, but his corneas couldn't transition quick enough from the pitch black to make out anything more than the shadows and dark spots just in front of him.

"I swear to God, when I find you," he muttered, blindly taking a step forward right into a rack and smashing his nose as he fired off another wild round.

Kal stealthily moved himself and Benny to the back of the room, staying as small and inconspicuous as possible. *Hopefully he runs out of ammo soon. I like my chances of taking him on one-on-one with the element of surprise. Plus, he's only got one arm and a bad eye.* Kal's conundrum was that he did not know how much ammunition his enemy was carrying. He had surprised them all earlier with the C-4, and for all Kal knew he had enough bullets packed inside his jacket to keep firing all night.

The room lit up again and a bullet fragment splintered a chunk of wood only feet from their hiding spot. *He just got lucky, he doesn't know where we are,* Kal reassured himself, peeking around the side to see if Marcus made any progress locating them in the desperate game of hide-and-go-seek.

The next shot bounced 20 feet to their left and nowhere near their vicinity. *He still has no clue.*

Marcus screamed in anger once again. "Kal! Are you listening to me, Kal? You once asked me what my last name is. It's Adler. My name is Marcus Adler. It's German. Do you know what Adler means in German?"

Kal wasn't paying attention to him anymore, though. Something caught his attention in the last brief burst of light. The way the racks were perfectly aligned in the vault reminded him of something—one of the few things from his old apartment in Atlanta that was always in perfect symmetry.

"It means eagle, Kal. Eagle. You see, I was destined to discover this piece of history from the moment I was conceived by my parents. I am intertwined with the Freedom Eagle. We stand for the same things, and you, of all people, are not going to stop me from my destiny."

*Of course, the dominos!*

The wooden racks lined up like two giant rows of dominos standing on their ends, organized in one of the simpler patterns Kal used to make for fun. He stood at the edge of the first row, Marcus all the way at the end. If he could somehow push over the one closest to him, it might start the same kind of chain reaction, resulting in the last one falling on top of the unsuspecting gunman.

"My bosses originally hired me to find the Eagle many years ago and I made the mistake of partnering with our fat friend out there," Marcus continued. "After many months with little to no results I was forced to dial up the intimidation. He unfortunately then decided to secretly collaborate with your friend, Dunning, behind my back, and that was not going to work."

Kal felt around and grabbed the lowest shelf of the rack he was hiding behind, bending down to use what strength was left in his legs to generate all the leverage. Nasty, jagged splinters from the old redwood dug into his fingernails as he pulled, causing it to slightly move, but not give. He quickly tried again but was met with the same result.

"You and Dunning really had no clue what was going on. But if it's any consolation, Ashworth really did believe that I would let you all go. I think he actually even considered you his friend."

Kal's entire right leg was throbbing in pain now. He could feel the kneecap float around the joint as freely as a dinghy on the high seas every time he moved, his mind pleading for him to quit and not risk any more permanent damage.

*One more time, one more shot, that's all I have left.*

"You really shouldn't have been so trusting, Kal. You were my little lab rats, running through the maze to find my piece of cheese. And I thank you for that."

Kal gritted his teeth, turned around so his back faced the stubborn rack and squatted, reaching down to his butt to both lift and use his body weight to simultaneously push. The heavy structure initially put up a fight again, but only crepitated in resistance until the mooring snapped underneath, slowly allowing it to be tipped over.

"Found you!" yelled Marcus, firing several shots toward Kal and the sudden cacophony, elated his prey exposed himself. But the chain of events were already set in motion, and just as Kal hoped, the first wooden rack fell squarely into the second, knocking it loose and into the next, and so on. The thunder of smashing timber started building, becoming almost cataclysmal and filling up the dark room with a deafening roar—to Kal it seemed like the entire place was coming down on top of them, and he dropped to the ground, reaching for Benny. But by the time he finally found his friend it was already over.

Kal turned the light back on and looked around, revealing a disaster zone. The row of racks which stood for more than a hundred years now resembled a giant pile of kindling hacked to bits and strewn across half of the vault. The light cut through the giant mushroom cloud of dust the pileup created, but Marcus was nowhere to be found on the other end.

*It worked, it got him! I can't believe it actually worked! He's buried under all of that.*

"I got him, Benny," he said, so excited he pumped his fist in the air. "Let's get the hell out of here."

Before he could lift his unconscious friend up, however, he was disheartened by a bellowing laugh emanating from across the room. "Very crafty, Kal, but once again it looks like you missed your target."

He scanned the vault, focusing on the second row of untouched shelves to his right, from which Marcus stepped out of the shadows. He simply moved a few feet out of harm's way when the destruction began, and now walked to Kal with his gun chambered and ready to fire.

"It's really a shame things couldn't have worked out better between us, you had to fight me every step of the way," he waxed. "In the end it's the same spirit that endeared you to me that will be responsible for your death. Your light trick isn't going to work again."

What Marcus Adler couldn't have possibly known was at that exact moment, a small crack, created at the spot where the last wooden rack missed its target and smashed against the wall, had slowly spread and sheared up through the ceiling at a seismic rate, through the main chamber where the overhead dome was still breaking apart, through the layers of rock, soil, and sand comprising the solid earth underneath the open field in Old Sacramento, and finally piercing the top layer of sod, exposing itself to a full night sky of brightly shining northern California stars.

The open fissure sat bare to the world for several seconds, unsure of its next move, when a lonely dew drop resting on a single blade of grass a few inches away was pulled downward by the force of gravity, splashing to the turf—an act of nature so regular that to try and estimate how many times it happened during the average human second would be impossible. Although microscopic in weight, this slight collision was all that was needed to give the fracture the direction it needed. And with the simple act, the crack relieved itself of all of its lower pressure, collapsing the entire field and raining hundreds of tons of sediment down into the chamber where Marcus, Kal, and Benny's drama was playing out.

Kal never knew what hit them—one minute Marcus was approaching in the vault and the next darkness engulfed them like a thick cloak. There was no warning, no sound, no shaking, just deafening silence. He found himself pinned down and struggling to breathe, as if he were underwater, only his clothes were relatively dry and his mouth was filled with dirt. He used a couple of swim moves to free his arms from the clutches of whatever was holding him back and worked to loosen his head, finally comprehending.

*It collapsed, the ceiling finally collapsed. I gotta get out and find Benny.*

Luckily only loose soil fell directly on them, knocking him to the ground and burying his body from his torso up but leaving his legs partially exposed. He was able to free himself within seconds by violently wriggling and extracting his head like a scared ostrich. Never having let go of the cracked but still working lantern, Kal spit out a mouthful of soil and attempted to get his bearings.

The new landscape was dramatically altered beyond his imagination.

Almost three-fourths of the vault they were in was destroyed, reduced to what resembled a rolling hillside rising all the way to the exposed street level, bespeckled with large boulders, rocks and debris. The earthen walls had crumbled on three of the four sides, covering and blocking off the double doors to the main chamber, which by all accounts did not exist anymore. Kal looked up and could see patches of night sky and moon—they were no longer under the cover of the grassy field.

*Benny!*

He immediately panicked and felt around for his friend, positive he was buried alive. Instead, Benny miraculously lay almost totally unscathed within feet of Kal, shielded by a massive rock that rolled and nearly crushed both of them, but instead transformed into a small retaining barrier holding back the tidal wave of dirt that should have swallowed them whole. The truth was both men were still alive due to the disinclination of a lone, partially standing wall to collapse. Because of their proximity to it, the spot they were in ended up being the safest location during the cave-in.

"Wh-what's going on?" Benny asked, still semi-coherent. "What happened?"

"We are two of the luckiest SOB's in the world right now, Ben. How are you feeling?" Kal said, rushing to check on him.

"Still shot. Are we in the Underground?"

"Kind of. It's a long story. You lost a lot of blood and we need to get you out of here and to a hospital. We just have to climb out to the street up there. Do you think you can make it if I help?"

Benny gently touched his wound and grimaced. "I think so. Where's Ashworth?"

"He didn't make it," Kal said, his voice trailing off. Even though Ashworth had ultimately betrayed them, the manner in which he died was still deeply disturbing.

"Marcus?"

Kal turned the light and pointed to the spot where Marcus last stood. "He's under there somewhere."

Benny lifted his head and smirked. "Good."

Kal gingerly helped his friend up. They were both in bad shape—beat up physically and mentally. Neither would have tried to scale the steep canyon of the newly formed abyss under normal circumstances, but the literal light at the top of the Underground gave them newfound energy and hope. Kal shouldered most of the load on his one good leg, and the two slowly began working their way upward, using each other's weight to find consistent footing in the hodgepodge, still sinking and falling over several times.

They barely made it 10 feet from their original location when Benny suddenly stopped moving, almost sending Kal tumbling back down the slope.

"Kal, l-look," he stammered, pointing off to the hill.

"What? What is it?" he asked, not sure of what he was supposed to be searching for.

At first glance in the limited light, Benny appeared to be pointing to some sort of mutilated animal covered in dirt and blood. But it immediately became apparent to Kal that it was no beast.

It was Marcus. And he was still alive.

"It can't be," Kal gasped, amazed their antagonist once again cheated death. An instinctual twinge of fear gurgled up from his stomach—despite the obvious fact the man was incapacitated, the trepidation he could still cause them harm endured.

"Did not . . . see that . . . coming," gurgled Marcus, small reddish spit bubbles foaming at the corners of his mouth. He was laid out on his back with most of his body, sans his one good arm and head, covered in what Kal initially thought was dirt. A closer inspection revealed it wasn't just soil—Marcus's torso was pinned by a two-ton rock with no hope of excavation. He was enduring a slow and painful death.

"Look's like . . . I'm not going to be able to get out of this one, eh?" he managed to say, struggling to lift his hand. "But I still have the power."

"The gun, he has the gun," Benny said, wincing in pain.

"We could have changed history together," Marcus said with a smile, pointing the weapon directly at Kal. "But you wouldn't listen. This piece of metal is the only thing you respected. It's all anyone ever respected."

Kal put his hands up and nodded, looking around for anything to throw as Marcus cocked the gun.

"I really did like you, Kal . . . I think we could have been friends in another life, and that's the god's honest truth. But . . . I guess we'll now have to settle on meeting again in hell," he said, putting the weapon to his own temple and pulling the trigger.

The noise from the shot nearly knocked both men over in surprise.

"Don't look," Kal said as he helped Benny stabilize and keep his footing. "It's not worth it. We need to keep moving."

The two were silent as they trudged to safety, using each other as leverage to overcome the unsteady footing. Kal could now feel the fresh air from the early Sacramento morning rush into his lungs as they climbed to street level—only about 15 more feet and they were home free. To take his mind off the tediousness he thought about everyone he loved and missed: his parents, Elle, Dunning. He reflected on how much he and Benny had been through recently and how odd the fates were to create a friendship between them.

"Professor Dunning was right all along," Kal said, his breathing starting to labor from the exertion. "The evil that drove Marcus ended up being the very thing that destroyed him. He couldn't let go of the Eagle and he lost everything because of it. He didn't break us."

Benny slightly smiled—his concentration focused on making it up the hill.

"We did win, didn't we?"

"Just as soon as we get you to the hospital."

As they ascended, Kal felt the urge to say a word of thanks but realized something was suddenly wrong with Benny. He was struggling to take the slightest step and straining to speak—it was if his tongue had become too big for his mouth.

"Ben, are you okay? Benny?" Kal asked as his friend slipped out of his grasp and began tumbling backward down the slope.

"Benny!"

# CHAPTER 37

$K$al pushed the button on the bed to adjust his mattress, raising his upper body to a semi-seated position, and looked out the nearest window down to Sutter's Fort.

He thought it ironic that the horde of police and medical personnel that seemed to flood Old Sacramento almost the second he stepped out of the massive crater took him to Sutter General Hospital for care, one of the modern buildings overlooking the fort's white walls. It had been just a few days since he spent the night there hanging upside down with Deacon Barry searching for him. Now, he could see a different group of school kids moving about the historical park getting ready to take part in the same program.

Kal felt his heavily wrapped knee and gently itched a sensitive spot. The dull pain was annoying, offset only by a self-medicating button that coursed Vicodin through his body whenever he needed it. Doctors at the hospital performed surgery almost immediately upon his arrival to stabilize the joint and repair some of the major ligaments he re-tore before the swelling became impossible to deal with. Kal was looking at not only months of intense rehab, but most likely a few more surgeries to make sure he could walk normally again without a limp or permanent help from a cane or brace.

"I just can't wrap my ahead around the fact he's gone," he finally said, mindlessly staring at the fort.

"The other man you were hurt with? He sounds like he will be dearly missed," quietly whispered the older nurse attending to his I.V.

Kal closed his eyes and sighed. "He was so strong throughout the whole thing, even after getting shot. He tried to walk on his own a few times but the pain was too much. If only I hadn't let go of him when we were climbing out, he'd still . . . "

"I'm so sorry for your loss. Were you very close?"

"Sort of. Not really. To be honest I couldn't stand him most of the time, he was more a friend of a friend."

"That seems harsh. So he won't be missed at all?"

"He had a dad and a sister, but I'm not sure anyone will even notice. He just kind of floated through life a lot."

"It seems like you're almost happy."

"Not happy, just relieved. We had a lot of bad stuff happen between us. I think I can close that chapter and move on now. He was weighing me down."

"Oh, come on!" yelled Benny, throwing back the drawn curtain separating his portion of the room from Kal's. "This thing isn't sound-proof, I can still hear everything you guys say. Really, Kal? Isn't it a little soon to be joking at my expense? I'm still, technically, listed in serious condition. Check my charts, the doctor said I'm supposed to be taking it easy."

"Whoa, I thought you were still sleeping. It's rude to eaves-drop."

The nurse couldn't contain herself and began giggling uncon-trollably. "I almost lost it twice, I was this close to laughing."

Benny just shook his head. "You know, you guys are jerks. I al-most died down there. Don't you have any sympathy?"

"Nope," Kal said.

"Screw you," Benny said in mock anger. "I wish you hadn't caught me, you're going to be holding that over my head the rest of my life."

Kal laughed, "Listen man, like I told you before, don't thank me.

Thank Ashworth's scarf—you know, the one you were making fun of. That's what I ended up grabbing ahold of before you cartwheeled your way down to the bottom."

"I wondered why I had a rug burn on my neck," he said, gingerly massaging the back of his collar.

"I almost forgot. I was able to retrieve those things you asked for, Mr. Boyce," the nurse said, handing him a newspaper and his pair of pants before leaving the room.

"Thank you," he said, opening the Sacramento Bee to the front page. "Look at that Ben, we made it above the fold."

The collapse of an entire block of Old Sacramento and the death of two men had indeed been big news locally, even though the magnitude and breadth of the story had yet to be revealed. The Sacramento Police and local branch of the FBI had already visited Kal and Benny several times and were fully aware of the situation and what happened to Ashworth and Marcus, recovering both bodies almost immediately. At this point, they had only publicly acknowledged the cave-in was caused by a natural sinkhole and that two of the four men who were illegally exploring the famed Sacramento Underground at the time were subsequently rescued. It would be months before that particular section of Old Sac would be repaired and reopened and even longer before the entire story leaked detailing the incidents of that week, propelling Kal and Benny back into the national spotlight. But for the moment, they were content and blissfully ignorant to the tempest awaiting them.

"It's going to haunt me we never found the Eagle," Benny said. "And we never really proved Dunning was right. With the cave-in there's nothing left to show of the existence of The Verein besides that chicken scratch under the fort. The only real proof we had was that vault, and it's gone."

"Well, not everything," Kal said, reaching into the front pocket of the pants and pulling out car keys.

"Are those for the rental? What do they have to do with anything?" Benny asked.

"It's not the car that's important, but what's in it."

Benny's face was blank.

"Don't you remember what we found at the Judah Monument?"

"The Mark Twain letter?"

Kal smiled and twirled the keys on his finger. "I hid it in the rental car after we left the library, stuck the box under the back seat. I called over to Gio's place a little while ago and the car is still parked out front. No one has touched it because of the weekend."

"If I could get out of this bed I would come over there and kiss you!"

"Please don't. That letter—by one of the greatest American authors—not only proves the existence of The Verein and what they were trying to accomplish, as well as support every one of our theories, but all the signatures all on that last page make it an archeological treasure probably worth millions. Now Professor Dunning will get all the credit he deserves. His and Elle's name will be synonymous with The Verein and they'll forever be recognized in history books. Their deaths will have meant something."

"I'm sorry. I thought you said millions. That's funny."

"I did."

Benny's face froze before he reared back and yelled in happiness.

"Of course, we'll never see a dime," Kal continued.

"Wait, what?" Benny asked, stopping his celebrating prematurely. "Why the hell not?"

"This is a piece of history too massive to be sold or cheapened. It deserves to be in a museum for the public and future generations to research and learn about. It's what Professor Dunning would have wanted."

"But, I got shot, and nearly blown up a couple of times, and chased, and I fell from really high into some nasty water."

"I know. Trust me, it's for the best."

"Did I mention I was shot?" he said with a sigh. "Oh well. I was rich for about 10 seconds there. At least Elle and Dunning will get the credit. Do you think the Eagle was ever down there?"

"I don't know," Kal said. "I never saw a tag on the shelves. To be honest, it seemed like we were always just chasing a shadow. It would tease us to keep going but there was never anything definite. From Sherman to the Cannonball House to The Verein to Underground Sacramento—it always seemed like it was toying with us."

"So speaking of millions, the million dollar question is, after all of the stuff we went through, do you think it actually exists?"

Kal contemplated before finally smiling. "Yeah, I do. I do believe it exists. I guess it'll just be found when it wants to, on its own terms."

"I don't know about you, but after a few weeks of healing here I have some time off coming to me. We could start looking in that old abandoned trainyard north of the downtown," Benny said.

Kal laughed. "You didn't let me finish, I was going to say if it is found, it's not going to involve this guy. I quit. And this time I can honestly say I don't have one scintilla of regret for being a quitter."

He picked up the remote control to the TV and turned it on, flipping through the channels until he hit a music station playing the Muse's *Uprising*.

"Although, I did read about some old tunnels underneath that train yard. If we could somehow get access . . . "

# EPILOGUE

**Part I**

"It appears to be a rash, Otis. Let me give you some ointment and you'll be fit as fiddle and on your way," Dr. Callahan said. "And if you want it to stop spreading, don't itch it."

He reached into one of his cabinets and handed the old miner a jar of cream before following him out the door of his office and onto the wooden sidewalk. "I mean it Otis, don't scratch it or it might fall off."

Callahan ran his hand through the nest of mussed redness he called his hair and stopped to soak in the early Spring sun. It was a beautiful day in northern California and a crew of workers across the road noisily toiled on the first section of the brick wall the mayor and city leaders ambitiously authorized to raise the street levels to keep the city from flooding. Callahan had lived in Sacramento for six months and thought the whole idea was ludicrous, not to mention unattainable. But then again, he had yet to experience one of the devastating river swells the locals talked about so often.

As he headed back inside he noticed a horse and wagon careening out of control down Front Street toward him, the driver furiously thrashing the reigns and screaming. He stopped to watch, initially believing the man was attempting to slow the wagon to keep from crashing, but when it got within earshot he realized the driver was yelling his name and accelerating his horses.

"Doc Callahan! Doc Callahan!" screamed the man, amazingly pulling the wagon to a dead-stop right in front of his office. It was Tom Wallace, a farmer who lived outside of town along the American River near the foothills. The doctor delivered the Wallace's first child a few months prior and was very familiar with the family.

"Tom, what's the matter? Are the wife and baby okay?"

"They're fine," he answered. "It's the guy in the back that ain't doing so well." Tom hopped from his driver's perch into the bed of the wagon, where an unconscious man lay covered in a blanket with a blood-stained towel over the crown of his head.

"What happened to him?" Callahan asked, climbing in to examine. He lifted the blanket to reveal several long, drawn out cuts on the man's upper chest—his breathing was very shallow and he appeared near death.

"I was out tending to my orchard, minding my business when this here wagon we're sitting on came on drifting through—no driver in sight. It scared me at first, thought it might be some kind of ghost or something. When I finally stopped the horses to check it out, I found this fella in the back, all passed out."

"Looks like he was attacked and robbed," Callahan said, checking the man's pockets and looking around the wagon, which was devoid of anything valuable. "I don't know how much longer he has."

"That's not the worst of it, Doc," said Tom. "Look at his head."

The doctor slowly pulled back the towel and recoiled in horror—the man's scalp was cut clean off his skull, the wound in the early stages of infection.

"For the love of Christ, let's get him inside."

The two gently carried the injured man off the wagon, into the office, and onto a bed in one of the back rooms. He appeared to be young, probably no older than 20, but his age was hard to pinpoint with the injuries to his head.

"The only thing we can do for him is wrap the wound and give something for his pain, hopefully he doesn't suffer too much. You say you've never seen him before?"

"Never. Looks like Indians got him, though."

Callahan concurred and carefully took off the man's coat to get a better look at the wounds to his chest. He instantly recognized the shirt the man was wearing, as well as the pants and boots.

"These are army-issued," he said. "I used to own a pair just like these when I served at Bull Run."

Memories of mangled body parts and gruesome hospital conditions came flooding back to Callahan. It had been three years since he was discharged from the Army after mentally breaking down. He moved out West to escape injuries like these, but they had now found him.

"You were in the Army, Doc? I didn't know that."

"I try not to remind myself," he said, attempting to take off the pants to check for any other wounds. But before he could undo the top button, the man suddenly became lucid and frantically grabbed Callahan's arm.

"The wagon! Where is it?" he rasped.

"It's okay, son," the doctor said. "You're safe now, you've been gravely injured."

"Where am I? Where is the wagon?"

"You are in my office in Sacramento. I'm a doctor. The wagon you were on is parked outside safe and sound. What is your name?"

The man did not answer but instead reached into his pants toward his crotch and retrieved a crinkled envelope sealed by a partially melted wax stamp. "Must take this to Hopkins. Please, Hopkins, hurry."

Callahan grabbed the letter and handed it to Tom. "He must mean Mark Hopkins. Take this over to his store as fast as you can, see if he's there. He might know who this man is."

Tom hastily ran out of the store to the Huntington, Hopkins & Co. Hardware store located just a few blocks away in the Big Four Building. Doctor Callahan gave the man some water and medicine and tried to calm him, this time taking a different tact.

"What's your name, soldier?"

The man showed surprise at Callahan's question. "How did you know I was in the army?"

"It's the pants and boots, they're a giveaway. I spent five years wearing some just like those."

"Wh-where did you serve?"

"I was a surgeon in the 5th Michigan Infantry Regiment under McClellan. How about you?"

"The 7th out of Illinois, was fighting down in Georgia under Sherman."

"Georgia? That's a long way from here. What's your name, son?"

"O'Neal . . . Private Jonathan O'Neal."

The doctor laughed, slapping his knee. "A good Irishman, eh? My last name is Callahan. We're probably related somewhere down the line."

Private O'Neal wasn't laughing, however. He was gritting his teeth through the pain and struggling to stay conscious. Callahan knew he had to keep him awake—the young man was likely to soon go under permanently. "So what are you doing all the way out here in California? You decide to try your hand mining since the war is almost over?"

The private stopped moaning and opened his eyes wide. "The war is . . . is over?"

"Just about. Grant's got the Rebs running, I hear. You helped the winning side, son."

O'Neal began to softly weep before composing himself and talking purposefully, taking the doctor aback.

"We were on a secret mission from General Sherman. Four of us were supposed to deliver a special crate. The Lieutenant wouldn't say at first what we were doing, exactly. I'm not sure he even knew where we were going, except it was out West. It took us only a few days after leaving Macon before we knew the Rebs wanted whatever we had real bad. A group of them chased us all the way to Missouri. They got Lester first, then Caleb Turner a few days later. The Lieutenant was so worried about the crate that he built a secret space for it under the floorboards—you can't see it unless you're really looking. It's a beautiful bird, probably the most pretty thing you've ever laid eyes upon. It took us weeks of slow travel and we thought we were in the clear once we reached Utah. But they somehow found us again outside of Lake Tahoe and caught me. Skinned and tortured me to try and get the Lieutenant to come back."

The young man was openly sobbing now, and the doctor tried to comfort him by placing his arm on his shoulder. He didn't seem to be making a lot of sense, babbling about a bird and a secret mission.

"And he did, he did come back for me. I told him not to, because it was a trap. But he did it regardless—said I reminded him of his kid brother. He handed me that letter, told me to take the wagon and get the bird to a Mr. Hopkins in Sacramento. He held 'em off while I got away. The last thing I saw was them murder Lieutenant Joseph, one on five. It wasn't even a fair fight."

Callahan tried to calm the private down. He was worried the stress of reliving his ordeal would be too much.

"Excuse me, Doctor. Might I have a word with you?" asked a voice from outside the room. Tom had returned to the office with a well-dressed gentleman, who was now trying to garner his attention. Callahan motioned for them to step out, closing the door behind him and leaving the private alone.

"How do you do, Doctor? It's a pleasure to meet you. My name is Dylan LeBay, I'm a representative for Mr. Mark Hopkins. How is the young man doing?"

"Not well. Lost a lot of blood and the wound to his scalp is already festering. He's close to death, most likely."

"That is truly a shame. He is a contracted employee of ours through the military and I would like to have just a few moments with him alone, if that's agreeable?"

Callahan pondered the request for a second and decided against it. "I don't think that's a good idea. He needs to rest. Any more stress might be too much for him to handle."

"I understand, Doctor. But it really is paramount I talk to him—it has to do with his family. If he is truly on death's doorstep, there are some things I need to find out from him."

Tom nodded in agreement with LeBay. "If it's about his kinfolk, he should really speak to him, Doc."

"Alright," said Callahan. "But only for a few moments."

LeBay slipped into the room, quietly closing the door behind him. The doctor and Tom could hear muffled conversation between the young private and the well-dressed businessman as they waited patiently. Then there was silence. LeBay finally walked out of the room with his hat in his hand.

"I'm afraid he's passed."

"No, dammit!" said the doctor. He rushed into the room and checked the man's pulse, but could not find anything. He gently closed the private's still-open eyes with a sweep of his hand.

"If it's any consolation, he drifted away mid-sentence, didn't seem to be in any pain. I'll have someone from my office come by later to make the funeral arrangements, if that's fine by you." LeBay asked, walking out.

"Now wait a second, I demand to know what's going on here. Who is after him and what was he bringing you?" Callahan asked.

LeBay stopped at the doorway and smiled back. "This man and the men who died with him are heroes to their country and this state— he was reassured of that before he passed. Their contributions will aid future generations in ways I couldn't begin to describe to you. What I cannot do, unfortunately, is give you any more details or answers to satisfy your queries. Just know, each of these men's families will be taken care of. I left some compensation for your troubles on your entry table. Good day."

Callahan followed him outside, where he noticed Private O'Neal's horses and cart were gone. "Hey, his wagon is gone! He mentioned something about a secret space and a bird."

"Ah yes, the wagon. We've already taken possession of it back at our supply store, since it was our property. As far as a bird?" LeBay said with a crooked smile. "I really don't have any idea what he could be talking about. He was probably delusional from the pain. Take care, doctor."

And with a nod and a skip in his step LeBay headed down the

sidewalk as Callahan watched, finally turning his attention to the men working on the street.

"Stupid thing is never going to work anyway. Lifting an entire city . . . ridiculous."

\*\*\*\*

Six months later and nearly 2,800 miles away from Sacramento, Michael Joseph held his youngest daughter Abigail in his lap and retold a tale from his youth in which his older brother Joshua, the soldier, saved him from drowning in the local creek.

"He was so brave," he said. "He couldn't swim but because he was not scared of anything he jumped into the water and pulled me out by my britches. If it weren't for him, you wouldn't be here today."

When the story ended, Molly looked up at her father and asked, "Daddy, where is Uncle Joshua?"

"I told you, honey. God gave him a special mission. He had to transport a secret treasure across the country, and once he finished, he was allowed to join heaven with the angels," he answered, looking out across the vast acreage of his new farm. "But if you squint hard enough at night, I think you can probably see him up in the stars."

"Okay, daddy," she said, jumping out of his lap and running off to join her sister in play.

She would spend her entire childhood and teenage years on that farm, later marrying a banker when she turned 22 years of age and moving to Colorado to start up her own family. One of her six children had a son, whose daughter wed a man named Boyce and produced several offspring. The youngest of those boys, Marvin, married a teacher named Diane and settled in the northern part of the state in the 1970s. They had only one child, a boy they named after their love of the Hawaiian islands . . .

Kalei.

## Part II

Laurent McNeil pushed his shopping cart over the lower, train-only half of the double-decker I Street Bridge, a historic, solid-steel truss running 30 feet above the muddy and fast-flowing Sacramento River.

The most recent Capitol Corridor Amtrak engine running to the Bay Area just passed, giving him at least a half hour to reach the safety of the Sacramento bank before another train came through. It was not easy jostling the cart over the wood ties while simultaneously keeping a vigilant watch for a 150-ton piece of steel, especially on a hot summer night like this in the Valley—past 9 p.m. and still 90 degrees out.

Making his way over the river and into the abandoned Union Pacific Railyards, he immediately parked the cart in its usual spot, hidden behind a small shed under the elevated I-5 freeway so that no one passing on the roadway overhead could spot it, and began looking for anything worth collecting. He was technically trespassing on Union Pacific's land, but figured the company didn't care about any of the leftover junk still on the property or they would have removed it when they cleared out of town decades earlier.

The place actually gave Laurent the creeps every time he made a collection run, but because it was so fertile in terms of finding valuable scrap metal and other odds and ends he continued to brave the once-a-week trek. Sitting on almost 250 acres of mostly undeveloped dirt adjacent to downtown Sacramento, these long abandoned railyards were once the home of the western terminus of the Transcontinental Railroad, and before that, Theodore Judah's Sacramento Valley Railroad. It was at one time the largest railroad facility west of the Mississippi, but with the decline of rail it now had sat vacant for many years. There were rumors that entire train engines were buried in graves all over the yard, but he had yet to find one.

Laurent at one time heard rumblings the city was moving closer to finally redeveloping the area, which would almost double the size of Sacramento's downtown with residential and commercial properties and even perhaps a new sports and entertainment facility—meaning his days of hunting here were dwindling.

He made a beeline toward a group of multistory, brick warehouses that once housed the repair and production of steam engines but now were the only remnants of the once-mighty facility. He'd discovered a small tunnel in the central building several years earlier leading to an subterranean network running throughout the grounds like a maze of gopher holes, even extending south underneath the current, more modern rail terminal and into downtown Sacramento. There were times, initially, when he found himself so lost exploring that he thought he might die underground, emerging after days with no food and barely any water. But he eventually mastered the complex, learning every twist and turn. He usually stayed in the tunnels directly underneath the Railyards because they were the most fruitful, but occasionally ventured downtown to see if anything was salvageable, although that area had been picked clean a long time ago.

Today, he was focusing on a new vicinity underneath Old Sacramento in a section of tunnels he discovered almost three weeks prior but hadn't been able to venture into because of a giant sinkhole. The place had been crawling with cops and construction crews day and night for a week, but they were now cleared out, and Laurent figured it would be void of any human presence, especially on a Sunday evening.

Armed with only a flashlight, a cane and a large canvas bag, he descended into the depths of the Underground and quickly made his way south. He found moving quickly through the cramped space saved wear and tear on his 45-year-old back as well as precious time, and within minutes he had maneuvered near the California Train Museum in Old Sac ready to start scavenging.

*That's weird, that wasn't here before,* he thought, turning to a section of tunnel with a large gash in its lower wall. Always inquisitive, he wiggled through the opening, blindly stepping inside, and realized he was in a new section of tunnel—different than the ones he normally traveled in. Narrower, and running deeper into the earth, this particular passageway was composed of brick and stone and appeared to be carrying a small stream of water to an unknown destination. He followed it for about 20 feet until the floor disappeared into a large chasm, cascading into darkness.

Laurent looked down with his light and spotted a dirt hill just underneath the abyss that sloped for another 20 feet. He weighed his options and decided to go for it, carefully lowering himself and then sliding through the dirt on his backside. As he reached the leveled-out floor, he became acutely aware there no longer was anything over his head—he was now outdoors and in some sort of canyon.

*I'm in the part that collapsed, the sinkhole.*

Two giant earth-moving cranes kept watch overhead at street level on both sides of the block, surrounded by temporary fencing and flashing caution lights to keep tourists in Old Sacramento from getting close. Some of the debris from the cave-in had already been cleared, but it was obvious the work crews were taking their time so as to not weaken any of the surrounding building foundations.

*As long as I'm down here, might as well look around awhile. Could be some neat stuff.*

Laurent picked through the dirt with his cane, pulling up chunks of broken concrete here and there and the occasional piece of rusted metal, none of which had any real value. After only minutes of futile searching his paranoia kicked in and he decided to vacate the premises before someone spotted him, heading back up the slope toward the tunnel he dropped through.

The ascent in the extremely rocky terrain proved to be much more difficult than the trip down, however, taking him 15 minutes to make it just three-quarters of the way to the summit. Mere steps from the peak of the hill he nearly lost his balance, slipping on a patch of soil and subsequently latching onto a semi-buried boulder in a desperate attempt to keep from sliding all the way back down. He held on for dear life and only regained his footing with the help of his cane, eventually straightening himself to continue upward, unaware the rock had been loosened from its tentative perch.

He pushed off to finish the last few feet of the climb and felt the ground give way as the boulder, roughly the size of a beach ball, seesawed and began rolling down the hill, accelerating until it was traveling at a high rate of speed. It leveled off on the floor of the canyon and smashed into a section of the earthen wall still upright from the initial cave-in, shaking the ground so violently that Laurent was sure another collapse was on the brink.

He frantically struggled to pull himself up into the safety of the stone tunnel, not wanting to chance getting crushed by what he was positive was an avalanche and only looked back when he felt totally secure.

What he saw immediately sent him scrambling back down.

*Looks like that boulder just knocked down an entire wall of copper!*

The precious metal was fetching a boatload of money on the market at the moment, and judging by the size of the piece laying on the canyon floor, he knew he could probably make out well.

*Definitely copper,* he concluded after nearly killing himself in the rush to climb back down. He carefully extracted the fragment from the soil and turned his attention to the remains of the smashed wall, which appeared to be supporting some sort of hinged door built into the earth. Laurent reached up and brushed the large chunk of metal, noticing an animal imprinted on it, the details very ornate.

*Gotta be worth a lot.*

He gently jostled the broken hatch to open it, but instead bent the copper away from the wall.

"What the?" he yelled out loud.

Sitting in a medium-sized cubbyhole behind the door was a dusty statue of a gold-colored bird, covered in fake jewels.

"Well kiss my black ass and call me Obama. This has got to be worth something," he said, quickly digging it out and wiping it off.

It was extremely heavy, and in his opinion, looked like a knockoff piece of yard art he'd seen sitting on front lawns in well-to-do neighborhoods. *Probably made with cheap metal meant to look like gold—somebody will buy it, though.* He picked up all the pieces of copper door and threw them in the canvas bag along with the bird and slung it over his shoulder, determined to get back to the cart, no matter how long the climb.

An hour and several bucketfuls of sweat later he popped out on the street level of the railyard complex, exhausted with his back close to seizing. He had almost left the statue behind several times because of its weight, but the idea of making a few extra bucks kept him trudging along. He happily dropped the bag into his cart and pushed it toward the bridge to take back over the river to the city of West Sacramento, dead-tired but pleased with a successful haul and ready to sleep for the night.

Prematurely assuming he was home free, it only took three steps on the bridge to realize a major obstacle still presented itself. The weight of the copper door combined with the statue made it nearly impossible to push the cart between the rails on the span. He was forced to lift and pull the front over every individual tie, and knew he didn't have the remaining strength to continue the entire length. To make matters worse, the 11:30 p.m. train from San Francisco was due to roll through soon.

He labored on, however, with a sense of determination, managing to struggle halfway across the connection before his body finally surrendered, unable to pull the cart any farther.

Figuring it was best to get home with something to show for his efforts on the night rather than nothing at all, he opened the bag and pulled out the statue. He pried off a few of the faux jewels using his hunting knife and tucked them in his pocket, *just in case*, then carried the statue to the edge of the bridge and let it sit there as if it were a genuine bird ready to spread its wings and fly, before finally kicking it over, sending it free-falling into the water with a large splash.

"Probably didn't mean nothing to nobody, anyway," he said, spitting in its direction before continuing on his way. "More trouble than it was worth."

The *L'Aigle de la Liberté* hit the surface and quickly descended though the darkness, enveloped by the murkiest of water, until it landed with a gentle thud on the base of the riverbed. It rested there for a brief moment, then slowly sank into the mud floor, vanishing within seconds until all traces of its existence were gone.

The Freedom Eagle had finally found a permanent place to rest.